FUGITIVE MOON

Ron Faust

A TOM DOHERTY ASSOCIATES BOOK
NEW YORK

FUGITIVE MOON

A Forge Book
Published by Tom Doherty Associates, Inc.
175 Fifth Avenue
New York, N.Y. 10010

Forge® is a registered trademark of Tom Doherty Associates, Inc.

ISBN: 0-812-52259-1
Library of Congress Card Catalog Number: 94-46342

First edition: April 1995
First mass market edition: March 1996

Printed in the United States of America

0 9 8 7 6 5 4 3 2 1

To Eleanor Wood

Out on the margin of Moonshine Land,
        Tickle me, Love, in these Lonesome Ribs!

Is it the gibber of Gungs or Keeks?
        Tickle me, Love, in these Lonesome Ribs!

Anoint him the wraithest of wraithly things!
        Tickle me, Love, in these Lonesome Ribs!
'Tis a fair Whing-Whangess, with phosphor rings,
And bridal-jewels of fangs and stings;
And she sits and as sadly and softly sings
As the mildewed whir of her own dead wings, —
        Tickle me, Dear,
            Tickle me here,
        Tickle me, Love, in me Lonesome Ribs!

—James Whitcomb Riley
The Lugubrious Whing-Whang

PART ONE

—‹◊◊◊›—

Give me chastity and continence, only not yet.

—Saint Augustine

1

I am feared and loathed in certain quarters; I have powerful enemies. Two years ago on the Oprah Winfrey Show I said that lady psychologists were the Jesuits of this century. I believed that I was being witty. Oh, Christ, even now I receive poison-pen letters written in pastel inks, and often my name is fouled in psychofeminist books and lectures. First I am pitied and then excoriated. Pity, you know, opens the gates for invective. I didn't realize then that lady psychologists controlled opinion in America—I thought it was the Jews—and so I was flippant when I should have been sanctimonious.

And now—curse my tongue—I am in trouble for slandering the diseased. Remember, I said that if shrewdly exploited, a convulsed body or fevered brain was worth more than an MBA. Damn! The diseased are not without influence. And they have a Sicilian sense of honor and a hard-nosed calculation of their perquisites. It doesn't help that I too am diseased; in fact, that makes my apostasy appear all the more vicious. Tomorrow I will try to repair the damage by saying some good things about Jesus on the Good Morning, America show. (My Doppelgänger laughs—get thee behind me!)

Maybe you read my ghosted autobiography. Maybe you saw me laugh and weep on the Geraldo Rivera show. Maybe you remember when I was a wild flamethrowing kid intoxicated by my gift and by a tendency toward madness. Time has cooled my smoke, and prudent doses of lithium carbonate abort my higher and more hazardous manic flights.

When you see me on the field or street or black hole, you do not see all of me. The best and worst parts have been electrically and chemically amputated, and now I am a condensed and expurgated edition of the original—a pocket Teddy Moon.

Friends and teammates and ex-wives call me Moon or Moonman. My kids call me Daddy. I silently address myself as Theodore in moments of anxiety: *Watch out, Theodore, or those lawyers will crack open your long bones and suck out the marrow.*

In cities all over America I hear police and ambulance sirens howl like wolves during the night and I am thrilled and jittery, feverish—I yearn to go out and again run with the barbarians. My ears ring, there is a fizzy sensation the length of my spine—symptoms of imminent exaltation, incipient anarchy. But a hit of lithium and a few pages of Epictetus or Marcus Aurelius more or less civilize me.

I have a video cassette of my appearance on the Phil Donahue show and every now and then I hook up the VCR and review my astonishing public crack-up. On the tape I am hilarious and piteous, a possibly dangerous buffoon—the kind of man you will cross the street to avoid.

The ironic thing is that I appeared on that show (and many others) while supposedly educating the public about manic depressive psychosis. That is, I was in a detestable oily way discussing my first crack-up while id-deep in the second. What a joke. What shame.

And it was on a radio talk show in Denver that I calmly announced my intention to fund and build a multimillion-dollar psychiatric research institute upon the Trinity Site in New Mexico. Brains instead of bombs. I was another idealogue of compassion. On that tape my voice is casual, persuasive. The proposal does not sound too outrageous. I knew that when a soul goes public it is better to have a good front than a good heart.

There were earlier symptoms (I stopped taking medication in San Francisco); but that was really the beginning of my legendary three-month-long roll, my manic disintegration, during which I soared higher and higher, faster and faster, heedlessly bombing and strafing the civilian population, until finally I crashed and burned in Chicago. At the end I was truly mad, a hyena.

Only two crack-ups, one heroic and the other not. I am quite healthy now, thank you. Don't let them tell you that I cracked up again last summer. And don't listen when they imply that I now and then stuffed the equivocal corpses of transsexuals into hotel laundry chutes. Not true. Not once. Look, stay away from the supermarket tabloids: they'll scorch your brain, they'll calcify your heart, they'll shrivel your loins.

I am not now nor have I ever been a serial murderer. Trust me, Jocko.

God bless. Ciao.

2

We had been commanded to report early to the New York ballpark, but the important team meeting turned out to be nothing more than a forty-minute lecture by a Dynamic Motivational Catalyst. The DMC had been hired by Fungo and Mr. Haugen, the club's general manager, to inspire us with positive self-assertion and winning attitudes. Leroy "Red" Girt was a lanky, long-necked man with knuckly hands and size-fifteen wingtip shoes. He wore a shot-silk suit that flashed rainbows when he moved. A big smile and tiny green eyes. His diction and accent betrayed his rural Oklahoma origin, and so did his unbuttoned tent-show oratory and his technique of associating Jesus with himself and the success-therapy he espoused. How can you argue with Jesus? Sincere eye contact. Moral bullying. "Jesus was a winner and you can be a winner too."

Dynamic Motivational Catalysm was a stew of evangelical Christianity, social Darwinism, and right-wing rectumtude.

The players morosely sat around, half undressed, smoking or drinking Cokes, autographing baseballs, illegally tampering with bats, kneading gloves, exchanging glances—what kind of horseshit will we have to endure tomorrow? I watched the black players. There was a kind of smoldering violence in their boredom. I liked the way their eyelids drooped. Only the lower halves of their pupils were visible. Hooded Mau Mau glares.

Fungo, Prosper, MacDonald, and the Garcia kid seemed truly interested in the tactics of DMC, although Garcia understood little English. Lately he had complained of an infection on his foot-fingers.

Braverman, making a fuss about it, opened his top shirt button and pulled out a gold chain and Star of David. A hex on all of this Jesus talk. Braverman had not worn the Star of David until last year when Prosper and MacDonald had appeared on the scene wearing their big gold crosses. A clash of symbols.

"It's easy to be a winner," Red told us. A finger snap. "Easy. Do you know why? I'll tell you why. Because there are so many losers in the world. People who lose, who can't win for losing. Think about that. If we was all winners, every one of the five billion of us on this itty-bitty planet, Christian and infidel—why, there wouldn't be enough to go around. We'd be lucky to be eating barley gruel and driving a mule. Lucky! Barley gruel, maybe an itty pile of rice, greeny taters, grass, locusts."

Red Girt paused dramatically and swiveled his eyes like prison searchlights around the room. Then he crossed his right leg over his left and an iridescent glow shivered through the fabric of his suit.

"Now, I'm going to tell you something. Not many people know this. Here it is—are you listening, guy? If you are a loser . . . if you are a loser then the other man will be living in that big mansion you always dreamed of owning, and that fellow will be driving the car you always coveted, and he'll send his kids to the fine schools you'd picked out for *your* sons and daughters. Do you see it? You maybe won't end up eating barley gruel—a man can be a failure, a parasite, in this great blessed America and still not end up eating barley gruel. But listen, *you* won't ever own that dream castle, or drive your Cadillac automobile, or attend your son's graduation at Oral Roberts University."

He bowed his head and pretended to brood for a time. Then: "And you single men . . . ? That other fellow just might marry your woman, the wife you was meant to possess! Do you see it? You paying attention? It's as simple as barley gruel and prime rib; a Cadillac or an itty-bitty Jap car; a beautiful, decent, moral wife or some slut from the warehouse district."

I sensed a stare and turned: Buckley, of course. His bland, unblinking, empty stare. Poor me, was Buckley at it again? Once or twice a season Buckley selected a victim and commenced staring at him for weeks, sometimes months. Wherever you were, whatever you were doing, you might look up and engage Buckley's inhuman blue-eyed stare. It was uncanny. He spent enormous energy in this eerie private joke. Step out of an elevator or hotel room or remote restaurant and there was Oliver, silently staring. He rarely talked to his victims. He arrived and departed silently, staring.

"Hey, baseball's like any other game," Red Girt was saying. "It's like the business game and the politics game and the stock-market game and every other game you can think of. The game of life. One man has got to win and a thousand has got to lose. Hear that? Are you going to lose, guy? What about you? Was Jesus a loser? Was Jesus a quitter?"

He shuddered at the thought and his suit emitted more rainbows.

"Listen, what would you think if Jesus was on your team and he came to bat in the last of the ninth with two out and the winning run on second base. Would you worry? Blast no, you wouldn't worry. Why, you'd grin as big as that, and think—the run is home. That run is home! The money is in the bank. Honey, put on your best, pack the Caddy, we're going to Walt Disney World, because Jesus is at bat and Jesus doesn't choke. Jesus Christ does not choke! Play on Jesus's side and you are automatically a winner."

Buckley was still staring at me. Most of the black players scowled murderously, their eyes so hooded that they probably could not see more than their knees and patches of floor. But Fungo gazed at Red Girt as Plato must have once gazed at Socrates.

"Hey, are you listening, guy? You're maybe thinking: 'But Jesus ain't on our team, Jesus ain't batting cleanup.' Yes, Jesus is! You bet he is! Because if Jesus is in your heart then you are Jesus. Did you hear that? I'll say it again. If Jesus is in your heart then you are Jesus Christ Almighty and you are invincible!"

Braverman got up and slouched off to the shower and toilet rooms. Maybe his sensitive Jewish ear could hear the remote drumming of hooves and the first faint cries of the advancing Cossacks.

"Let me tell you a story," Red said.

This was mad. I knew madness from the inside out and the outside in, and this was mad. The clubhouse was now like the asylums I had known. Depressed, silent, passive people. Men with tics. Men seething with a resentment that could neither be swallowed nor expressed. All cowed by a slick redneck in a chromatic silk suit. Ah, but behind Red Girt were ranked the Legions of Fear—God and America and Success and Love and Orthodoxy, and the stern feudal lords who signed our paychecks.

I got up and followed Braverman into the other rooms.

He was washing his hands at one of the basins. He turned off the tap, dried his hands on a towel, then leaned close to the mirror and studied his reflection.

"Moon," he said. "Do you think I look too Jewish?" His breath clouded the glass.

I said, "Neither too Jewish nor insufficiently Jewish. You are just right."

"Thank you."

"Do I look too Gentile?"

"You're my friend. I don't like to hurt friends."

"I understand."

Braverman stepped away from the mirror. We watched each other's reflections.

"What do you think of the revival meeting in the other room?" he asked.

"Hey, guy, I dig it. It suits me just fine. I've never believed that God should be denied admittance to schoolrooms and locker rooms, boardrooms and rest rooms. What are we hiding? Listen here, Braverman, I beseeched the Father and he put the buzz back in my fastball. I implored the Son and my portfolio prospered. I invoked the Holy Ghost and now my breath is sweet. Hey, guy, that's what the religion game is all about."

"Hey, goy, I didn't enjoy it as much as you."

"That's because you people think of the deity as Yahweh. No way, Braverman. Wake up. Yahweh's a foreigner, he speaks with an accent, he's got a terrible temper. He alienates people. It's hard for Americans to dig Yahweh. Be reasonable. How would you like to see someone named Yahweh come up to the plate in the last of the ninth with two out and the winning run on second?"

Braverman smiled sourly. "The other day Frank Prosper told me that Jews were without athletic talent."

"Well, that's true, guy. You people brood too much. You think dark thoughts. You fool around with violins."

"I said to him, 'What about Hank Greenberg? What about Sid Luckman? What about Sandy Koufax?'"

"Did you remind him that the Virgin Mary was a Jewish mom?"

"And Prosper said, 'Really, were they Jews? Incredulous athletes.'"

"Well, there you are."

Braverman walked past me and paused at the door. "Yahweh would hit one into the upper deck," he said.

"Have a nice day, guy."

I went into one of the toilet stalls, locked the door, and sat down. Home, safe, free—no one harangued a man who was ensconced on the Kohler throne. This was humanity's last refuge, the only remaining sanctuary. Here one could be deaf to the rabid exhortations of priests and patriots, politicians and psychologists. Aye, this is where the Moonman delivered his stillborn ideals.

3

I shagged fly balls in deep center field during batting practice. That was something I had done about one hundred and fifty times this year, counting spring training. Catching fly balls was as satisfying as any of my minor compulsions. I was good at it too; I had the predator's dispassionate eye and heart. I walk down city streets with my eyes lifted, alert for falling babies. My all-time fly-ball record was one hundred and ninety-three, in 1987, and I only dropped one finally because a flashy romanticism had invaded my austere, classical style.

This evening the ball would rise high into the sky before I'd hear the whipcrack report of the bat and its dull echoes, and it kept climbing past the stands and banks of light until it was no bigger than a starpoint; and then it began to descend, accelerating, expanding, tinted pink by the spinning seams, and finally snapping in my glove like a firecracker. Each was as sweet as a first kiss.

Later I went into the clubhouse, toweled off, and put on a clean sweatshirt.

Oliver Buckley, sitting on a bench, watched me.

"Did Blas tell you?" he asked.

"Tell me what?"

"God knows it isn't any business of mine."

Two years ago Buckley had been struck on the cheek by a ninety-mile-per-hour fastball and there had been nerve damage; now his right eyelid drooped and the right half of his mouth was less mobile than the left. It gave him a loopy, sardonic expression which suited his personality far more than had the prior bland symmetry.

"Maybe I shouldn't be talking about it," he said.

"You aren't."

"Blas denounced you to the police."

"He what?"

"He talked to the cops about the girl-guy who was murdered at our hotel in Cincinnati and stuffed into the laundry chute. The cops figure you for the killer because of your unfortunate history of mental disorders. It's unfair, it's a pity—Christ, they won't let a man forget, will they? But there it is. The homicide people are watching every move you make, listening to every word you utter."

Buckley was lying, of course; this was another of his mind games. Or was it?

"Bullshit," I said. "I'm not worried."

Buckley smiled with one half of his face. I had not fooled him. He planted little hooks in your brain. Some of the hooks were safely encysted; others festered and caused paranoid fevers.

I got a fresh package of chewing tobacco from my locker, and when I returned Buckley's expression had changed.

"How does it augur?" he asked.

"It augurs well."

"Yet a mouse by yearning becomes not a bat."

"So the elders have spoken."

I was the only person who enjoyed Buckley's peculiar language games; they irritated everyone else, which was the intent.

"Hence?" he said. This was Noble Savage Tongue.

"Yet the cuckoo lays her eggs in the nests of other birds."

Buckley slowly rose to his feet. His lopsided face was rigid—this was his expression of "steely character." Softly he said, "Ah, does then Brother Cuckoo sing like noble Brother Nightingale?"

"Nay."

"Thus we forget the old songs," he said, and he picked up his glove and left the clubhouse.

Spooky Oliver. He also spoke New Age Tongue, a psychomystical drool; and Sage Oriental Tongue, a patois cluttered with parable and paradox and reverberating with the profound clamor of one hand clapping. He claimed that it was his life's goal to be the first to utter sentences of perfect Negative Meaning. Phrases so banal that they possessed antisense and ignited synaptical firestorms in the cerebral cortex. "Shadow words, Moon," he once said, gnawing on his pipe's stem. "Almost here. Less is more, eh? Almost here, Moonman."

It was not merely matters of abstraction or inversion: Negative Meaning existed, it was an actual all-consuming vortex of antirationality. No thing escaped. The lights dimmed. You spoke the right words in the right order and annihilated vast areas of knowledge and erased thirty points off everyone's IQ. And Buckley told me that we were both prophets of Negative Meaning; he in a theoretical way, and I because in my maddest periods I'd babbled a word-salad that had nearly purified the language of content.

I went down to the dugout. It was almost dark now. Fans were streaming through the entrances and then fluttering down among the seats like brightly colored confetti. They made a lot of noise. I resented them; I regarded them as intruders.

"Goddamn," Brieschke was saying. "Goddamn, is this our national pastime? Well, is it? It is! Moon, for Christ's sake, will you put your fucking cap over your fucking heart tonight when they play the fucking national anthem? For me? Just this one time?"

"You're carrion, Brieschke."

"Well, that's who I am. That's me. Don't expect me to change. Take me as I am. Relate to me as carrion or forget it."

I walked to the other end of the dugout, away from the steps and water cooler and bat rack and coaches. My cleats made a pleasant clacking sound on the concrete. Heel and toe, clack clack clack. Coaches and over-the-hill ballplayers carried around dead weight even if they were not fat, and their cleats made a dull, crunching noise. I figured that this would be Bob Brieschke's last year; there was a discernible crunch, a mortal crunch, in his cheery clack clack clack.

"Move over, rookie," I said to Dickie Brackett. "You got my place."

I sat in the dugout throughout the game, expertly spitting tobacco, commenting on the action sport announcer's style, and telling vicious lies. I spun a really fine slander for the dugout troops, a legend of lust and lycanthropy on the golden sands of Malibu where I had once, so I claimed, spent a lascivious weekend with a fa-

mous movie star. "When I left she told me that I had
ruined her for lesbian relationships." No one listened except for a couple of kids who had come up from the
minor leagues for the tail end of the season.

I enjoy telling lies and I'm very good at it. All of my lies
have a beginning, a middle, and an end. They strain toward the universal. They are Ideas in the Platonic sense.

4

Some time ago I spent two weeks at the Cintrons' country home in one of those nasty Latin American republics, a Garden of Eden turned deliquescent. The hacienda, a big Moorish-style building, was located in the highlands several thousand feet above the capital city. There were ninety acres of coffee trees, as much pastureland, a miserable worker's village, and all around a palmy, ferny forest spattered with orchids and hummingbirds.

Toward the end of my visit Blas had to go down to the city on family business, and I was left alone with his father Esteban—a big-bellied mestizo—and the servants. But that evening Blas's sister, a beautiful and languidly stupid young woman, arrived for the weekend.

The three of us drank too much wine with dinner and too much brandy afterward, and when Elena Cintron came to my room at one in the morning I was still drunk and incapable of refusing her gift. We were naked, sweating and mindless, triumphal, when Esteban and three of his peons broke through the door.

"My own girl child!" Esteban cried. "My little baby!"

I recall being roughly dragged from the bed, slapped and cuffed; and I remember Esteban shouting and his brandy-stinking breath and the way globules of spittle seemed to hang suspended in the light. And then I was dragged down the stairs and across the veranda and down more steps into the mosquito-humming night where I was forced to kneel, advised to pray, and then Esteban pressed the muzzle of his revolver against the base of my skull, cocked it, waited and waited, and then finally pulled the trigger. A click. Amigo! He roared drunkenly, hauled me to my feet and embraced me. Dragged me back into the house for another drink.

It was a joke, you see. The girl was not his daughter after all, but only a whore he'd hired for the occasion.

Esteban was still drunk, crazily vain, and very dangerous. The louder he laughed and the more sincerely he declared himself to be my friend, the more I feared him. At dawn he slept. I dressed, sneaked outside, drove one of the farm vehicles down to the airport, and caught the first flight out of the country.

Blas had not been involved in the joke. "That's just Papa's way of kidding," he later told me.

"He's insane, Blas."

"You bet."

We flew to Chicago after the game and arrived at our hotel a little after two A.M. Blas broke the seal on a liter of rum and half filled two water glasses. He drank at least a pint of booze every night now, said that he couldn't sleep without it. He seemed near the breaking point; sometimes you could see the violence swimming around deep in his eyes.

"I don't like this town," he said. "I don't like the people. Loudmouths. They think they know it all."

I said, "Chicagoans and New Yorkers know all that is knowable. Los Angelenos know all the rest."

He lit a cigar and moodily smoked it. "Why do people call me a Mexican? I'm not a Mexican."

He nervously twisted the ends of his moustache. When he was more than usually tired, like tonight, his accents became stronger: he spoke English with a Spanish accent and Spanish with an American accent. When I first met Blas eight years ago he was a chubby, baby-faced kid; but over the years he had successfully willed himself to be lean, brown, fierce-eyed.

"Hey!" Blas said.

I looked at him.

"Are you listening?"

"Sure."

"Bullshit. You just had one of your fade-outs."

"Did I?"

Occasionally I experienced a lull in attention, a dreamy instant that was usually accompanied by déjà vu. Doc Whillans, my shrink, suggested that I might now and then be buzzed by that form of *petit mal* epilepsy called "short stare." It could be, he said, a side effect of the electroconvulsive torture I'd endured at the snakepit. My poor martyred brain.

"I asked you why people call me a Mexican when I am not Mexican."

"Mexican is a generic," I said.

"Piss on you," he said, and he went into the bathroom.

Prosper and MacDonald, Crusaders for Christ, were staying in room 1014. I dialed the extension: their phone rang five or six times and then I heard MacDonald's gentle, sleepy voice.

"Truth is stranger than crucifiction," I said, and I hung up the receiver.

My problem lately was that I was always conscious of my consciousness. At the moment, though, I didn't know if I were crazy or not, happy or not. Still, I was not bored: I knew that my sense of stasis was pure illusion. Even while I slept I was being hurtled into new realms. Time was a perpetual conveyance; whether you moved frantically or remained still, you were carried on at the same speed. Death was waiting. (I'm on the toilet, Death, I can't come out right now.) And so I was unanchored, unmoored, swept along in the cosmic drift. Free to perform good or commit evil. Free in more trivial ways as well: free to wear hideous bikini briefs beneath my trousers; free to wear a gemstone in my earlobe; free to obey commands issued by the Legion of Fear.

When Blas returned to the room I said, "I know about it. Buckley told me."

"Told you what?"

"He told me that you denounced me to the homicide detectives in New York."

"For what?"

"About the transsexual who was murdered in the hotel. The cops think I did it."

"Did you?"

"No. Of course not. Jesus. It's disloyal to ask."

"Maybe you don't remember killing the girl-guy."

"Blas, I didn't kill anyone."

"Well, would you remember if you did?"

"Certainly. My memory has been quite good lately."

"Lately, huh? Maybe so, maybe not. But how would you know if you forgot something? It's been *forgot.*"

"Do the cops really believe that I killed that creature?"

"They're very curious about you. They think the killer might be someone with the team."

"That's stupid. There must have been five hundred people staying at that Cincinnati hotel."

"Sure. But what about the one killed in Philadelphia?"

"No."

"Yes."

"No."

"Another transsexual was killed at the hotel in Philadelphia while we were staying there. Same *modus operandi,* the cops said. Sexually violated, strangled with her panty hose, and dumped down the laundry chute. They found her next morning tangled in all the bedsheets and towels. Twenty-six years old, a dental assistant. A beauty, the cops said. A really luscious transsexual person."

"Blas, this is really all crap, isn't it? Something you and Buckley cooked up to torment me with?"

"Cops said the one in Cincinnati was quite feminine, too, except she had very big hands and feet."

"Well, if . . . I'd guess Kopfhammer."

Blas chewed on his cigar. "Yeah. Maybe Fungo."

"Sure, I can see Fungo doing something like that. Maybe Buckley. Oliver is a very strange man."

"Maybe Buckley. Maybe you."

"Blas, you really don't believe that I killed anyone, do you?"

"I keep an open mind."

"You trust me enough to sleep in the same room with me."

"I ain't no transsexual," he said. "And I sleep with a gun."

Sometime before dawn I awakened with a familiar panicky buried-alive feeling. Hallucinations were materializing out there in the darkness. Spectral orchestras began to tune up.

5

Blas was gone when I awakened. I got out of bed, crossed the room, and opened the satiny gold drapes. The room was on the ninth floor. I watched the continuous flow of traffic below, cars peeling off and other cars joining the flow, and after a time it seemed that the streets were moving like conveyor belts and the vehicles upon them were motionless. Across the boulevard there was a cement walk, a low seawall, and a sandy beach. Lake Michigan stretched on until water and sky fused in a bluish haze.

After breakfast I took a taxi to the Art Institute, which was showing one of those traveling schlock exhibitions in some of the first-floor galleries. It was called Homer's Gold: The Bloody Treasure Hoard of Ancient Illium. I paid my admission and entered the first of the rooms. It was dark except for the brightly illuminated cases scattered here and there, each of which contained a few coins or pieces of jewelry lying on a bed of black velvet. The room was crowded: ordinary-looking but obviously unbalanced people stood five- and six-deep around the cases. No one spoke or moved. It was ghastly. The faces, lighted from below, seemed to float disembodied in the general gloom. I had stumbled into a convocation of the Undead. Get out of here, Theodore, before these gold-crazed shades catch a glimpse of your Patek Philippe wristwatch.

Back in my room I switched on the big RCA black hole and spun the dial. Ah. A talk show had as a guest a woman who was pregnant by artificial insemination—sci-porn at its coldest and driest reaches. Another guest, a lady psychologist who was on the show to promote her book about the tragedy of clitoral impotence (classy psy-porn), stated that artificial insemination was certaintly a viable alternative. An actor chewed on his knuckles and muttered, "Gonna put us out of business." The host, a deadly sincere fellow with cashmere hair, seemed intimidated by the women's smiling ferocity.

Smiling, "We don't really need men, you know." Gendercide!

There was an empty chair onstage and I filled it with an imaginary sperm donor, a deep-voiced macho—perhaps black—who wore an executioner's hood to conceal his identity and who talked intelligently about creativity chromosomes and sensitivity genes.

Two years ago I had appeared on the same show as a militant altruist, a fervent advocate of mental health, and as a celebrity athlete peddling myself and my ghosted autobiography, *Safe at Home*. I knew very well that sex and violence were not the only through tickets in pop-America; disease will also carry you to the end of the line. I was one of the anointed, one of the afflicted.

I switched off the black hole and tried telephoning my first wife, Patsy. She lived in Iowa. Patsy Moon. A wo-moon. A woeman. There was no response at what had once been my home, and a clerk at the bookstore told me that Patsy had gone out.

I called another ex-wife, Pamela Moon, at another former home, this one in Oregon. Ashley, my four-year-old daughter, answered the phone. The boy's name was Whitney. Pam had given them soap-opera names.

"Hello, Tadpole," I said.

"Daddy?"

"Tadpoles grow up to be ugly frogs, you know."

"It is Daddy!"

"Only I can break the evil spell, the tadpole-curse placed on you by a wicked witch." Her mother.

"Hi, Daddy."

I heard a voice in the background and then my daughter said, "It's Daddy number two, Mommy."

Daddy number two?

Pamela came on the line. "Moon?"

"Shit."

"What do you think you're doing?"

"I thought I was talking to my daughter. Put her back on the line, and then I want to speak to the little bugger, what's his name."

"Whitney doesn't talk yet."

"He says 'Daddy.' And he can say 'caca' or something, can't he? Is the kid retarded? He's nearly two years old, Pam, he should be saying 'caca' or 'bye-bye' now, shouldn't he?"

"Are you drunk?"

"Let me speak to my kids for a few minutes."

"I'm getting the children ready for their naps."

"Naps! They'll get narcoleptic if you let them lay around all the time."

"Moon. . . ."

"Listen, what is this Daddy number two crap? Are you really teaching my kids to regard me as Daddy number two? I'm their biological father, Pam, remember that. Who's Daddy number one, that creepy dentist with the long black hairs in his nose and ears? Look, if he's going to be regarded as Daddy number one then let him start paying some of the bills."

"I won't talk to you when you're like this."

"But I don't want to talk to you, I want to talk to my kids."

"Moon, isn't it about time you finally faced the truth? You're no good at nurturing and parenting."

The line went dead. My ex-wife; the mother of my ex-children. It was not the lack of justice that I minded; it was the lack of shame for the lack of justice. I resolved to kidnap the kids someday, when both could feed and wipe themselves and carry on an intelligent conversation.

I telephoned a woman in Newport Beach, California, an actress whom I had met while *Safe at Home* was being made into a television movie.

Five rings and then, "Hello?"

"Hi, baby," I said. "I've been thinking about you."

"And I've been thinking about you."

"What have you been doing, Carole?"

"Oh, you know, the usual."

"I'll be in L.A. in a few days. I want to see you."

"Mmmm. And I want to see you," she said.

"I yearn. I lust."

"Me too." A pause. "Is this Russell or Damon?"

"Come on now. Jesus."

She laughed. "I was only teasing. Hi, Moon."

"Were you really just teasing?"

"Of course."

"My vanity has been taking a beating lately."

"I'll baby your vanity. I'll pet it, I'll kiss it."

"Have you been good, Carole?"

"Ain't misbehaving. How about you?"

"I live like a monk."

"Yeah, Rasputin."

"Not so. I really need to see you. Abstinence makes the heart grow fonder."

"Have you been taking care of yourself?"

"Sort of."

"Eating well?"

"Pizzas and hamburgers and eggs and Beechnut tobacco. And steaks, slabs of meat so undercooked that the blood is still circulating."

"God, honestly Ted, please."

"Don't start."

"Really, you must learn to eat well. There's a delicate balance between psyche and soma. Both require scientifically valid nurture."

"I'm not listening."

"You're going to listen because I love you. Okay? So then listen. We ingest more than the simple vitamins and minerals and nutrients—we take into our being the spiritual traces of the foods we eat."

"That's true of you neo-Hindus, Carole, but I'm a pagan. Pagans got to have blood."

"Just listen. Eating animals is a barbarity not easily forgiven by either psyche or soma."

"I'm becoming depressed."

"People should be careful about what they put into their bodies."

"I should hope so. God yes. And they should be careful about what they put into their brains too."

"Please? For me, Ted? Stay away from junk foods."

"You ought to take that junk-food routine on the road. To Calcutta, maybe, or Ethiopia."

"That's not fair."

"We play four games against the Dodgers. Do you want me to get tickets for you?"

"Of course, yes."

"I miss you."

"And I miss you."

"Goodbye."

"Bye."

I telephoned Pamela's lover, the dentist, and persuaded his assistant to put him on the line.

"Dr. Abernathy here."

"Doc, you sleazy reptile, you absorb sunlight and piss darkness. You rub against schoolgirls who are helpless in your dentist's chair. Your nose is full of black hairs."

He laughed and said, "Hello, Moon, how are you doing?"

"Pretty good." I slammed down the telephone.

I turned on the black hole and watched part of the afternoon movie, a repeat of a television adaptation of *Billy Budd.* The story's appeal was broadened, so to speak, by changing the young sailor into a nubile, impish tomboy who was only masquerading as a man. She wore baggy male clothing, her hair was cut ragamuffin style, and she worked aloft as bravely as any of the tough crewmen.

I knew that there was no hope that Captain Vere would hang the perky little bitch and so I turned off the

black hole. Now I could hear impatient knocking at the
door. Hard knuckles on thin paneling, brisk, confident
raps, authoritative. That's how the Gestapo knocked on
doors.

6

I went to the door and looked through the spy tube: a man and a woman, their faces distorted by the lense, were standing in the hallway. Gargoyles. The man smirked and wriggled his fingers at the peephole.

I opened the door as far as the chain allowed. They held up police shields.

"Detective Sullivan," the man said. "Chicago PD."

"Detective Russo, Angela Patricia."

Emissaries from the dreaded Legion of Fear.

"You are Theodore Moon?"

"Yes, but you may call me scumbag."

Sullivan smiled. "That's how cops talk in the movies."

"A scumbag is a used condom," Angela Russo said. "We don't address citizens in such derogatory terms."

"May we come in for a moment? We are pursuing an inquiry."

I unchained the door and let them in. Angela Patricia Russo sat at the desk. She was plump, with black hair and soft brown long-lashed eyes. Sullivan stood with his back to the window. Perhaps he had stationed himself there to prevent me from crashing through the glass in a spectacular defenestration. He watched me, teasing the ends of his walrus moustache.

I sat on the edge of my bed. "Can I get you anything from room service?" I asked. "Coffee, a drink, a thousand dollars in tens and twenties?"

"Nice environment," Sullivan said. "Ninth floor, high enough to shut out most of the traffic noise. Close to the elevators, the refreshment alcove, the fire escape, the laundry chute."

"I never killed a transsexual in my life," I said.

"We aren't accusing you of any such deed. We are here merely to conduct some interviews at the behest of fellow police officers in other cities."

"Our brethren," Russo said.

"She screamed," I said. "I had to stop her screams, didn't I?"

"They told us he was a madcap, didn't they, Angela? They warned us."

"A master of merriment," Russo said. "A whirling dervish of quips and pranks and wildly demented fun."

I realized that I was gnawing at the calluses on the first and second fingers of my right hand, my pitching hand. I stopped. Those calluses were precious.

I said, "Have you talked to anyone else? Or am I the only suspect?"

"We intend to talk to some of your teammates and camp followers. But you aren't suspects—you're wrong there, sir. You aren't a suspect, Theodore. You are a citizen assisting the police in their official inquiry."

"Talk to Kopfhammer for sure," I said.

Russo removed a notebook and pen from her purse. "Again."

"Kopfhammer." I spelled the name. "And Fungo Gates. Blas Cintron, my roommate. Buckley. And Frank Prosper—I think that Prosper is probably your perp. Repressed guy, very religious, loves his mother too much. One of those spooky loners who one day picks up his assault rifle and goes off to a rendezvous with death."

"Cincinnati," Sullivan said. "New York. And now Philadelphia. Philadelphia, Hotel Louis XVII, August nine, the morning of, between the hours of midnight and five A.M. or thereabouts. Did you see anything unusual, Theodore? Hear anything that raises the hair on the back of your neck when you think back on it?"

"No."

"Were you in fact in your hotel room that night during the hours specified?"

"We played a night game. After the game I had dinner alone, got back to the hotel at about one."

"Can your roommate, Mr. Cintron, verify that?"

"No. Blas rarely shows up before five A.M. after a night game. After a day game too, for that matter."

"Have you ever dated a transsexual, Theodore?"

"Not to my knowledge."

"What about transvestites?"

"What about them?"

"You sound angry," Russo said from the desk.

"I'm not angry."

"When Phil used the words 'transsexual' and 'transvestite' your expression changed."

"It did not."

"It did so. Your voice changed too."

Sullivan chewed some moustache hairs for a time and

then he quietly said, "Do you despise transsexuals, Theodore?"

"No."

"Loathe them, regard them as like . . . like dirty laundry?"

"No."

"Ah. Then you love them."

"No."

"Which is it, Theodore?"

"Neither."

Russo smiled at her partner. "He hasn't been able to resolve the raging conflict, Phil."

"I don't have a raging conflict."

Sullivan was alert now. "No?" he said. "But isn't it true that on two separate occasions you were locked up for maniacal activities?"

"No."

"What? You categorically state that you are not a certified maniac?"

"That's *manic*, for God's sake. I have been diagnosed as suffering from manic-depressive illness. Though nowadays we prefer to call it bipolar mood disorder."

"Does this bipolar mood disorder refer to transsexuality?"

"No. For Christ's sake, no."

"He got angry again, Phil," Russo said. "The t-word."

These two cops reminded me of Oliver Buckley and Blas Cintron on those occasions when they united to torment me. Was this some kind of bizarre practical joke? Had my teammates hired a pair of actors—perhaps from the Second City improv group—to drive me deeper into dementia?

"You two don't seem like cops," I said.

Russo nodded. "We're the new breed of law officer,"

she said. "We're educated, articulate. We're warm, open, and caring."

"And we're tough," Sullivan said. "We can gun down a miscreant or deliver a baby."

"We practice holistic law enforcement."

It was silent then. Sullivan turned to look out the window. Angela Russo tapped the pencil's eraser against her front incisors. Tick tick tick. It was hot in the room.

"It was self-defense," I said.

Sullivan turned. "Tiffany, in Cincinnati. LaMenta in New York. And now Philadelphia. You were in all three cities, pal."

"So were millions of others."

"Tell him how we access it, Phil."

"We access it this way. A guy, a masculine guy, a male athlete, meets a girl in Cincinnati. Thinks she's a girl. Is a girl, actually, though not very long ago she was a man. A damned good-looking woman too. A charming woman. A sexy woman if you don't know that she was once a fellow named Edward."

Russo picked up the narrative. "Now, our athlete's not *always* a macho prick. He has a decent side. Married a couple of times, has a couple of kids, plays baseball, plays baseball for big bucks, may or may not have experienced bipolar mood disorder in the past. He meets our girl. How do you like the scenario so far, Mr. Moon?"

"What did Edward change his name to? Edwina?"

"Tiffany."

It was Sullivan's turn to carry the ball. "They meet, our hero and heroine. There is a powerful mutual attraction. They chat, they tease, maybe they dance. La la là. They like each other. The sexual tension is excruciating. They have a late dinner."

"Salad," Russo said. "Dover sole, saffron rice, asparagus tips. According to the autopsy report."

Sullivan continued. "They go to the guy's hotel room on—let us say—the twelfth floor. They have a couple of drinks. They disrobe. Her skin is like glowing alabaster. Her breasts look breathtakingly real. She is gorgeous in the moon-drenched ambiance."

"They fuck," Detective Russo said.

"Right, they fuck. And afterward they maybe smoke a joint and talk. They possess a special rapport. They are mutually supportive as they cuddle in their postcoital triste. The woman confesses that she is a guy who recently had a sex-change operation. What happens? The macho athlete runs amuck. Doesn't that sound logical, Theodore? He has just boffed a girl who eighteen months ago was a hairy, sweaty male. He is outraged. This is too close to dreaded homosexual activity for a man of unresolved conflicts. All of his elaborate repressions and defenses have been violated. In his rage, he takes her panty hose from the floor and . . ."

". . . And the nightmare commences," Russo said.

It was a good story. They watched me carefully.

I said, "All right, that's Cincinnati. What about New York? Does the guy pick up another transsexual by accident? Not likely, Sherlock."

"No," Sullivan said. "This time it's deliberate. He is a hunter now, a predator. He has tasted the forbidden fruit. He kills, and kills again. He goes looking for transsexuals. Maybe there's a place in New York where they congregate, a transsexual cafe. He finds her. LaMenta."

They watched me.

"It was an accident," I said.

"We wonder," Sullivan said, "if you would be willing to come down to the station with us."

"Am I under arrest?"

"No, no, it's purely voluntary."

"Then I won't go."

"This is a laugher, Theodore. We're goofing off today. We're just killing time, chiseling the taxpayers. It will be a fun afternoon. We'll take you through the Cook County Jail and show you some real bad guys, maniacs. Pardon me. You can meet our captain later and chat with the boys. Just sit around, bullshit, you know. Tell riotously funny cop stories. How about it?"

"I don't think so."

"It's strictly up to you, Mr. Moon," Angela Russo said. "Say the word and we're out of here."

"The word."

"Look," Sullivan said, "we'll drive you through some rotten neighborhoods, prowl around the Projects in a police vehicle. We'll let you operate the lights and siren."

I was tempted.

"Come on, we'll go down to the station and take a few samples and then we'll bug out and have some zesty cop fun."

"What kind of samples?"

He chuckled. "Oh, nothing much, don't worry. Some hairs."

"Some scalp hairs and pubic hairs," Russo said.

"And torso hairs. A leg hair, you know. Maybe the lab guys will vacuum your body if you don't object. That's about it."

"No fingerprints?" I asked.

"Hey, yeah," Sullivan said. "Now that you mention it."

Russo nodded slowly. "Phil—just a notion—but while he's there he could maybe give us a sample of his saliva." To me she said, "You just spit into a paper cup. Anybody can do it."

"And that's all?" I asked.

They looked at each other.

Sullivan said, "Maybe the lab guys will want to scrape your fingernails."

"It's like a free manicure," Russo said.

Sullivan slapped his cheek gently. "Shit, I forgot."

"Blood," I said.

"They won't invade a vein," Russo said. "Maybe just prick your earlobe or something."

"And then what?" I said.

"That's all."

"Phil . . ."

"I promise, Theodore."

"Phil, you forgot . . ."

"Yep, I forgot again."

"He doesn't have to do it."

"Of course not. No one has to cooperate. This is America."

I said, "You want to biopsy my liver?"

Sullivan laughed. "Naw, nothing like that."

"Forget it," Russo said. "It was just an idea."

"It's only, maybe you could give us a little sperm. A squirt of the old seminal fluid."

"The lab guys give you a jar," Russo said, "and a dirty magazine if you need one."

I stood up. "Well . . ."

I walked them to the door. When they were out in the hall I said, "Sorry I couldn't be of more assistance."

"Thanks anyway, you snotty scumbag," Russo said.

I closed, locked, and chained the door, then went back and turned on the black hole. The local news was on. The anchorman, a superior specimen of the Undead, was saying, "Two people were killed and one was injured in the blaze."

I sneaked past the beds and bathroom and down to the door, and placed my right eye to the peephole. A huge, magnified eye, pathologically dilated, stared back at me.

The network news came on. There was ten minutes of a war taking place somewhere, and then a reporter from the affiliate in Philadelphia appeared on the screen. He was standing in front of a hotel. A murdered transsexual, Courtney Corbett, nee Charley Clabbert, had been found buried beneath half a ton of dirty bed linen in the basement laundry room. Courtney had been sexually violated and then strangled with her own wide-mesh panty hose. This was the third such transsexual murder during the last week. A new serial killer had arrived on the American scene. A psychological profile of the murderer indicated that he was probably a man suffering from unresolved conflicts. An FBI spokesman advised all transsexuals to take special precautions during the days and weeks to come.

I jumped up and returned to the door. The eye was gone. I went out into the hallway. The laundry chute was located in a recessed section of the wall: to the right and left were doors, one to a broom closet and the other opening into a small room containing a sink and mop buckets. The visible part of the chute was an aluminum strip about a yard wide. I opened the oven-type door and stuck my head inside the shaft. My breathing was amplified by the empty vertical space. I looked up, wary of descending laundry. Looked down. You could not see very far but the chute probably ran the entire height of the building.

Laundry dropped from the floors above might fall past with a hissing whisper. A transsexual, falling at thirty-two feet per second and accelerating, would rush by with a reverberant bang and clatter, a tinny din. I wondered: say a citizen was passing along the corridor at the same instant a body hurtled noisily down the chute—would the citizen be able to observe the Döppler effect?

I barricaded myself in the room, crawled into bed, and pulled the covers up to my chin. I was innocent, probably.

Young galguys plunging down laundry chutes. I wondered if I had ever unknowingly boffed a lithesome transsexual. How many were out there, anyway? Sitting demurely in bars and restaurants, walking tap-tap-tap in their high-heeled shoes while the wind lifted their skirts, standing hip-shot on street corners, at the beach posing provocatively in French-cut swimming suits. Flaunting their hormonally and surgically altered bodies to unstable men. Tempting men made dangerous by unresolved conflicts.

Tiffany, LaMenta, and now Courtney. Who was next?

I was starting to breathe whoop-whoop-whoop, asthmatic with anxiety. Please. I wouldn't hurt a fly. I picked up the telephone and punched out the extension numbers to Red Girt's room.

Three rings and then he said something like, "Hah. Rad chere. Watcher doon?"

"Leroy?"

"Yar."

"I saw you, Leroy. I saw you there at the laundry chute. You son of a bitch, she was just a sweet little thing, she never meant nobody no harm."

"Moon? Is that you, Moon?"

I hung up the telephone. Every demento knew how to transfer his guilt and fear to another. It's a survival tactic.

Now I could sleep while Red muttered in Oklahomese and paranoidally paced his room.

I awakened with a monumental signal of virility. Patience, noble root.

7

~~~

I groomed myself with precision; dressed with insidious intent. Cruel gunfighter's moustache, boyishly tousled hair, a cologne—Lord Byron—whose scent was reputed to cause the instant lubrication of female loins. Loafers, gray slacks, pale blue shirt, red-striped tie, and a blue blazer. A pocket handkerchief for display and for drying tears. You have shot the Moon, my dear . . . henceforth life will be without savor.

It was only eight-fifty. I decided to investigate the hotel's two lounges; it was not rare for females to seek the company of swift, clean-limbed athletes at the source, so to speak, only an elevator ride away from Moonglow.

Oliver Buckley was on the elevator when it stopped at my floor. Today he was wearing one of his many Salvation Army suits; he bought clothes at mission shops in slums all over the country. This was a charcoal chalk-striped double-breasted suit from the thirties. With it he wore spats and a gray fedora. A gold chain dangled from vest pocket to vest pocket.

The doors hissed shut and we began to descend.

He said, "Do you have an agenda?"

"What? Agenda? No, but I got concepts."

He shook his head.

"I got concepts, scenarios, criteria. I got goals, realistic goals."

"Won't do. Report immediately to your Agenda Control Authority."

The door hissed open and I was decanted into the lobby. A man and a woman entered the elevator and, as the doors were sliding shut, I heard Buckley say, "Sir? Madam? Do you have—"

Kopfhammer was sitting alone in a jungle of potted plants. He smiled when he saw me, swiftly stood up and approached.

"Hey, Moon, do you want to go to a movie?"

"No, sorry, I read the comic book."

Dick Kopfhammer was a huge, dumb towhead who had taken a liking to me; he told others that I was his best friend on the club, a great guy, and would be his best man when he got married in November. This was inexplicable since I hardly knew the kid and didn't want to know him better. Even more baffling, when drunk Kopfhammer went berserk and tried to kill me. He never remembered the dark side of this duality.

"Do you want to go out to dinner with me, Moon?"

"Sorry, I've got an appointment. In fact"—I shot my cuff and frowned at the Patek Philippe—"I'm late. Some other time, Hammer."

I figured the odds at nine to five that Kopfhammer would soon be arrested for killing the transsexuals. He was a brute. Last spring he'd confessed to me that he had raped "a half-dozen or so" women since puberty. ("But they weren't sex crimes, Moon. They were crimes of violence.")

I tried the Blue Room first. Yes, a trim girl in a print sundress sat alone at the bar.

I sat on the stool next to her. I smiled. "This air-conditioning is not good for my arm."

"Oh?"

"I'm a baseball player."

"Are you really?"

"Yes."

"You look like one."

"I am one."

"You aren't a Cubbie."

"No."

"What is your name?"

"Oliver Buckley."

"Oh, yes." She nodded vaguely, uncrossed and recrossed her legs. She was short of tooth and long of leg.

"Most people call me Buck."

"Okay . . . Buck. My name is Terri, with an *i.*"

"Can I buy you a drink, Terri?"

"Well . . . all right. Thank you, Buck."

Few women, even athlete-stalkers, were eager to meet let alone copulate with the unpredictable Teddy Moon. They presumed that it would be an ugly encounter even if they escaped alive and unmutilated. (Though I did have my own kind of female fan, women who wrote me long, incoherent letters in crayon, and who usually enclosed peculiar amulets or kinks of pubic hair or Polaroid snatchshots.) I thought that someday, sooner or later, I would manage to get Oliver Buckley involved in a paternity suit.

"And what do you do, Terri?"

"Actually, I'm an educator."

A schoolteacher. "I see that you're married."

"What? Oh, my rings. Well, you see, I am married but my husband and I are presently in the process of divorce. We failed to relate in the deepest man-woman context and so . . . but Earl's been very supportive."

"Any kids?"

She shook her head and daintily licked the Old Fashioned dew from her upper lip. "No, Earl and I decided to postpone the regenerative process until we both had established our own complete and separate identities."

"Ah."

"The trouble was," she went on, "Earl is predominantly a left-brain person while I am right brain."

"I see."

"I am a creative person."

"I can tell that you are," I said with greasy sympathy. She was pleased. "Really? How can you tell?"

"It's like an aura around you. A creative glow."

"I think you are a sensitive man."

"Yes, I believe that is true."

"Do you ever cry?"

"Often, copiously."

"Earl never cried. Earl isn't vulnerable, and that's why I had to leave him. I can see that you are a vulnerable man."

"Indeed."

Fresh drinks arrived and she removed the plastic sword and gently nibbled the fruit—snick snick snick—with her little white teeth, like milk teeth, and her upper lip was cutely everted. Her lower lip was rosy and plump, a fat jalapeño pepper, inviting my teeth. Pink gums and tongue. No evidence of pyorrhea.

"Earl is a goal-oriented person while I am people-oriented. I'm interested in the individual human ecology."

"God yes," I said.

"I'm enhancing my human contacts now. I'm networking."

"God yes! Listen, Terri, the musicians will be starting soon. Let's go up to my room where we can seriously talk—dialogue, interface. Discuss parameters and things. I like to talk to creative souls."

"I find it difficult to resist charisma."

"I've got a bottle, and if you're hungry I can send out for egg rolls or something."

"Egg rolls! Oh, I love egg rolls. I love Oriental food. I love all things Oriental, the food, the culture, the straw hats, acupuncture . . . I'm Orient-oriented."

"How about it, Terri?"

She smiled. "I can't say no to an Alpha male."

We necked in the elevator. She was squirmy and her mouth tasted of maraschino cherries and Angostura bitters.

The room was hot. I telephoned the hotel services and ordered ice and mix. Terri prowled the room like a visiting cat, exploring closets and corners, sniffing, looking into the bathroom and beneath the beds. Satisfied, she kicked off her shoes, turned up the air conditioner, and opened the drapes. Blas's portable radio was on the table; she intently twisted the dial until finding the station she wanted.

> *I'm gonna beat them ideas*
> *Outta your head,*
> *Gonna beat them strangers*
> *Outta your bed.*

> *Gonna beat this game*
> *Called looooove.*

"Johnny Midnight," she said. "A poet of the streets."

"A savage troubadour," I said. "An apostle of senti-mental nihilism."

She smiled. "I like the way you talk."

"So do I. You should hear me when I really get going, Terri. I'm a motor mouth." That was true: when manic I was possessed by *furor loquendi,* and was then always fluent, often eloquent, and sometimes intelligible.

> *Ain't gonna hit you no more,*
> *No, baby, no.*
> *Gonna hit the road.*

The bellman arrived. I mixed two potent drinks. She sat on one bed and I on the other. Our knees touched. We chatted. We related, maybe even bonded.

Terri believed that some men and women were the seed of ancient astronauts, and a few of these hybrids still tread our own ecological planet. Jesus and Shakespeare and John Lennon were such men. She showed me her thumbs. Extra-long thumbs were a sign of godblood. My mind wandered. Patience, noble root. The California disease had metastasized throughout the body politic. And then I heard her say, "I was ashamed of my own body. I had to learn how to get in touch with my body."

"I'd like to get in touch with it, Terri."

She smiled.

"You're a state-of-the-art tomato. I'd like to invade your space and provide you with a little quality time. I'd like to pay homage to your individual human ecosystem. You require a little hands-on management."

"You really talk strange."

"I'd like to give you a little data input. I'd like to vector your sector and expand your conceptual mode."

My smooth lewd patter aroused her.

"It's terribly hot in here."

"Let us shed our superfluous garments," I yelled, and I removed my blazer, tie, and shirt. "Clothing is basically totalitarian—left brain." I took off my shoes, socks, and trousers. "What are we trying to hide?"

She gracefully stripped down to her pants and bra.

"Aphrodite," I crooned.

"Let's dance, Buck."

"You bet."

She danced well, lithe and cool, self-intent. She moved over to the window and watched her reflection in the glass, and then turned and danced past the beds. She slowly, erotically advanced toward the full-length mirror on the door, moving in tempo with both the radio music and a subtler interior rhythm. I could see a shadow of pubic hair through her translucent white panties. Hallelujah!

I got up and began my own clumsy ape-dance. I followed her and suddenly my image appeared in the mirror, a hulking apparition. We both watched her reflection. I leaned down and lightly bit her shoulder. Yum. She twisted away and danced lightly, leisurely across the room.

"Boogie," I said. "Boogie boogie."

I ducked into the bathroom, took my overdue dose of lithium, smeared my armpits with deodorant, then boogied down the room and rejoined my Terri. Lawdy, Lawdy.

"Ain't this fine, honey?" I said.

We paused, sweating, while the disk jockey read a cou-

ple of commercials (Terri's body now still, her face blank,
as she awaited reanimation), and then the jockey played
a hit by the new English group, Corpse; Terri snapped
her fingers one two three and then swiftly went through
gears until she had achieved full kinesthetic expression. It
was wonderful.

Terri removed her pants and bra, I bailed out of my
bikini briefs. We indulged in a simulated—no touching—
copulation. My root saluted. She edged past me and
danced down the carpet. At ease, soldier, this isn't pay-
day. I followed her smooth, rounded haunches down toward the mirror.

> I was keepin' faith, baby,
> But you was keepin' score.

Yin and yang, we danced. Finally, sweating and shiv-
ering, we tumbled onto one of the beds and coupled
fiercely—pelvic assault.

"It was great," I said. "It was never better."

She was too joyously depleted to reply.

We showered together (she was without visible herpes
stigmata), returned to the bed, and enjoyed a restrained,
contemplative reprise.

"That was right-brain humping, Terri," I said.

Just before leaving she looked in her purse and cried,
"My God, what a fool!—I don't have enough money for
taxi fare."

I gave her one hundred dollars. She lived far out in the
Northern suburbs.

I turned on the black hole and watched the David Letterman show. His guests tonight were dull: an hysterical
comedienne and the author of a diet book. It was much
more fun to be a guest on the Letterman show—or any

other show—than to watch it. This was the wrong side of the camera. Here and now I was one man, time-and space-bound, but on that show my image had been divided into twenty million homunculi. Twenty million Moons had been spectrally reassembled on twenty million bright screens. One weak man had become a powerful mob. It was only multiplication but it felt like immortality.

Still, I had not given one of my better performances on the Letterman program. I was last out, and my manic filibuster had been frequently interrupted by commercials. Also, I had appeared with Burt Reynolds and Mother Teresa; there was no chance that I could shine among stars of that magnitude—supernovas.

I turned off the black hole and walked over to crank open a window. The lights, white and red, were an intricate braid on the street below, and I could hear the rumble of traffic and, somewhere to the south, the wailing of a siren. The whole city seemed to be throbbing. The air smelled of deadly chemicals. There would be sex tonight; hundreds of new citizens would be conceived in cars and rooms and parks and tenement hallways. And there would be blood spilled, gallons of it, as duels were fought all over the great city—sordid *affaires d'honneur*.

All of the lady psychologists were in their sleeping environments now: they were enjoying a sleeping experience, they were relating to their mattresses. Politicians slept with rictal grins and open hands. Elderly night watchmen slept in hard chairs, their gummy tortoise eyes slowly opening and closing at ten-minute intervals. Members of the Legion of Fear never slept.

I didn't sleep either, for a long time. I anxiously wondered if cute little Terri was a transsexual. Doubt had entered the Garden of Eden. Life would never be the same.

8

When I awakened all of the room lights were on and Blas, who wore a wrinkled three-piece suit, was smoking a cigar and muttering. "Jerk," he said. "Freak."

I was reminded of some advice by Marcus Aurelius: "Begin the morning by saying to thyself, I shall meet with the busybody, the ungrateful, arrogant, deceitful, envious, unsocial."

Blas ceased pacing when he saw that I was awake. He leveled the barrel of his cigar at me.

"Why are you in my bed?"

"This is my bed."

"Why is the other bed rumpled? What are those stains?"

"They're Rorschach blots. What do you read in them?"

He tilted his head. "Premature ejaculation."

I laughed.

"Moon, you soil your bed, you lie in it."

He resumed pacing. Beard stubble speckled his chin and cheeks. His moustache had not been trimmed in a week. He had that haggard, desperate look that you see on men in police photographs.

"What time is it?" I asked.

"Six-thirty."

"What evils did you commit last night?"

"The usual—drunkenness, fornication, blasphemy, bearing false witness. . . ."

"The evils of banality. Are you still drunk?"

"Yeah, but coming down."

"Which do you like more, Blas, the nighttime debauch or the daytime remorse?"

Eyes narrowed, he puffed his cigar. "Who was the whore?"

"She wasn't a whore, exactly. No sir. She was a moon-lighting schoolteacher. A user-friendly bimbo. A priest-ess of Negative Meaning."

"I don't want to hear any of that Oliver Buckley bull-shit."

"Right," I said. "Oliver can be a bore."

"I was with a girl too. I picked her up when I was drunk. This morning—she was ugly. But clean, anyway, very clean."

"Fasthideous," I said.

"Do you need to use the bathroom? I got to shower and shave."

"Why now? Where are you going?"

"To Mass."

"Do you want to have breakfast first?"

"No."

"Do you intend to eat God on an empty stomach?"

"Enough, please." He stared pensively at the ash on his cigar and then, without looking at me, said, "My father is going to be in Los Angeles when we get there."

"Thanks for warning me."

"Moon, I know you don't like my father. I guess I can't blame you after what he did. But remember that he was drunk."

"Sure, Blas."

"He's not the way you think he is."

"What way is he?"

"He's really a great guy."

"Good old Esteban."

Blas went into the bathroom.

Until the night of my mock execution Esteban had been courteous, even friendly in that formal and over-solicitous Latin American way. Honor depends in part on one's hospitality. But Esteban did not wholly subscribe to that civilized code.

He was a widower. No one I met during my visit ever mentioned his wife, Blas's mother, an eerily beautiful adolescent whose picture hung in every room of the hacienda. She had borne Blas at fifteen, Blas's sister at sixteen, and had died of typhoid at seventeen. Sometimes, looking at her photograph, I had sentimentally imagined her to be alive, a nun perhaps, now safely cloistered in some ancient stone convent.

One day we were sitting on the veranda, and he said, "I am a ver' sad man, yes sir, a ver' unhappy man, a tragic life have I lived."

It was a smoky tropical twilight, hushed and humid and hot, the perspective so flattened that the mountains appeared to be a single translucent chain rather than several chains with each higher than the preceding. Fires burned below us, geometrically lighting and shadowing the workers' shack village. I could smell coffee and burning animal fats.

"Ver' tragic, yes sir."

"Yes?" I said, only half listening.

"Greatly have I suffered."

I made a noise in my throat.

"Hugely, desperately, tragically. Like Jesus have I suffered. Like sweet Jesus on the cross nailed."

I looked at him.

"The life she tastes like vinegar."

I laughed then. At the time I thought he was merely an upper-level bureaucrat, a grafting functionary. I did not sense his power because it was not personal; he possessed little force as a man, only that which the state and his enormous wealth had conferred on him. And I had failed to intuit his intelligence, his cunning. I saw him as a clown. I laughed, and he stared at me, his upper lip peeled back as if he shared my mirth, and I believe it was then that he planned my "execution."

Blas was still in the shower. I dressed, took an elevator down to the lobby where I bought the two daily newspapers, and went into the coffee shop. I defiantly consumed two breakfasts of ham, eggs, toast, and coffee. Trichina. Caffeine. Cholesterol.

Tempo, the *Tribune*'s feature section, had a long article about the lasting psychological damage incurred by teenaged victims of incest. There were several luridly described case histories and an illustration of a luscious little Lolita cowering in her frilly froufrou bed. A huge sinister shadow was projected on the wall behind her. Here comes Daddy! It was superb child porn. It made the reader wish that he could establish a meaningful incestuous relationship. Perhaps I ought to visit my sister after the season. Get drunk and kick down her bedroom door.

"Hey, come on, Nance, don't knock it until you've tried it."

On the religion page I read about a minister who practiced and preached the "theology of self-esteem." Feeling good about yourself, Jesus?

In the *Sun Times*'s Living section there was a piece about a man who died of cancer, but not before videotaping sixty hours of bathetic instruction for his young children. The man seemed to presume that he would be both dead and alive: "I'll be watching you all the time, and loving you, and praying for you. . . ." Just what the kids needed: a didactic ghost, a visible and audible superego. A vulture eating their brains.

What's on the tube tonight?

Pop, you know, telling us we got to take good care of Ma and each other.

Okay, you roll a joint, I'll make the popcorn.

The waitress, a weary woman in her seventies with yellow hair and a carmine mouth, asked if everything was all right.

"Perfect," I said. "I'm ready to face the world."

"I'm glad someone is," she said. "Face it for me too, will you, honey?"

"Done," I said. I left her a twenty-dollar tip. I earned more money than was decent; and I half believed that dollars were negotiable in the spiritual realm. Generosity was a hedge against the rancorous forces that manifested themselves in my nightmares.

9

It was one of those clear, bright days that commence as October and gradually retreats to August. Deep blue sky, an angled sun, long shadows. I fooled around in the outfield during batting practice, jogging a little, chewing grass, running under easy fly balls and screaming, "I got it! I got it!" and letting the ball bounce twenty feet behind me. "Way to go, Kopfhammer," the other pitchers yelled. "Nice, Hammer, thanks again." Young Kopfhammer turned routine fly balls into doubles and triples. Then he whined: the sun, the lights, the wind, a goofy spin on the ball, fate. Why me?

Nearby Jonah Hardy fielded a line drive on the first hop, lobbed the ball toward the infield, and walked my way. He was a big man with a disproportionately small head and an Adam's apple like a goiter.

"Gawd, Moon, what is this stuff?"

"What stuff?"

"Gawd, all this horrible scummy, slick green stuff all over the ground."

"Grass. That's grass, babe."

"Guh-rass."

"Grass."

"Grrrasss."

"Better."

"But what they do with the plastic?"

"Well, grass is a kind of plastic, big guy. An experimental plastic, one might say, one of nature's lamentable errors. This is a backward town and they still use grass in Wrigley Field."

"What's that stuff over there?"

"What stuff? Where?"

"That slimy green stuff on the wall."

"Oh, that's ivy."

"But Gawd, it's kind of wet and . . . nasty . . . and like . . . like it's alive!"

"You're a dupe of the old pathetic fallacy, babe. You're a simple lout. But I don't hate you—I pity you."

Jonah had a trick of making bird chirping noises deep in his throat. He sneered at me and then chirped all the way into the batting cage.

I got along well with the blacks on the team: most of them regarded my psychotic episodes as a cunning form of rebellion.

Jonah had played a small role in my first crack-up, the one that became known as The Story. A few years ago I had been standing in the outfield with him and he'd said, "I'm gonna hit a couple of home runs today for sick kids." I said, "That's noble, big guy." "Yeah, I'm gonna pop one for a pale leukemic, jerk one for a paraplegic. But, Moon—did you ever stop to think that the pitcher's mound looks like a grave?" I considered that while he continued. "It's a terrible responsibility. Did you ever wonder where they put all the sick and crippled kids who were promised a home run and the hero failed to deliver?"

Now there was nothing unusual about this exchange; it was the standard wry bullshit; but at that time all of the seams in my life were beginning to open and the world was pouring in—I was ripe for an obsession.

Two days later I went out to pitch a couple of innings and I saw that Jonah was right; the pitcher's mound did look like a fresh grave, and the seventeen-by-four-inch rubber resembled a small marble slab that had not yet been engraved with the name and dates. And for a moment I imagined, I saw, a crippled child beneath my feet, a pathetically pale boy with dirt in his mouth and eyes.

We completed our first circuit of the league. I pitched badly. My obsession expanded, multiplied: crippled children beneath the mounds at Montreal and Pittsburgh and San Francisco; an old Confederate soldier in Atlanta; a young bride, clutching her bouquet of chrysanthemums, in Cincinnati; a distinguished old gentleman who wore a tuxedo and top hat in St. Louis; Madame Curie—somehow—beneath the mound in Houston; and at home the worst, a tangled pile of emaciated, charred corpses, the victims of some unimaginable atrocity.

It was there, at home, that I came in to relieve Berry in the eighth, threw two wild pitches and left the mound. I walked in circles, squeezed the rosin bag, spat, adjusted my cap, rubbed the baseball, and then tried to sneak back to the grave. But I couldn't; my legs rebelled.

Rizzo called time, removed his mask and walked out to me. "What's wrong?" I shook my head; how could I explain that I considered it a desecration to throw baseballs from on top of a mass grave, the site of one of our nihilistic twentieth-century crimes?

The infielders drifted toward me, Fossey, Blas, Garcia, Brieschke. The pitching coach came out, then Fungo, and then the home umpire. I pushed through them toward the mound but my feet halted at the incline. I looked down at the marble slab—the rubber—and saw that it was blank like all the others. The crowd was jeering now. The players and umpire were impatient. I searched for a friend among the ring of cold faces. Blas! My friend, my roommate, seemed to be gazing sympathetically at me. I grabbed his arm and led him away.

"Blas," I said, "listen." And I lowered my voice because I suspected that the murderer might be a member of the team or an umpire. "Blas, there are bodies buried beneath the pitcher's mound. It's a grave."

He stared at me, grimacing with what I assumed to be revulsion and moral outrage, and then he smiled. He looked intently at me, smiling, and then he staggered off like a wounded man, howling with laughter.

That was the beginning of The Story, of which the graves were only a part. I learned to embellish The Story with a few authentic details and many perverse comic inventions. I wished to please. Eventually The Story slipped away from me and became the property of others, many others, and even a fat commercial enterprise. And so, with my complicity, an internal revolution was turned into The Story, and I was denied what might have been a significant experience. My second crack-up was much more fun but just as futile.

I saw Braverman jogging toward me.

"Get thee behind me!" I said, making the sign of the cross with my forearms.

"Fungo wants to see you."

"Where is he?"

"In the clubhouse office."

"Fungo is always on my ass."

"Fungo is a mad dog. Fungo really should be exterminated, Moon."

Since I was certifiably crazy, the players believed that I could be induced to murder Fungo. (Kill him, Moon! Don't be shy. You can do it. Kill the son of a bitch!)

Jim Gates was almost as broad as he was tall. He had a spade jaw, a wide mouth, and tiny, watery blue eyes. He looked like a fat troll, a cruel troll. Fungo was a petty dictator, a management lickspittle, a hairy bowlegged missing link.

He was waiting for me in the little clubhouse office, posed impressively behind the desk. He put aside his stage props, a yellow legal pad and yellow pencil (Fungo wrote in a childish scrawl, and always with a gnawed three-inch pencil stub), and stared at me for ninety seconds. Fungo believed that a hard stare establishes moral superiority. Weak men cannot outstare strong men. Men who blinked or averted their eyes implicitly confessed that they were the sort who did hideous things to schoolchildren or sold atomic secrets to Iran. And so he stared.

But I upset his calculations: I had been stared at for many hours by the best starers of all, mental patients, loonies with shit in their pajamas and zeros in their eyes; and so, by squeezing my brain half as dry as Fungo's, I could outstare him every time.

I waited, savoring the power that Fungo, by his own code, had granted me.

He surrendered by speaking first. "Union agitator!"

The team, probably as a joke, had elected me their union representative.

"Bolshevik!"

"Hey?" I said.

"Well? Ain't you a Bolshevik?"

"Define 'Bolshevik' for me and I'll tell you."

"Smart guy," he snarled. And then, afraid that he might have flattered me, he said, "You ain't so goddamn smart."

"Fungo. . . ."

"What's this I hear from the league office about days off?"

"I wrote to the league office, Fungo. We never get our off-days, you always call a special practice."

"Always the wise guy. Why can't you be sincere for once."

"And you go crazy with fines. It's a good thing athletes are so dumb. You'd never get away with fining an industrial or clerical worker for being late or making a mistake. Someone is going to sue one of these days, Fungo—maybe me—and fines are going to be declared illegal."

"You never give the straight answer, do you? It's always the sidestep, the shuffle, the duck, the tricky dodge, the smear. Words, always words with you, ain't it?"

"Yes," I said.

A blank stare. "Crazy stuff! You bitch all the time in public. Not keeping the matter inside the organization where it belongs."

I nodded.

"Well?" Fungo said. "Thinking of the tricky words? Where are the slimy words, Moon? Come on, come on."

"Is this some kind of trial?"

"Oh, trial, good. I knew you'd find the greasy words."

"Fungo, just why in hell did you call me in here?"

He leaned back in his chair. I was angry now; he was

happy. "Yit's a mute point," he said. "Yit's yall yapples yan yoranges."

"Fungo. . . ."

"Yeah?"

"Have you ever heard the word 'sadist'?"

"More dirty words!" he shouted, showing his eyeteeth and hairy fists. "I called you in here because you're pissing in the waterhole we all got to drink out of. You're lowering the morale tone around here. You bad-mouth the organization, you bad-mouth America, you don't even put your hat over your heart when they play the fucking national anthem! You even bad-mouth Jesus!"

"Aw, shit," I said. Fungo was yet another jock who'd found Jesus at the same time as his liver got hard and his penis soft. And Fungo's theology was unsound: he believed that Mary Magdalene had been the mother of Jesus.

"Is that all?" I asked.

He swiftly arose and stalked around the desk, then stood threateningly at my shoulder. A short two-hundred-pound troll in a baseball costume. Hairy arms, blue jowls, leaky blue eyes.

"I called you in here to have it out," he said. "Between you and I. Man to man. I'll close the door and lock it and swallow the key."

"Hold your water, Fungo!"

"If you got the balls."

"Fungo. . . ."

"But you ain't got the balls."

"Fungo, few persons know this, but I killed a man in the institution. I went berserk. God. They couldn't pull me off the poor old man. I turned into a slavering beast with the strength of ten."

He smiled down at me.

"Really, it's true. The institution wants to hush it up. It took six powerful attendants to subdue me. Fungo, the coroner was talking about werewolves."

"Get the fuck outta here," he said, tapping me lightly, almost affectionately, on my ear. He was magnanimous. Victory temporarily sweetens even the sourest stomach. When aware of his impotence, Fungo was a ravening animal; but let him gnaw on your soul for a while and he became a jolly old uncle.

I arose with dignity, and walked straight and proud from his office; but inside I was slinking.

Back onto the field. Numb first, then humiliated, and then enraged. Why hadn't I jumped up and smashed Fungo's chops? I was fifteen years younger, five inches taller, ten pounds heavier, and in superb physical condition. So why hadn't I accepted his invitation to fight? Well, because I was a civilized man. Because Fungo was an imbecile. Because I had been deemed crazy in the past and would again be deemed crazy. Because I earned eight hundred thousand dollars per year. And because Fungo, no matter how stupid, was a representative of authority. The unseen power, the silent leverage, the mysterious Legion of Fear.

Later, just before the game started, I returned to the locker room to get some tobacco, and found Leroy Girt there. He was wearing his shotsilk suit again, and his rusty hair erupted in three or four wet cowlicks.

"Howdy, Red," I said.

"Howdy, son."

"I sure like that suit, Red."

He winked and smiled. "You a winner or a loser, son?"

He told me that the Club had extended his contract; he would continue to travel with the team and provide individual or group Dynamic Motivational Catalysm.

"I used to be a loser, Red. But one day I got fired up, got down off the cross and started kicking ass."

Len Sharkey, who hoped to become a television anchorman when his bench-warming career ended, sat hunched near the center of the dugout, muttering into a baseball. "The candidate's been shot!" he said in a soft, outraged tone. "Lord God A'mighty! He don't appear to be moving. Dan, a candidate of this here proud nation's been shot down by a weasely loner what emerged from a mob of patriotic wish-wellers to put a slug in the guts of our beloved candidate."

I walked to the end of the bench and said to Dickie Brackett, "Move over, rookie. You got my place."

10

~∾∾~

At the end of the seventh inning I walked out to the bull-pen, sat down next to Frank Prosper, and tuned into the latest installment of the bullpen coach's season-long monologue. "Hey, lookit dere, Berry th'owin' crost he body again. I tol' him, but no, do he listen?" The coach, Jules Hebert ("That pronounce ay-bare, rookie"), was an old Cajun.

"Lookit dere, dat man slide straight into de base when de th'ow comin' from de right side. Why doan he hook to de leff? All dese baserunner who never learn to slide, where do dey come from, hey?" Jules had been a pretty good catcher during the days when ballplayers wore baggy wool uniforms and knew how to hook slide and throw to the right base—the golden age.

"Dere he go," I said to Prosper.

"Hebert, he goin'," Prosper said.

Prosper and his good friend Paul MacDonald were the born-again twins, members of the Association of Crusading Christian Athletes, and they proselytized aggressively among the team. Braverman and I were their special objectives: Braverman because he was an infidel Jew, and I because I boasted of my paganism. They were two healthy, well-groomed young men, the type who ring your doorbell on Saturday morning and ask if you would spare a few minutes of your time in order to learn the Truth. Prosper was married and had two angelic little girls. MacDonald was engaged to a female evangelist whose orgasmic voice and abandoned posture, whose sexuality, had raised the hair on my arms when I'd seen her preach at a tent show outside of Atlanta. Prosper and MacDonald had taken me there, expecting my atheism to crumble when I encountered the Truth in that particular form.

I said, "Tell me, Frank, does the soul occupy space?"

His forehead wrinkled. "It occupies the mortal body until it is redeemed by Jesus."

"Then the soul is tangible, it occupies space and exists in time."

"The soul is immortal."

"Ah, then it occupies space, the body, but is independent of time. Does it have substance? Can it be measured or weighed?"

"Why do you talk such garbage, Moon? None of that stuff counts. All that counts is our lord and savior Jesus Christ. Only Jesus is real."

"That may be true eschatologically, Frank, but not epistemologically."

I had only the vaguest notion of the meaning of those

words, and Frank no notion at all; but the stately parade
of syllables, laden with centuries of somber mystiscience,
made him anxious.

Braverman and I had gradually been wearing him
down, confounding him; Braverman with Talmudic ped-
antry and I with ancient heresies.

I decided to test him with the great Arian heresy. "You
believe that Jesus is the son of God?"

"Jesus *is* the son of God."

"Well, then God the father is older and greater than
Jesus the son. God created Jesus. Then it must be that
Jesus is subordinate to God."

He stared at me.

"God and Jesus may not be of the same substance. Is
one a part of the other or are they separate wholes?"

"You're an animal," said Prosper.

"Indeed."

It was a pleasant afternoon, cool in the shade, with a
mellow crowd, and nearby a nubile ballgirl who postured
charmingly, crouching in a way that invited bestial assault.

Prosper was silent for a time and then he asked,
"Moon, do you ever pray?"

"Only in schools."

"Be serious."

"I don't pray."

"Not ever?"

"Never."

"I don't believe that."

"Well. . . ."

"Tell me. Lord man, you do not have to be ashamed of
prayer. Rejoice in it!"

"Well, Frank, sometimes I repeat Saint Augustine's
prayer. 'Give me chastity and continence, only not yet.' "

Prosper sadly shook his head.

"Kiss me," I said to the ballgirl, but Prosper thought I was speaking to him: he spat and then vigorously rubbed his mouth with the back of his hand.

"Boy," he said, "you are wickeder than anyone knows."

11

—✺—

After the game I showered, toweled off by my locker, and began to dress.

Nearby Red Girt, in his Technicolor suit, and Fungo, Prosper, and MacDonald, still wearing their uniforms, were discussing the recent stay-of-execution of a mentally retarded sixteen-year-old killer. Red Girt was passionately in favor of capital punishment. Fungo said he'd personally enjoy torturing and strangling the "animist" who could do such things. Frank Prosper approved of capital punishment only if the miscreant's soul was saved before it was dispatched to hell. MacDonald was stubbornly opposed to state-imposed death: only God had the right to take human life.

Red Girt, smiling and drawling, said that scripture counseled that one should give unto Caesar that which is Caesar's. "And if Caesar says to fire up the hot seat, I say hallelujah! Amen."

I appreciate inconsistency in others as much as in myself and so, without malice, I approached the theologians.

"So," I said, "you'd like to see the kid fried, Red?"

"You bet, son. Pan fried, stir fried, I don't care. Dipped in milk, egg, and cornbread batter and deep fried in smoking oil. It don't matter how. Fried."

Fungo scowled at me; Prosper and MacDonald, accustomed to my heretical inclination, waited.

"You're in favor of capital punishment, Red?"

"I surely am, my friend."

"You believe that the legally constituted state has the right to—"

"The duty."

"The right and the duty to impose the death penalty on those whom it judges to be in violation of the applicable laws."

"Well, sir, I can't talk as pretty as that—but yes."

"Then you have to agree that the Romans were legally justified in executing Jesus."

Red Girt was delighted. He feared neither the Sophist thrust nor the dialectical ambush; he'd learned all about such rhetorical devices during the long years in shabby tents and dim auditoria while he struggled to become the Führer of Dynamic Motivational Catalysm. He smiled, aw shucks, and prepared to eviscerate me in debate.

"Well, son—"

But Fungo let out an anguished moan, placed his palms against my chest, and pushed me halfway across the room. Fungo could not endure the menace of ideas unconnected to doctrines. Ideas as toys, the tools of play. Ideas and words, that is, free of morality. Because for the primitive Fungoid mind words have the power of acts and ideas are the tribal glue. Fungo knew me and, in a sudden uncharacteristic flash of intuition, he recognized Leroy "Red" Girt—another slippery slimy wordtwister!

"Asshole!" he screamed. Everyone in the locker room froze. "Atheist pig-fucker!" His face was swollen and mottled red and white. "Queer whore!"

"Now, Fungo . . ."

He advanced. His arms were short levers with a fist at the end of each. Apeman, primal hominid, gland-mad Fungo.

I did not consciously elect to hit him; that decision had been marinating in my dreams for a long time and so the act itself seemed inevitable, the fulfillment of prophecy.

"Outside agitator!" Fungo shouted.

It was like throwing a good fastball except my arm did not describe much of an arc. I used a modified pitching motion, shifting my weight, pushing off my rear foot, and desperately throwing an overhand right. There was a meaty sound, a dull crack, and Fungo staggered back a few paces and sat down. His face was crooked. There was something wrong with his face, it was asymmetrical now, and he began to whimper in fear and pain.

"He was smite!" Red Girt said in a panicky voice.

Fungo, his legs sprawled out in a vee, his face crooked, breathed hard and fast and there was a whimper in each exhalation.

"Jesus, Fungo," I said. "Hey, I'm sorry." I was sorry for a moment; I had broken his face, made him whimper. But at the same time I was proud and relieved; it was out in the open at last—Teddy Moon had not been totally cowed by the Legion of Fear.

I glanced around the clubhouse. No one moved. Red Girt had closed his eyes. Fossey giggled nervously. Oliver Buckley, seated naked on a bench, contemplatively regarded his scrotum. No one moved to help Fungo or sub-

due me. I was at the center of the tableau. Werewolf
Moon. My preemptive first strike had captured their
wonder and respect.

There was an asthmatic wheeze in Fungo's whimper-
ing. Was he going to die?

I stalked out of the clubhouse, caught a taxi on Wave-
land Avenue, went to the hotel and hurriedly packed,
rented a car at the desk—a black Mercedes—and drove
west out of the city. Maybe a fugitive. An outlaw, gallant
but doomed. Doom /Moon. The Ballad of Teddy Moon.
What word rhymed with Fungo? I knew that there had
once been a major league pitcher by the name of Van
Lingle Mungo. Mungo / Fungo. I couldn't concentrate;
there was too much traffic and everywhere I saw triangu-
lar signs commanding me to Yield—bulletins issued by
the Legion of Fear. Write the ballad later. Sardonic
smile / the last mile.

I was as happy as a truant schoolboy. What did out-
laws do? They slept in a woman's white arms before
going out to face the execration and the bullets.

Thank you, ma'am, I'm surely grateful for your
pleasurin' me, and I don't mind dyin' whilst knowin' that
I left my seed in your proud belly. Tell little Jody that I
wisht I'd knowed him. Tell him that I said he should obey
his ma, drown the runty pups, and don't let the sow eat
her farrow.

I caught the tollway west toward Iowa. Iowa, Ne-
braska, Colorado, New Mexico—the Alamo Ranch
Sanitorium was located in New Mexico. I ought to go
there and give my shrink Doc Whillans an opportunity to
justify my behavior. But he probably would not; the old
Doc was no longer a true believer, he'd lost his faith, and
no doubt he'd tell me that I must take responsibility for
my actions.

Low on gas. I left the tollway and entered Dixon, Illinois, the dismal little town that had once echoed with the sonorous chuckles of Ronald Reagan.

I cruised past the shrine where he had spent his adolescent years. It wasn't a stable, it wasn't a log cabin, it was just an ordinary frame house. Well, gosh. If he could do it why couldn't I? There were going to be more actor Presidents and anchormen Presidents and athlete Presidents—why not the Moonman? I was half kidding but my stomach burned: I really wanted to be President, or better yet, the benevolent dictator of the world.

This was manic thinking. Had I neglected to take my lithium? Crazy, yes, and yet my prospects at the moment were no worse than Hitler's after the failed beer-hall *putsch*.

I got ten dollars' worth of quarters at the gas station and headed for the pay phone. My first wife, Patsy, said yes, why not, she would have dinner with me tonight as long as I was passing through town.

"Pick me up at the bookstore at about eight," she said. "Sober."

I called the Alamo Ranch Sanitorium and was connected with Dr. Whillans.

I said, " 'Canst thou not minister to a mind diseas'd; pluck from memory a rooted sorrow . . . ?' "

There was a silence. "I forget what comes next, Theodore. I'll look it up."

"Hi, Doc."

"Theodore, how are you?" Phlegm crackled like static in his throat. Whillans was in his early seventies and looked like the aged Einstein, with sagging, wrinkled skin and rheumy eyes and a corona of wild white hair. It was a resemblance that he cultivated, although he was not resentful if someone said that he looked like Mark Twain.

"I'm okay," I said.

"Fine, fine, glad to hear it. Really?"

"I'm all right. But I'm very tired. It becomes harder each day to make the required gestures."

"Yes, yes, God, I know."

"Hypocrisy is hard work."

"Indeed, nothing is more enervating."

Dr. Whillans was a heretical psychiatrist. He had started out as an orthodox Freudian, passed through Reich and Jung and Szaz and Laing and finally emerged as a rather befuddled humanities professor. That is, he'd lost his vocation and all he had left to offer patients was sympathy and a kind of classical resignation. ("Never mind, my dear, it has always been so. Remember poor Antigone.")

"Actually," I said, "I am having a problem. I thought I'd maybe come to see you."

"Have you been taking your medicine, Theodore?"

"Yes. I forget sometimes, though."

"Don't forget. Are you drinking?"

"A little."

"How little?"

"A little too much."

"Theodore, you and alcohol are like gasoline and a match. Have you been getting plenty of rest?"

"I don't sleep well."

There was a considerable pause. "What can I tell you? Take your medicine on schedule. Don't drink. Get plenty of rest. And cultivate your inhibitions."

"Right."

"Lily has been asking about you. Do you remember Lily?"

"Certainly."

Lily was a patient who had become infatuated with

me. She was not pretty—too pale, her features too sharp and anguished—but she had lovely long blond hair. Once she had cut off her hair and braided me a bracelet that covered my wrist and half of my forearm. It was an effective conversational gambit at bars and parties, but it itched, particularly in humid weather.

"Bring Lily a gift, Theodore."

"All right."

"Do it."

"I will, I promise."

"She watches the baseball games on television, hoping to see you. She doesn't understand that you don't play for all of the teams, only one."

"I swear, I'll bring her something—my ear, maybe."

"Last week Dewey Yankhe told me that all mental illness is a result of the class struggle."

"Really?" Dewey Yankhe was the "political prisoner."

"And so he's devising something he calls Therapeutic Dialectical Materialism."

"You ought to try it. On Dewey."

"Yes. Well, you know that you are always welcome here."

"That's something that both comforts and worries me."

He indulged in a little emphysematous laughter. "Goodbye, Theodore. Keep your dobber up."

PART TWO

One can only conclude that this
is indeed a great wall.

—*Richard M. Nixon*

12

<hr/>

Patsy, behind the counter, was wrapping books for a pair of students. She smiled and wriggled her fingers at me. I wandered back into the store.

It was a narrow, deep room stuffed carpet to ceiling with shelves of books, with more books arranged on oak tables and in wire racks. A helical iron stairway led to a loft that Patsy grandly called the mezzanine. Paperbacks up there, and shoplifters, and a coffee urn. Bookstore coffee. There is bookstore coffee just as there is hospital coffee and truck-stop coffee. There is bookstore music too, usually J. S. Bach.

I strolled down book-walled aisles. "In the beginning was the Word." In the middle and at the end too. There was even a word for this incontinent discharge of words: logorrhea.

There was a small section of serious books, but the rest

of the store was filled with brightly packaged illiterature. Sci-porn and psy-porn; ghosted celebrity autobiographies like my own; diet and exercise and cat and get-rich books; women's lib and racial minority polemics; quack medical and religious manifestos; Oriental mysticism; crackpot fantasies (astrology and pyramidology and Atlantis and the Bermuda Triangle and ancient astronauts and astral projection and flying saucers and assassination conspiracies); and truckloads of psycho-enlightenment merchandise; vice and advice; and of course the novels . . . novels about spies and Eyes, jogging and flogging, Nazi plots, Commie plots, killers with ice-blue eyes, sex, sex and money, sex and power, wizards and lizards; sentient vegetables from Neptune's moons, aching virgins, Homeric elves . . .

The bell above the door rang as the students left, and then Patsy, slender and pretty, smiling, was walking toward me. Her blond ponytail bounced as she moved.

We embraced and I kissed her beneath her ear. Nostalgia, and an unexpected pique of lust, made me prolong the embrace. She stepped back and gave me a slanted, speculative look.

"I'll change in the back room," she said. "I won't be long."

"I'll browse."

"You can autograph copies of your book for me."

"Do you still have some?"

"They're in front, on the discount table."

"You expect me to sign discounted books?"

"Just sign them, okay?"

There were seven copies of *Safe at Home* on the discount table. ("The moving document of an athlete who grappled hand to hand with his demons and scored a heartwarming triumph!") I wrote on the flyleaf of each:

"Reader beware—I changed my image but not my ways. Theodore J. Moon."

I was ashamed of the book. Three hundred pages of vain drool. I vowed that someday I would really write my autobiography, by and for myself, and make it as true as I could; that is, I would never lie to serve my myth but only to injure an enemy.

Mostly I regretted that I and my ghost had romanticized madness by converting my desperate psychotic episodes into a kind of slick spiritual odyssey. A quest, I mean, from which I returned a better and wiser man.

But it is difficult, once your mind has exploded and you can no longer clearly distinguish between inner and outer worlds, fantasy and reality, to afterward regard yourself as a player in some existential melodrama—the victim as hero or the enslaved as rebel or the stupefied as prophet. Madness is not a radical repudiation of modern society, a kind of saintly protest. Neither is it an authentic way of perceiving a mad world. It is not even the cross of the sensitive. It's hardly anything at all. It is a little like Oliver Buckley's Negative Meaning.

I returned unenlightened from my two excursions into madness: I learned nothing, accumulated no hoard of insights and truths, no vision of beauty. The first time I came back slowly, in small increments, a thick-witted alien. The second time I returned abruptly, not too stupid, with shit in my pajamas and a keen curiosity about the result of the last World Series.

Patsy emerged from the back room wearing a black cocktail dress. She had let down her hair, applied makeup. She carried herself differently now. Her expression had changed. Woman. I watched her walk briskly down the aisle and then climb the stairs to the loft. The Bachground music ceased; lights were extinguished.

Safe at Home. My ghost, a Bendzedrine-gobbling hack by the name of Russell P.G. Kell, had thought of the title. "This guy has been through hell but now he's safe at home." Kell usually referred to my literary persona as "this guy" or "the bozo.".

The TV "docudrama" extracted from the book and scheduled to be shown around World Series time was also titled *Safe at Home.*

Patsy, presaged by the scent of lilacs, was now at my side. "Ready?" she said, as women always say when they have kept you waiting.

We went to the town's best restaurant, a place with a French name, white linen tablecloths, silverplate utensils and candelabra, and a ladies' menu that omitted the prices. We ordered drinks, Patsy a glass of white wine and I a lethal martini.

"Do your lovers take you here?" I asked.

"I call them Johns."

"Ah, yes, an exquisite *truite au bleu,* an exotic herbal liqueur, and then off to the sack."

"Are you going to get weird?"

"Do you have many lovers, Patsy?"

"You've been sweet until now."

"Do you?"

"Do *you?*"

"Womoons, I call them."

She smiled maliciously, pleased that I was jealous, glad that I wanted her, and yet uncertain in what way she could exploit her unexpected power.

"How is wife number two?" she asked.

"Jesus. Getting ready for Halloween, I suppose."

This pleased her. I knew she would not mention my two kids; a sad and wistful part of Patsy regarded them as rightfully her children, the pair we had hoped to have.

She had miscarried twice during our marriage; the second had left her infertile.

I said, "When we met, Pamela was a nice girl with just enough bitch in her to make her fascinating. You know, unpredictable, volatile. But the bitch side kept maturing while her other side dwindled."

Patsy opened a menu. Her mentioning Pamela had been a tactical error; she had not come here to talk about other women, particularly the one who had succeeded her.

"Of course, being married to me accelerated her decline. For sheer survival she had to become meaner and meaner as I got crazier and crazier. It was reciprocal."

Patsy ran her forefinger down the menu's columns.

"Do you think you'll ever marry again?" I asked.

"I doubt it."

"I probably won't. I'll never regret our four years, though."

"I'll never regret three of them."

The candlelight flattered her, softened the angularity of her features and almost succeeded in turning her prettiness into beauty.

"It's nice to see you," I said.

The waiter arrived: Patsy ordered a winey veal concoction baked in a pastry shell—*haute cuisine du Iowa*—and I asked for the house's best steak. I also ordered two more drinks and a bottle of wine to be served with dinner.

I said, "Once, in Texas, at a restaurant called Le Château, I ordered their prime New York cut steak. It was a fine piece of meat too. But it came to the table covered with gravy."

She smiled.

"Texans pour a gray mucilage over everything—beef,

pork, lamb, even fish as far as I know. They eat biscuits with gravy for breakfast."

"Do they?"

"When you meet a Texan he says, 'Hah you!' And when you leave he says, 'Bah now!' The Texas girls are pretty, though. The best food in America is served on both coasts and in New Orleans. The most beautiful women are in the South and California. The ugliest women call the Midwest home. Present company excepted, of course."

"Relax, Moon, you don't have to be interesting."

"But I feel interesting."

"Didn't they warn you not to trust your feelings?"

"I regard myself as a brilliant amateur student of America. A pop-Tocqueville. A hard-eyed investigator of the squalid and tawdry."

I paused while the waiter brought our fresh drinks. Patsy seemed embarrassed; I was talking too fast, too loud.

I drank half of the martini. "Seven months a year I buzz all over the country, from coast to coast and border to border. It's a beautiful country. I mean, the land is beautiful, the towns and cities are junkyards. The people—the people are haunted. On the edge of panic. There's a furtive look in the eye, a tendency toward rage, a tremor in the hand that holds the whiskey glass or hypodermic."

Patsy was skeptical. "Maybe you're describing yourself, Moon."

"Probably."

"Listen, why are you here? Why aren't you with the team?"

"Long story, angel."

"I have time."

"Read about it in tomorrow's newspapers."

"Oh, God. News or sports section?"

"Sports, I suppose."

"What did you do this time?"

"I protested Fungo Gates's habitual incivility."

"What does that mean?"

"Fungo was Moonstruck."

"Talk straight."

"I punched him."

"Oh, Moon."

"Really, it isn't important. Forget it tonight, read about it tomorrow."

"Are you okay?"

"I'm fine. Don't I act all right?" I wanted to know.

"Well, I wondered. How do you feel?"

"Good. Honestly, I'm not going to throw food around or stand on the table and harangue the customers." Which was something I had done a couple of times, though never while married to Patsy; and not since commencing my lithium program of mania control. I was tamed, the barbarian subdued and maybe even gelded.

"Is there going to be trouble?"

"A lawsuit, probably. Brute he-men like Fungo sue faster than swindled widows."

"And your baseball career?"

"I don't know."

She gazed intently into my eyes. "Are they going to say that you cracked up again?"

"Sure. But I didn't."

"Oh, Moon, damn it, Moon."

She averted her gaze and little frown lines, dimpled brackets, creased the skin between her eyebrows. Patsy was troubled by inconsistency: she believed that a person should be a coherent whole. Everyone possessed anarchic impulses, sinful drives, irrational desires, but all should be dominated, kept locked in the skullbox by force of will. And why not? I puzzled and disturbed her because I was many Moons.

She had never seen me when I was truly mad. Wisely, she had left me when it became apparent that she was to be a passenger in my swift decline. And so she had seen me wild, loud, vulgar, agitated, arrogant, but not mad. She had been humiliated by the adulterous Moon; slapped by the vicious Moon; bored by the garrulous Moon; exasperated by the lying Moon; and alienated by the Moon of trivial enthusiasms, artificial emotions. Patsy had been hurt but not badly. She still liked me and worried about me, which meant that she had discovered one or two sympathetic Moons among the disagreeable multitude.

The food was served, the wine opened and poured. Patsy began to daintily excavate her veal pot pie while I savaged a great bloody slab of meat. I was ravenous. Stabbing and hacking. Kill, eat. You could not trust the ascetics. Elevate the organism with a platter of hot grub and the spirit was sure to hitch a ride. The tablecloth around my plate began to resemble a late Pollock.

"We must not forget our animal natures, Patsy."

"I won't easily forget yours," she said.

"You know, someone is trying to frame me for the murders."

"Stop. I don't want to hear any more."

"You heard about those three transsexuals who were murdered? In Cincinnati, New York, and Philadelphia. Tiffany, Courtney, and LaMenta? Well, I think I'm being framed."

"Moon, for God's sake, Moon, who would want to frame you for murder?"

"I have my suspicions."

"Sure you do," she said scornfully. "Probably that silly Legion of Fear of yours."

"No. The Legion of Fear is clumsy, brutish. They employ intimidation and force. This is the work of the Illuminati."

"The what?" She stared at me, breathing fast and shallowly. "I'm going to scream."

"This shows the subtle hand of the Illuminati. Their plots are always brilliant, delicately nuanced, elegant in simplicity."

"Please," she said.

"Not all of the Illuminati are Gnostics, and not all Gnostics are Illuminati, but there is a significant connection."

She covered her mouth with a palm and emitted a high, thin nasal keening, a sound she made when trying to suppress hysterical laughter. No one could laugh as uninhibitedly as Patsy when the mood was on her. She laughed like a banshee. I considered it sport to provoke these breakdowns in public places.

The other patrons' interest in our table had not diminished.

"The Illuminati," I said, "are everywhere—and nowhere."

She abruptly rose from her chair and hurried toward the ladies' room. I extracted a piece of veal from her pastry, drank her wine.

When she returned five minutes later her expression was stern and disapproving, but hysteria remained in her eyes and her voice.

"Don't say anything weird for a while, okay?"

"All right."

"The Illuminati. Moon, you aren't half as crazy as you like to pretend. Nor," she said, her voice rising as the correlative became obvious, "nor half as sane."

13

~~

It was cool and misty outside now; vapor drifted past the streetlights and the moon had deployed a double corona. Condensation dripped from the trees. I could smell the earth of Iowa, musky and sour.

On our walk to the car I said, "Patsy, you know the trouble with you women?"

"Shut up," she said. "Never mind."

"It's hormones. You have the wrong kind of hormones."

"Male chauvinist."

"I hate that. It's stupid."

"Sexist."

"Dumb. A sexist is a guy who turns roosters into capons."

"Male chauvinist pig, nyah nyah nyah."

I said, "A few Novembers ago I visited Oliver Buckley

in Texas. We hunted doves and quail and drank lots of good whiskey. One day I was driving down a twisty road, coming around a blind curve, and there was a car coming at me from the opposite direction. A woman stuck her head out the window and yelled 'Pig!' Can you imagine? 'Pig!' And so I yelled out my window, 'Whore!' "

I waited for Patsy to ask:

"What's the point?"

"I drove around the corner and ran into a four-hundred-pound pink and black pig. Wrecked the car."

Her smile was slow to arrive but it lingered at the corners of her mouth and in her eyes.

I had made up the story but it was the kind of thing that should happen. It was art in that sense. The story made Patsy happy. It took her mind off petty earthly concerns and let her penetrate, however briefly, the veils of the Cosmic Consciousness. Temporarily we shared a single vision. That pig had not died in vain.

We went to Patsy's—once our—house. It was smaller than I remembered. After you reach thirty everything is smaller than you remember. I was much smaller than I remembered being.

She had changed things, of course. Modern paintings on the walls, a lighted aquarium, many books, and delicate, uncomfortable furniture, the kind I and my roughneck friends would have turned into kindling in six months.

She served coffee in the living room. She was a little tense, wary, now that we were alone.

I said, "If we're both free in five years let's remarry."

"It is to laugh."

"I'm serious. I should be burned out by then, a docile husk."

"What kind of woman wants a docile husk?"

"Many do."

"I suppose you'd know."

"Do you need money?"

"No."

"You didn't get much out of the divorce settlement." This house, a car, a small cash amount.

"You didn't have very much then."

"I do now. It's odd how even small-time celebrity breeds money. I earn my baseball salary, but the celebrity money just oozes out of the telephone. It rings and a voice asks if you'd care to write a book. Have a TV drama made out of the book. Make a commercial, endorse a product. Invest in a business coup. Go on a winter lecture tour. Take a bit part in a movie. Sign autographs for children at an exorbitant fee. Patsy, it's incredible how much one can profit out of a colorful disease."

"I imagine."

Patsy was not interested in money beyond what she required to live in moderate comfort. She believed that to talk about money was vulgar; to possess a very large amount, shameful. (But Pamela's eyes dilated at the mention of money, and her upper incisors descended like tiny guillotines into her lower lip.)

"The TV production company asked me to play myself in the TV dramatization of *Safe at Home*." That was not strictly true: I'd insisted on testing for the role and had impersonated myself capably, so I thought, but the studio brass informed me that I was too frantic, too emotional. (Did they want a brooding, laconic manic? Yes.) They hired a forty-year-old ham who threw a baseball like a five-year-old.

"I refused the part," I said. "God knows I've made an ass out of myself in the past, but I had to draw the line somewhere."

"Listen," Patsy said, suddenly alert. "Am I going to be portrayed in your sleazy movie?"

"No. My first wife isn't mentioned. They didn't want to confuse the audience."

"You put me in your sleazy book."

"In a couple of chapters, and only in a favorable light."

"There are no favorable lights in that travesty."

"Pamela is being portrayed in thé movie as the saintly, long-suffering wife and mother."

"How could you leave me for that whore?" Patsy said evilly.

"It wasn't like that." It wasn't either; she had left me months before I'd even met Pamela. But what is chronology to women? They have long been familiar with the eeriest aspects of the space-time continuum.

She was arranged on the sofa in one of those tortured female positions, the upper half of her body sitting almost erect, the other half lying down. They are supple.

"I lust," I said.

She knew it.

"I yearn."

She nodded smugly.

"I want. I need."

She watched me.

"Take womoon."

"Yeah?"

"Man take womoon. Fiercely. Gently. Womoon receive man."

"You are such a jerk, Moon," she said complacently.

"Man take woman-thing to love-place. Yes. Good. I like. It is right. My heart is squeezed. My root takes notice."

Impatiently she arose and climbed the stairs, saying, "I'll be in bed. The door will probably be locked. But maybe not."

"Man break door. Crush walls. Kill dragon. Take wo-moon."

She was standing naked by the window when I entered the dark bedroom. She half turned and quietly said, "Shut up, blabbermouth."

After midnight I was awakened by a thunderstorm. I went to the window. The lightning was constant, dozens of separate forked bolts that combined into a flickering web. The thunder was continuous too; it sounded like the detonations of the final war, the ultimate holocaust. Rain lashed down and burst white like popcorn on the street.

"Moon?"

"Father Sky is vexed," I said.

"Moon . . ."

I returned and sat on the edge of the bed. Patsy's skin was feverishly warm.

"Come back to bed."

"I'm going to leave soon," I said.

"Leave?"

"After the storm. I'm on my way to New Mexico, to the nuthouse there."

"Do you have to go?"

"I think it's best. I want to talk to the Doc."

"Can't you at least wait until morning?"

"I won't be able to sleep. I might as well get out on the road."

"Oh, Moon. Damn it, Moon."

"I'm sorry. I'd like to stay. You know that, don't you? I'll come back and see you when I get things straightened away."

"All right."

"I'll call you from New Mexico."

"No you won't."

"Yes I will."

Patsy, embracing me tightly, cried while we stood on the front porch. Goodbye. And then she became angry. "Don't come back to see me," she said. "I don't want you to come back ever."

"I'll visit you within a few weeks."

"Just go away."

She let me kiss her.

"What folly!" she cried, laughing and crying, and she went into the house and slammed the door.

I drove to Interstate 80 and entered the river of light that flowed swiftly through the city and then emptied into the vast estuary of darkness to the west. Passing trucks threw up long roostertails of water. The traffic gradually thinned. Later, when the pavement appeared reasonably dry, I pushed the Mercedes up to ninety miles per hour. I could afford traffic tickets but I could not afford to poke along at the legal speed limit; my shrink was a thousand miles away and we both were aging at a terrifying rate.

After my first crack-up I was confined for seven weeks in a state-operated snake-pit, a theater of Grand Guignol, where my depression was treated by opening a circuit between my brain and an electrical outlet. Torture therapy, but it seemed to work in a curious way: after the first three in a series of sixteen electroshock treatments I became quite cheerful, a grinning fool, and I would shuffle around in my oversized slippers saying, "I feel pretty good. I'm happy." I remember that, but I do not recall much more about the period. I was crazy, I was constantly drugged, and my brains were fried. I do remember that there was an entire ward of the Undead, refuse left over from the lobectomy days. And there are images, incidents, that occasionally rise dreamlike to my consciousness; but five or six months of my life, the time just before, during, and after that crack-up, were cleanly erased by Commonwealth Edison.

My wife Pamela, her mother, and their lawyers tried to keep me in that institution while they maneuvered to gain control of my assets. But my lawyer finally secured my release and personally escorted me to the Alamo Ranch Sanitorium in southern New Mexico.

By that time I myself was a member of the Tribe of the Undead, a zombie in a filthy bathrobe, incontinent and incomplete, embracing doom. "This is a good place, Moon," my lawyer told me. "They won't bother you. You can walk out any time you want."

You could walk out anytime, but to where? The Ranch was located on a vast desertic plain with here and there an isolated rocky hill, a butte, a mesa, or small volcanic cone; and all around the remote horizon there were gray, furrowed mountains, and beyond them higher mountains, and then finally mountains that could be clouds or clouds that might have been mountains—a huge amount of space compressed into my eyes, my poor brain. The sky, day or night, was a hole torn open to expose infinity. It was enough to blind a man.

You could have seen the fireball of the first atomic explosion from my west window. One of the patients gave me a piece of trinitite, a greenish stone that had been melted and transformed in the blast.

On the desert there was a primal silence, a vertiginous

sky, a stone-cracking heat. Every animal seemed to possess needlelike weapons and dangerous toxins. Scorpions hung upside down on old adobe walls. Rattlesnakes left their tracks—mysterious runes—in the dust. I saw scorpions, rattlers, tarantulas, eight-inch-long centipedes, black widow and brown recluse spiders, and what might have been a Gila monster. One night I was bitten by a kissing bug and my lower lip swelled to twice its normal size. This was a terrain that matched my inner landscape.

Even the vegetables were hostile. Cacti, ocotillo and barrel and prickly pear; and crucifixion thorn; yucca, creosote, nettles and burrs, grass that sawed holes in my socks.

Sometimes I would walk far out onto the desert at night, wary of the nocturnal rattlesnakes, oppressed by the stars. Too many stars were visible in that clear dry air—an excess of suns. Other worlds, maybe better worlds. Or Christ, maybe worse worlds.

The nights were comparatively cool: stars pulsed, the moon palely illuminated that barren moonscape, the coyotes yipped and keened and yammered—a chorus of sly devils. They challenged the institution's slob dogs, teased them, like calling to like, and like morosely declining the call. Dazed, frightened, lost, I sent telepathic postcards into the ether: is there a deity out there? Gone, left no forwarding address.

Now the storm had passed to the east and the radio reception was good. I spun the dial, trying various late-night talk shows from all over the West. After-midnight America, vampire and werewolf America, was astir and afoot and maybe even aloft. You could hear agony in the static between stations: high-frequency screams, barely audible moans, death rattles, laughter like the sound of wind through dry leaves.

Night people telephoned the stations and inarticulately exalted or denigrated their special demons. They all tried to sound intelligent and rational—"scientific"—and all failed. Some of the callers were obviously psychotic; many more were crazy in subtler, more cunning ways, and then it took one to know one. I knew them. They were my people. I had twice been a citizen of their surreal realm—a prince, in fact.

On other stations the fly-by-night evangelists were peddling Jesus to invalids and insomniacs. Buy a touch of Grace. Purchase surcease to pain and fear and sorrow. Jesus reads all of your cards and letters, he surely does, and he thanks you for your contributions. Even a dollar helps. Each dollar drives another nail into Satan's coffin. Jesus needs more nails, folks, more dollars, to wage holy war against the devil's evil army.

Paranoia contaminated the airwaves. Hatred seethed through the night. Madness slithered out of the radio speakers and perched on my shoulder.

14

I ate a late lunch in Albuquerque, drove on through the southern edge of the city and past a few small towns, and then headed straight south on I-10 into the heat and desolation. There was not much traffic. Dead animals lay alongside the road, jackrabbits, a coyote, a thick black snake. Ravens erupted from the road as my car approached, and in the rearview mirror I could see them settle back down to the carrion. The edges of the road narrowed with perspective and finally converged far ahead in a heat blur. I pushed the car up to one hundred and five miles per hour and at that speed the country appeared to undulate. Hills were born; arroyos suddenly opened; volcanic cones sprouted above the horizon.

It was about sixty miles to Socorro; I stopped at a bar there and ordered a beer. Half a dozen scruffy redneck types sat at the bar. Sobs and twangs issued from a jukebox.

I drank my beer, took my change to a wall phone and dialed the Ranch's number. The desk connected me to Whillans's office.

"Yes?" he said.

" 'Canst thou not minister to a mind diseas'd; pluck from memory a rooted sorrow . . . ?' "

There was a long pause; I could hear a typewriter clacking in the background. Then Whillans said:

" '. . . the patient must minister to himself.' "

"It's me, Doc. I'm on my way."

"Where are you calling from?"

"Socorro." Succor.

"Are you all right?"

"Well enough. Can I have the cottage?"

"Of course. All of your things are still there. Are you really all right, Theodore?"

"What's for dinner?"

"Creamed chipped beef on toast."

"I'm looking for a tax deduction."

"Benefactors of this worthy institution are often lavishly wined and dined."

"How about a barbecue out by the grove of cottonwoods? Spit-roasted cabrito."

"Short notice. Remember that our servility is commensurate to the size of the check."

"Big check."

"Done. Seven o'clock."

I bought two bags of groceries at a Socorro market, a case of beer and a liter of good scotch malt whisky, cigars, and a fat paperback thriller—*The Red Eagle Parameters*. I drove south for an hour and then turned off the Interstate, passed through a shabby little town bisected by the Rio Grande (a narrow mud ribbon in the drought), and then I followed a county road that ran directly east toward the San Andres Mountains. After twenty miles the road crossed a set of rusty railroad tracks, hooked to the left around an adobe ruin that was gradually melting back into the earth, curved right, ran straight for three miles, and then passed the stone gate pillars of the Alamo Ranch Sanitorium. I went on past the huge main building and the "parade grounds" and pulled up in front of one of five stone cottages. Home. My halfway house between the institution proper and the world.

Inside, I opened all the windows, plugged in the air conditioner and refrigerator, unpacked the groceries, killed a couple of scorpions, inspected the living room, bedroom, bathroom, and sat down on the desk chair. Home. Jesus.

None of my possessions had been disturbed. Three hundred-plus pages of typescript lay on the desk: a few mad essays, what I had written of my autobiography before the publisher took it away from me and gave it to a ghost, the first act of a play titled *Pope Bob,* and the fragment of a novel—*White Thighs.* My stereo set and cassettes were in the corner.

I found the portable black hole and VCR in a closet along with some clothing, a glove and several baseballs, a pearl-gray Stetson, and a pair of ostrich-leather cowboy boots I'd never worn. My books seemed to have survived the hordes of beetles and moths.

I opened a can of beer and went to the window. The brilliant light, the heat, the stillness, combined to give this place a surreal aspect. And the sanitorium's main building contributed to the effect; it looked like a Disney cartoon version of a fairy-tale castle.

The Ranch had once been a great luxury hotel and spa, built by the Santa Fe Railroad in the nineties of the last century. Some of America's richest and most powerful families, footnotes in the history books, traveled thousands of miles for the dubious privilege of bathing in the resort's sulfurous hot springs—a prologue to hell. The hotel and spa were then a kind of secular Lourdes. But the Depression put an end to the nonsense; the railroad closed the spur line and, looking for a tax break, donated the establishment to a monastic order.

No doubt all of the gilt and plush, walnut and ivory, the rococo elegance, were removed by the order and auctioned off: still, I like to imagine a humble God-intoxicated young monk, a man like Saint Francis, silently eating his bowl of barley gruel beneath the six crystal chandeliers in the great dining hall (while, perhaps, on the stage a choir sings the *Te Deum*); and later my ascetic wearily climbs the central stairway (as wide as a two-lane highway) and shuffles down the richly carpeted hallway to his cell, the Sun King Suite. Then he kneels and in anguish prays, "Father, I find myself thinking more and more of the World. My cabbages will not grow in this alkaline soil. My faith cannot survive in this old whorehouse. Free me from my vows." And I like to think that this same sweet, pious monk is now president of one of the country's television networks.

In the late thirties the property was sold to a group of patriotic Texas businessmen who established a military prep school on the site, the Alamo Academy. The fortress decor remains in the iron spear fences and gates, gatehouses, the huge flagstone quadrangle, and incongruously, in the dozens of artillery pieces still scattered over the grounds, their muzzles cocked menacingly toward the dangerous high ground to the east—Apache country. The lease forbids Dr. Whillans to remove the cannons. The patients do not seem to mind them except for Dewey

Yankhe, the political prisoner, who regards them as evidence that the Alamo Ranch Sanitorium is an integral part of the American Gulag system.

The military academy was a profitable enterprise for many years, but in the early sixties the black ink turned red, and the facility was closed. Rats nested in the Sun King Suite; rattlers slithered among the chapel pews; lizards darted in and out of cannon barrels.

And then in 1979 the Texas businessmen loaned the complex to a charitable foundation—Dr. Whillans.

"So there it is," Whillans liked to say. "From luxury hotel to monastery to military school to crazy house. Alter the order slightly and you have the genealogy of civilizations."

15

⦁⦁⦁

At seven o'clock I left the cottage and walked north across the desert. The temperature was still close to one hundred degrees but the dryness of the air almost instantly evaporated my sweat. I knew that tonight when I returned to the cottage my face would be dusted with tiny salt crystals and my hair would have the texture of dead grass.

The desert gained in color as the sun declined, and each plant replicated itself in shadow. The powdery soil was reddish, the sky ultramarine. And there was a hush; even the cicadas were silent.

The vast space permitted me to grow a little. The clarity of the air, detailing each grain of soil, cleanly etching the cacti and creosote and wrinkled folds of hill, allowed me to dream of a comparable inner clarity. In the desert my isolation became innocent solitude.

The Ranch buildings diminished behind me; the grove of cottonwoods gradually enlarged. Beneath the trees I could see a pickup truck, a pair of miniature figures, and a spiraling braid of smoke. The white smoke writhed ecstatically against the egg-smooth sky. I heard a latent music in this silence, unborn songs, like the rhythms I sometimes detected issuing from machines and moving water and the wind. I saw myself describing a line as insubstantial as smoke across the desert, linking my past and future confusions.

Tom Lopez, a forty-year-old who looked sixty—his face was as parched and furrowed as the land—was tending to a spitted kid. His twelve-year-old son assisted him. They shyly greeted me, shaking my hand when I offered it, staring out over the desert as we forced our way through the reacquainting small talk. There was a washtub filled with ice and beer; Tom got out three cans, snapped them open, and passed one to me and one to the boy. He rolled a cigarette then and we leaned back against the pickup truck, drinking beer and smoking. It was relatively cool in the shade of the big cottonwoods. I learned that I was an hour early; I had forgotten to adjust my watch to the time change.

We discussed the weather (it had been terrifically hot and dry since May), and the events of the summer. Muriel Pietsch, an inmate, had given birth to a baby boy in July. Five male inmates claimed paternity. We laughed. Louis Gryz had signed himself out of the institution in June but had returned three weeks later, claiming that he had robbed half a dozen convenience stores in El Paso. No one believed him, and yet no one had been able to determine where he had got the twelve hundred dollars he carried. We laughed again. Dewey Yankhe, the political prisoner, had written another batch of letters about his unjust incarceration, and the Ranch had received an inquiry from Amnesty International.

Tom's son watched me intently, a persistent stare that would have annoyed me if I hadn't understood its genesis. I was used to having small boys stare at me that way. Billy was prospecting for secrets, the source of what he blindly assumed was my great strength. The fact that I was one of the Ranch's dementos only served to deepen the mystery. Primitives and children believe that physical prowess is connected to virtue.

And then, during a lull in the conversation, the boy blurted out, "My team won the Little League Championship." He turned away from my gaze and sipped his beer. "But there are only six teams in the league."

"What position do you play, Babe?"

"Pitcher. I used to be an infielder but this year I wanted to pitch."

"Well, maybe we ought to play catch tomorrow morning. How does eight o'clock sound?"

"Sure." He was very shy now and sorry that he had spoken; playing catch with a major leaguer was an enormous responsibility.

"We'd better tend to the cabrito," Tom told his son.

I got another beer from the tub of ice and sat with my back against a tree. An apparition was moving across the desert. I could not make it out at first, and then I saw that it was a man carrying a big stringed instrument, a double bass or cello. He was holding it by the neck so that it appeared as if the instrument were walking alongside. He passed through a patch of creosote shrubs, crossed a shallow depression where his legs vanished from view, and then ascended to level ground. Dr. Bloom. He held the bow in his left hand, the instrument in his right.

Bloom approached, breathing hard, tenderly leaned

his instrument and bow against a tree, and turned to me.

"Theodore. Bless you for rescuing me from institutional cuisine."

I got up and shook his hand.

Dr. Bloom was a tall, awkward man who wore thick-lensed glasses and a hairpiece that did not match the color and texture of his natural hair.

"So you're back here again, are you, Theodore?"

"It seems that way."

"Back again. You're a recidivist."

"Well, sure, but only with consenting adults."

He grinned. "A recidivist, Theodore, is a person who—"

"I know what the word means. I was joking."

Dr. Bloom was both a staff member and a patient, and it was often difficult to judge when one function ceased and the other commenced. He was a former psychiatrist. Dr. Bloom had successfully practiced psychiatric medicine in Buffalo for eighteen years (perodically taking long vacations to "recoup his energy"), and then one morning he had announced that he could not go on. And he hadn't. That is, he refused to work, talk, eat, bathe, move. He was confined, improved after a time and released, regressed, improved again and fell back, until Dr. Whillans had "salvaged" him four years ago.

Whillans said that Dr. Bloom was still a fairly competent therapist if given a short work week and assigned to a certain type of patient and, of course, properly supervised. At least, Whillans said, the man did little harm, an assertion that could not be made of a high percentage of the profession, the mob of Don Juans and messiahs and pop-slicksters, etc.

"Are things going badly for you?" Bloom asked.

"Not at all. I lost my job. I'm suspected of being a serial murderer. I'm fine."

"Come on."

"Actually, I feel very good."

"Well, hell, Theodore, feeling very good is symptomatic of your disease in the ascendant phase."

"I don't care. I feel good except when I feel bad."

"I wish Whillans had given me a crack at you."

"Whillans didn't want me to submit to conventional psychoanalysis. He says that all of us nowadays know far too much about ourselves and almost nothing of humanity."

"Yet another dumb epigram. Whillans isn't a scientist, he's a nineteenth-century literary man."

"Well, so was Freud, basically."

"What? Oh, here now, that's utter nonsense." Dr. Bloom believed in Freud in the same uncritical way as Dewey Yankhe believed in Marx and Frank Prosper believed in Jesus. To question one article of the faith would be to threaten the entire structure.

I said, "Freudian analysis works on the same principle as the other demonologies, except that a priest or sorcerer casts out the devils in just a few hours while the psychiatrist requires eighteen years."

"Whom are you quoting now?" he said angrily.

"Whillans."

"Whillans, Epictetus, Plato, Shakespeare—you're a parrot, Moon, a muscular recording device. You can perform clever little tricks like hurling baseballs at high velocity and memorizing verses. Perhaps someday you'll learn to think and speak and act for yourself."

"Doc, I used to think and speak and act for myself all the time—that was my trouble. Look what it got me, electroshock convulsions, straitjackets. Listen, there were periods when I'd wake up every morning and I was totally new, and the world was new. I invented them both. I existed wholly in the present moment. No one was ever freer. I said what I pleased, did what I wanted to do, acted in strict compliance with my emotional whims. I was crazy. Now I'm trying to live as if something had been learned during the last five thousand years."

"Forget it. You're a thug."

"Don't call me that."

"Thug thug thug. Thugathugathugathug. Thugaroo."

"Doc," I said, "I'm not going to let you pull rank on me. We're equals, we both have histories of mental illness."

"We are not equal. I am a psychiatrist, a scientist."

"Psychiatry isn't a science, it's rogue philosophy."

"Who said that?"

"The Moon."

After a long silence he said in a sulky, injured tone, "You never even told me a dream, not one dream."

Dr. Bloom, like sorcerers and shamans and gypsies, believed in the significance of dreams.

"All right," I said. "I'll tell you one of my dreams."

"It's too late."

But I knew that it wasn't too late. Dr. Bloom hungered for your dreams: he devoured them and digested them and finally regurgitated them for analysis.

"In the dream," I said, "I am very happy. It's a cold morning. I can see my breath, feel the icy cold. Apparently I work for a car dealer, new cars and trucks, used cars, there is this enormous car lot. Maybe five hundred vehicles. Cars can't sit for too long, you know, especially in cold weather. The batteries run down, the oil turns to sludge, it's bad for them. My job is to start the vehicles and let them run for a while."

Bloom's eyes were half closed, perhaps in ecstacy, and his lips curved in a sweet half smile.

"So I got into a car, a Buick, and started the engine. I left it running and started another car, a Ford. The exhausts were smoking. The engines were running roughly because of the cold. I started a truck then, a Dodge, and then a nifty little sports car. Five little Jap sedans. A Fiat. A Renault. Then I had three rows of brand-new cars, all red. I got in one, started it, got in the next, started it, like that, maybe forty cars, Doc. In and out, in and out. The entire car dealership was vanishing in the exhaust fog. My fingers and toes were cold. Next was a big camper, a Winnebago. I had trouble getting that one going. A bad solenoid, I figured. Next to it was a Corvette. I got in the Corvette and—"

"Theodore, stop. Wait. Aren't there any other people around this car lot?"

"I don't think so. I sat in the Corvette for a time and ran the heater. I was really getting cold, Doc. Next to the Vette was a Cadillac. I got out of the—"

"Theodore. Did you ever work for a car dealer?"

"No. Now, I still had maybe four hundred and fifty vehicles to start before I can knock off for a cup of coffee."

"Theodore."

"Yeah?"

"Does anything occur in your dream other than the starting of five hundred vehicles?"

"Well, sure," I said. "Later I have to switch off the engines when they're warmed up, and return all the keys to the big cork board in the office. Correct key, correct hook, or else things become terribly confused."

"Is this a true dream, Theodore? Are you tormenting me?"

"Don't you like this dream, Doc?"

"Is it a true dream?"

"Yes, I swear."

He smirked. I couldn't tell if it was a professional smirk or a private smirk.

He said, "During my long career, during my distinguished—yes, distinguished—career as a psychiatrist, I've heard only one dream that is even remotely like yours. The details were different, of course. The other dream was by and about a man who fitted components together on an assembly line for eight hours. But the two dreams are similar—absorption in an idiotic task, brain-numbing repetition, the stupidity, the fatuity. . . ."

"Who was this guy, Doc?"

"It doesn't matter. It won't help you to know about him."

"Hey, come on."

"Dreams aren't fate, Theodore. They aren't prophecy. They merely—if correctly interpreted—provide a map to the unconscious of the dreamer."

"Pretend that I believe that. Tell me."

"Rafael Maleparte was an infamous serial murderer—a monster. I'm a scientist, I shouldn't use the word 'evil.' But Rafael Maleparte was evil. I spent nearly fifty hours in his company. Fifty hours of hell. His tedious dream of working on an assembly line was the key I used to unlock the secrets of his miserable psyche."

"Oh, sure, that Rafael," I said. "He was basically okay. He just lacked self-esteem."

I stalked off to pee at the base of a cottonwood. Damn. Bloom had trumped my actual dream with an invented one. I liked his dream more than mine. It was derivative, but still—eight hours on an assembly line. You could kill a party with that one. You could kill a party or create a zone of silence and privacy in the tumult.

Pissing hurt. I'd first noticed the persistent drip and the stinging sensation this morning, but the pain had increased. The clap, probably one of those antibiotic-resistant strains that swiftly rotted loins, heart, and brain. Why me?

16

The others, staff and patients, began to arrive, walking in twos and threes or riding in the beds of the Ranch's battered pickup trucks. I greeted those I knew and was introduced to the others. Only a few of the patients were, like Lily, remarkable for their eccentricity. Most were tranquil (perhaps tranquilized); none were aggressive or disruptive (Dewey Yankhe was not among them); and all, I presumed, could be trusted to wield knives and forks in the socially approved manner. Doc Whillans would not have invited any stabbers or slashers, no droolers, no smirking coprophagists.

Lily stared at me whenever she believed that my attention was directed elsewhere, and quickly averted her eyes if I turned her way. She was excruciatingly shy, and like some mentally ill persons she seemed to possess an abnormal sensitivity to mood in others; she was attuned to the highest and lowest frequencies. One had to approach Lily with a pure heart, an untroubled mind. She would inform you, by bursting into tears or running away, that you were angry or fearful or sad.

I pretended to ignore her for about twenty minutes, all the while stalking, moving closer, and finally I was just a yard away. I drank beer with my right hand, so that she would see that I wore her gift, the hair bracelet, on that wrist, and then, without looking at her, I said, "Hello, Lily."

"Hello."

"How are you?"

"Oh, better, I think."

"It's good seeing you again."

"And you," she replied.

Lily had lost weight, was gaunt, and all the years of fear had erased whatever beauty might have been hers. Despair unfolded in the curve of her rare smiles.

I said, "I brought you a present. I'll give it to you tomorrow."

"I think they're going to kill me," she said softly.

"Who?"

"Mr. Yankhe told me so."

"Lily, I've warned you, everyone's warned you, not to pay attention to Yankhe."

"He said the Germans did it."

"Did what?"

"The Germans killed the crippled and sick and the stupid. He said that it's going to happen to us soon."

"Lily, poor Lily, this is America. If America ever goes bad we'll go around killing the swift and the smart."

My joke alarmed her.

"It's all nonsense," I said. "I promise you. No one intends to hurt you."

"Did the Germans really do what Mr. Yankhe said?"

"No, certainly not. People aren't like that."

She was silent, fidgeting, and then she said, "If people are not like that, how could Mr. Yankhe think of such a thing?"

"Dewey is a confused and frightened man."

"No, I mean—if Mr. Yankhe could think of such a thing, why then such a thing could take place. If it exists in his mind then it exists in the world."

"It just isn't so."

"And now, you see, there are three of us who can conceive of such a thing, such horror. Mr. Yankhe, you, and me. If three can imagine crimes like that then why couldn't millions?"

There was a raw patch on her left forearm and now the thumb and first two fingers of her right hand began plucking at it. It was like watching a hen peck at the raw flesh of another chicken.

"Look," I said. "We're going to have a spectacular sunset."

"I must be right," she said. "Thoughts are only unborn actions. If Mr. Yankhe can have the idea of our extermination, why then it's plain that others can have the same idea, and soon enough we'll be exterminated."

"Lily, I must see Dr. Whillans now. I'll talk to you later, okay?"

"All right."

"If you want to talk to me."

"I don't care," she said.

Whillans was autocratically, and ignorantly, telling Tom Lopez how to barbecue the kid. As usual there was the stub of a Camel cigarette smoldering below his weedy, nicotine-stained moustache. Some visitors to the

Ranch assumed that Dr. Whillans was a patient, another crackpot singing another incomprehensible song. But he was not at all mad; it was just that after fifty years spent among the mentally ill he had acquired their childish candor and spontaneity and swift mood changes. Whillans had acquired some superficial characteristics of the insane without submitting to the inner dynamics.

"Come on, Doc," I said.

We walked a hundred yards out into the desert and turned to watch the crimson and gold sunset. I could hear the smug chortling of quail off in the creosote.

"You've got to get rid of Dewey Yankhe," I said.

"That's easy to say. Dewey won't leave. He says that if he ever gets beyond the fence we'll shoot him down like a rabid dog."

"Jesus, Doc, is this your asylum or not? Do you let the patients dictate to you?"

"If I did, you'd be dictator by now. What's the problem?"

"Yankhe scared the hell out of Lily with his talk of an imminent final solution here."

"Oh, that. Yes. You know, I've often wondered if Dewey would be happier and healthier if he actually were persecuted. If I weren't constrained by certain ethical considerations . . ."

"Well, what about this?"

"I'll see what can be done with Dewey. Now, what about you? Why are you back here?"

I told him about my fight with Fungo Gates.

"Fight *and* flight, eh Theodore? Are you here as a patient?"

"No."

"Well, why did you come here, then?" Whillans's aureole of hair was glowing pinkish from the sunset. He took a Camel from a crushed package, lit it and let it fume between his lips.

I hesitated, then said, "Doc, I *like* it here. Does that make me crazy?"

"I'm not sure, Theodore. I like it here too, and I've often wondered if that made me crazy. How do you feel?"

"Okay?"

"Any anxieties, dread, sweats, hallucinations? A narrowing of your field of vision?"

"No. Well, I do feel some anxiety, but that's natural, isn't it? Only the Undead don't feel anxiety."

"Has your memory improved?"

"Not much. I don't think it's going to. I'm trying to learn about that period from the outside. People tell me what I was like and what happened, and it's almost like being there."

Whillans laughed, a phlegmy hack that ended in a cough.

"Listen, can we talk about something besides me while I'm here?"

"Yes, on my part with great relief."

"I'm sick of introspection. I'd like to put in at least one day during which I never once speak of or think about myself."

"Hah!"

"I mean it, Doc. Hell is subjectivity."

"Hell is standing around and defining hell."

"Hell is creamed chipped beef on stale toast." I withdrew a five-thousand-dollar check from my shirt pocket and gave it to him.

"This is a lot of money, Theodore."

"I can afford it. Anyway, it's tax deductible."

"But didn't you lose your job?"

"Maybe I'll play baseball in Japan."

"Just out of curiosity, Theodore—what is your salary?"

"Eight hundred thousand dollars per year, plus incentives."

"My God."

"I'm grossly underpaid, Doc. But I'm a risk because of my history. They never know when I'll go cuckoo again."

We rejoined the others. Bloom's string quartet played pieces by Brahms and Mozart. All four were sweaty and happy afterward; they had done a very difficult thing moderately well and were proud. There was talent among some of the insane, and intelligence. They, more than anyone, understood the magnitude of their defeat.

The sky was consumed by scarlet and coral fires and then turned as black as carbon. A few sparks—stars—remained. The pulsing coals of the piñonwood fire became our new sun.

We ate the smoky-sweet kid with cole slaw and chips and beans and 3.2 beer. I was commanded, as host, to give a speech. I could not think of anything appropriate and so I recited a poem I'd written during my *furor scribendi.*

> *All things are One*
> *and One thing is All.*
> *Dark is the sun and*
> *big things are small.*
>
> *Downward we climb while*
> *upward we fall.*
> *Time is not time—*
> *it's nothing at all.*

Less is More,
as we all know.
Three is four and
stop means go.

Naught is king,
zero's a lot.
Nothing is everything
that Everything's not.

The applause was hearty, and there were whistles and shouts of "Bravo!" My fellow patients seemed genuinely moved.

17

〰

Back in the cottage I pulled the drapes and turned on all the lamps. Cockroaches scuttled across the kitchen's linoleum floor when the lights went on. I managed to stun one with a kick and then finished him off with half a dozen whacks of a folded newspaper. Moon 1, roaches 0.

Someone had taken all the 150-watt bulbs that I'd installed and replaced them with 35's and 60's. A simple thief of light or a lover of obscurity? The same person had, like a pack rat, left me an object to replace my pilfered light: a cracked earthenware pot full of desert plants now sat on the coffee table. It contained twigs of crucifixion thorn, sprays of yellow gamma grass, and tiny yellow flowers. An austere bouquet.

I glanced at the litter of typescript, the product of my conversion from *furor loquendi* to *furor scribendi*. During the months of convalescence from my first crack-up I had literally written like a madman, polemics with titles like "*J'Accuse*," verse, poison-pen letters, fragments of a play and a novel, and the part of my autobiography that I had written alone, before the ghost arrived.

I sat at the desk and read every third page of my aborted autobiography. It was all the things that the editor claimed, dull, rambling, foolish, messianic . . . Even so, I preferred it to the ghosted version; it at least bore some relation to the busted puzzle that was my life.

My lawyer had proposed the book to several publishers. It's a natural, he said: big-league baseball player sees his career and family being destroyed by an insidious mental disease, valorously wrestles with his demons, and finally, against all odds and all the people who said it couldn't be done, he triumphs. A positive story. It had everything. Popular sport, family anguish, adultery, a devastating and yet very colorful disease, and lots of psychiatric mumbo jumbo—America's favorite mysticism.

At that time I was living stunned on the New Mexican desert. I picked cactus needles out of my hands and knees and wondered how they'd got there. My brain, infested with fire ants, itched ferociously. I sassed the walls, the stones. My life was one endless, scrambled, delirious day, and it required a singular act of faith for my lawyer to suppose that there could be any book at all, let alone one that ended with a heartwarming comeback. At any rate, diet, quiet, tedium, and lithium had fairly quickly restored my equilibrium, although parts of my painfully accumulated heritage, my memory, remained ash-dead. ("Ah, memories," Buckley had once murmured, avoiding my eyes. "That's one thing they can't take away from you.")

My editor believed the book should be colloquial and profane, a slangy romp through the vicissitudes of sport and mental illness. He advised me to read Ring Lardner for stylistic tips.

"Are you personally aware of any homosexuality in baseball? Do you know of any buggery among the athletes, rumors, even rumors of rumors?"

He encouraged me to write an exposé. Scandal was the ticket, sex and dope and racism. Sodomy, rape, bondage games, pedophilia, wife-swapping, bestiality. Anything like that. Incest, voyeurism. And dope: marijuana, cocaine, crack, heroin—any black players on the needle?—steroids, barbiturates, mescaline, LSD, angel dust, glue. Racial animosity?

I telephoned my lawyer and screamed, "Who are these people? Who have you sold my life to?"

I was assigned a new editor and two days later a sweating, overweight man arrived at the cottage door. "Hi," he said. "I'm your ghost. The sex and the dope are out. Sensitivity's in."

He rented the cottage next door and for several hours each day sat by while I spoke into his tape recorder. (Back again to *furor loquendi*.) He was sympathetic, like a psychiatrist, and he asked me psychiatrists' questions. "How did that make you feel?" "Were you resentful, Ted?" "Tell me more about that."

He smoked a pipe and all of his shirts were pitted with burn holes. There were fingerprints on the lenses of his glasses. In speaking, he dropped the *r*'s from words like "car" and "far," and saved them to put at the end of words like "idea" and "data." ("Give me more dater on the gel in the cah.")

At ten I turned on the black hole and watched the news. There was a clip of President Clinton, the latest in a long line of philosopher-kings; a corrupt congressman who proclaimed his innocence, his *purity;* automobile accidents; the tape of a female corpse being fished out of an irrigation ditch.

Then there was a feature, part of a series, on female cancers. Sci-porn. What bluenose could object to an objective discussion about the dangers of vaginal and cervical cancer? None, since health is the issue. And who can be blamed if, in the interest of health, a hypothetical penis is inserted into a hypothetical vagina and vigorously implemented? None, since such "penal" (said the TV reporter) activity can be a contributing cause of female cancers. Sex causes cancer. Prisons too, apparently, cause cancer. We had abstract politicians, abstract accidents, abstract crimes, abstract sex, abstract disease, abstract life and abstract death. Abstract art. We had it all.

And then the station provided abstract weather for the abstract viewers: cartoons and maps and flashing lights and satellite photos and prophecy-by-computer. It would be warm and dry again tomorrow.

I did not watch the sports news. My name might be mentioned. I didn't need that now; I was feeling sufficiently abstracted.

My hands were trembling. The window air conditioner had begun to sing, a distant a cappella voice now, but I knew that there was a full chorus waiting, and a symphony orchestra. Bubbles fizzed upward along the length of my spine.

I picked up the phone and dialed Doc Whillans's room. It rang six times, seven, and I was about to hang up when he answered. His voice was sleep-thickened.

"Sorry to wake you, Doc."

"I wasn't sleeping," he lied.

"Forget it. I'll talk to you in the morning."

"Theodore, what is it that you need?"

"Nothing. I was about to crack open a bottle of whisky and I thought—"

"You thought correctly, Theodore. I'll be right there. I saw that bottle in your cupboard and wondered if you intended to be greedy."

"Did you steal my light?"

"We need high-watt bulbs over here. These rooms are vast."

"I shouldn't have awakened you. We'll drink the scotch tomorrow."

"Nonsense," he said, and he hung up.

Whillans arrived in the two-piece gray sweatsuit he used for pajamas. He held aloft a pressurized gasoline lantern and his hair looked like a fright wig in the hard white light.

I held the door open. "Doc, I'm sorry."

"Don't be sorry. Get out the goddamned malt whisky. And a couple of towels. We'll go to the spring."

18

—〰—

The baths were located on the southern edge of the Ranch property. Whillans's lantern hissed like a deflating tire, and his loose sandals flopped against the flagstones.

"I don't know, Doc," I said. "This is an awfully hot night for a hot bath."

"I want to bathe, Theodore. Do you mind?"

"Do the chemicals really help your arthritis?"

"The heat does."

"Odd," I said, "that you psychiatrist bozos used to believe that arthritis was largely a psychosomatic disease."

"Theodore, it may be that the happy day is coming when we psychiatrist bozos will be replaced by pharmacists."

"Good news for the addled," I said. "You bozos can go back to reading chicken entrails."

I could see the building now. It was constructed out of

thousands of small panes of glass, like a greenhouse, and was scaled with moonlight. Many of the panes were cracked and broken, and the rest opaque with dirt. In cold weather steam filled the interior and billowed out through all the broken glass; there were days when the entire structure vanished behind a seething white cloud.

"I can already smell the water," I said. "Why do you think all those millionaires came here to drink and sit in that vile, stinking water?"

"Because of an ancient principle. If a substance smells and tastes evil, it must be good for you. Suffering is an essential part of the curative mystery. That's why I use placebos that taste like deadly poisons. My patients wouldn't respond to mint wafers or marzipan."

Whillans unlocked the door, entered ahead of me and flicked the light switch. A few bare bulbs were strung on a wire that ran the length of the center beam. Shadows filled the corners and spilled out onto the tiled pool apron. Cobwebs and dirt, rat droppings, and a chemical stink that burned my nostrils. It was very humid. The water, deep at one end and shallow at the other, was clear. That always surprised me. It should have been a nauseous yellow-green and coated with bubbling slime, with here and there a bloated rodent floating head down in the noxious soup.

Whillans began undressing. "Long ago, when these springs were just a natural pool in the rocks, the Apaches came here to bathe. They bathed here long before the millionaires. Do you suppose that has any significance, Theodore?"

"Sure. It means that, contrary to our expectations, aborigines aren't any smarter than millionaires. Or you."

He smiled. "Or you. Aren't you coming in?"

Whillans had a smooth, hard potbelly, a melon, but

elsewhere his skin was loose and sagging. Time had consumed his fat and shrunk his muscles and now he looked as if he were wearing a skin-sheath that didn't fit, that was one size too large for the bones and flesh beneath.

"Don't stare," Whillans said.

"Sorry."

"Your body will look like this someday."

"By then the cosmetic surgeons will be able to carve new bodies."

There was an underwater ledge running around the perimeter of the pool, and we sat on that, our heads poked through the water's surface. The water was very hot. Its fumes cauterized the mucous membranes of my nostrils, throat, and sinuses; I could feel my brain turning to white ash. A pump throbbed at intervals, and there was the gurgle of drains and the splash of fresh water rising from hell. Moths formed flickering coronas around the light bulbs.

"Ah," Whillans exhaled. "It feels good. Admit the truth, Theodore, it feels good."

I had forgotten glasses. I broke the seal on the bottle of scotch, twisted off the cap and took a swallow. Its flavor seemed tainted by the water's stink, it tasted medicinal. I passed the bottle to Whillans.

"You know," he said, "I drink very little these days. My body can't easily metabolize alcohol. I am poisoned for days. But I may drink immoderately tonight."

"Drink, then."

"I'll drink in thanks to your substantial gift, Theodore. The Ranch is deeply in debt and that's a constant worry. We beg and we borrow and sometimes we poach—in extremis Lopez shoots game for our tables. Valuable protein. And the little market in town donates to us their half-spoiled fruits and vegetables. One of the churches there helps. Your contribution is greatly appreciated."

"Doc, I believe that speeches should be made after the drinking, not before. They're delivered with more eloquence then, and are better received too."

"In the spring we eat the fruit of the prickly-pear cactus. Our own chickens provide us with eggs and the occasional soup. Our ovens supply us with bread. Rice is cheap. And luckily a few of the patients are enthusiastic anglers and bring us fish, though the river is very low this summer . . ."

"Okay, I get it. Tomorrow I'll write another check, one for—say, three thousand dollars."

"Cash is our chief problem. I can't ask our small, highly unqualified staff to work for room and board."

"You get another three thousand and that's it. Please don't try to extort any more. What is this? I phone my physician and a fund-raiser shows up. I'm feeling insecure right now, Doc. I might be going crazy again."

He tilted the bottle and his Adam's apple bobbed three times. He passed me the bottle.

"You aren't going crazy."

"How do you know?"

"It's my business to know."

"Don't you make mistakes?"

"Not anymore. I've made them all."

"Doc, there are people who suspect me of being a serial killer."

"Nonsense. You couldn't kill. You haven't got the guts."

I laughed but at the same time I resented his flip dismissal of my capacity for insensate violence.

"Pass the malt," he said.

I passed it and said, "Doc, would you choose to live your life over again?"

"God, no."

"If you could live your life over, would you change anything?"

"Only an imbecile would not."

"What would you change?"

"I would prefer to start out as a bitter cynic and finish as a wild romantic, instead of the other way around."

"Sure. What else?"

"I would be more active sexually, a goatish sower of seed."

"You'd like to be more like me and less like you."

"But most of all I should like to be born skeptical about all the claims made about man's nature. All the sappy lies. We've sold ourselves a bill of goods over the centuries, Theodore, we've created a ridiculous composite monster—*homo sapiens* as designed by a committee of lunatics."

I nodded. "Pass the juice."

Alcohol had affected me to the point where this strange steaming greenhouse, our immersion in the stinking water, and our conversation, had begun to appear hallucinatory. Perhaps it was like the drug user's contact high: this moment was so unreal to me that I connected it to past moments of actual madness. The sensation was mild enough to be pleasant. It was no more than a disorientation of time and place, and a confusion of sequences. I felt that I was filled with a magic that I could exercise if I chose. Once I'd been convinced that I could walk through walls, and even fly if my motive were pure. I don't know if I ever tried to fly; my memory of those periods is dim and riddled with holes. Magic was real for me then. And as I recalled, sitting there in the hot water, half hearing Whillans talk about Ranch affairs, there had been moments when madness had been profoundly beau-

tiful to me, an ecstatic fusion of the conscious and unconscious when I could not resist regarding myself as the
possessor of some kind of cosmic grace.

"Theodore, have you been listening to me?"

"You said that the institution will die when you do."

"That isn't what I said."

"It was something like that."

"Something like that," he said scornfully.

"Pass the sauce."

"*You* have the sauce."

We were both drunk. Whillans's eyes had rounded and
were rimmed with red membrane, and his stare was belligerent.

"I was thinking about when I was crazy," I said.

"I don't want to hear about it."

"You saved my life, Doc."

"*Mea culpa maxima.*"

"Shit, I'm still young, I don't need baseball."

"Don't whine."

"But you're my physician."

"And you, alas, are my patient."

"Pass the booze."

"*You* have the booze."

I drank and passed him the bottle. It was about two-
thirds empty now.

"I don't know what I'm going to do now, Doc. I've
failed as an actor, failed as an author, failed as a talk-
show celebrity, and I'll probably fail as a politician. And
now I'm out of baseball."

"Stop whining."

"I'm not whining. I'm superior to the situation. They
can't touch me deep, where it counts. Fuck Fungo
Gates."

"That's what I've been trying to say all my life, Theodore, but lacking your eloquence, I've not succeeded. But there it is, a luminous phrase. Fuck Fungo Gates. An incantation for our time."

"No offense, Doc, but you're feebleminded."

"No offense taken, Theodore."

"Pass the bottle, Feeb."

"Whoops," he said, and he dropped the bottle. It was filled with the evil chemical brew when he retrieved it.

"That was cruel," I said.

We got out of the pool and dried ourselves on the towels I'd brought. My skin was lobster-red and tingled in the relatively cool air. Whillans was very drunk; I had to help him dress.

We walked to the main building's front door. Whillans was drunk and perhaps sick, and he had to work hard to maintain dignity. In the hissing glow of the lantern his face sagged with fatigue, had a mournful aspect, and I realized how much it had cost him to help me tonight. I had used him unfairly.

He made a last tough effort to seem cheerful. "As Richard M. Nixon said as he stood atop the Great Wall of China—'One can only conclude that this is indeed a great wall . . .' "

19

~~~

I lay in bed for several hours, battling insomnia with images that turned ugly just as I began to doze; and then I got up, dressed, took two cans of beer from the refrigerator and went outside. It was cooling now and might even turn chill in the hour before dawn. The silence was total except for the remote static, the faint crepitation, of space itself.

I walked east across the desert. I did not need my flashlight; the sky was densely sprayed with stars, a powdery glow like foxfire in decayed wood, and the moon was bright enough to throw shadows. My elongated shadow preceded me.

Bristling cacti, yucca, creosote, sparse tufts of yellow grass. Each desert plant was cleanly defined by moonlight and shadow, isolated—a primitive might invoke the individual plant spirits at such a time. I tried speaking

Noble Savage Tongue. "Greetings, Brother Yucca, tall sentinel of the drear wastes." It lacked the reverent intonations of Oliver Buckley. "Greetings, Brother Prickly Pear, vegetable cousin of the formidable porcupine." Better. I imagined an encounter with a coiled rattlesnake. "O greetings, Brother Pit Viper, piercer of rodents, cunning drinker of moonlight—I walk in peace." ("O pass then, Brother Theodore," my rattlesnake replied in a voice that sounded like Buckley's, "go pacifically, mighty hurler of compact spheres.")

The land before me appeared level but gradually ascended toward the mountains. I could feel the incline in my leg muscles. My breathing accelerated. I began to sweat. And I wondered if I were—ignorant of deepest intent—stalking the site of my death. Maybe my suicide was an act impatiently awaiting consummation. Ahead of me, a mile in distance, half an hour in time, with each step and tick converging toward my extinction. I did not feel free enough to deny the possibility. It seemed that my footprints were implicit in the smooth earth; I had only to step into them.

The mountains were a dusty gray in the moonlight, with each crease and fold indicated by pools and cataracts of shadow. Beyond the mountains lay a stretch of the White Sands Missile Range. And to the northeast was the Trinity Site, where on July 16, 1945, the first atomic bomb was detonated. The desert was named Jornada del Muerto. That was one of the more crudely ironic juxtapositions of geography and incident. The Journey of The Dead.

The two cans of beer warmed in my hands. The incline steepened. I reached the foothills and continued climbing. Fatigue had hollowed me out, bells chimed faintly in the bloodrush in my ears, and my mouth was coated with a viscous scum. I spat, sucked my cheeks, spat again. I no longer felt that I was approaching some perilous assignation.

There were stunted junipers and piñon pines on the slope now, dark and gnarled, and their scents were like rich perfumes in the dry desert air. I turned, and was surprised to see how high I had climbed; the valley floor was far below, a vast lake of moonlight, and the trees and buildings of the Ranch complex were merely dark stains near the horizon. Its lights looked like low stars from here. A downhill current of air cooled my sweat.

I sat down, feeling absurdly proud of my trek. It was an action, no matter how gratuitous. The opposite of nothing.

I let the beer settle for a while and then opened a can and sucked up the eruption of foam. Ambrosia. I drank the first beer quickly and rationed the second.

It was almost five o'clock. I decided to remain here and watch the apocalyptic desert sunrise. It would be fairly cool then. I would not have to worry as much about treading on Brother Pit Viper.

I lay back on the hard ground. The night creaked and ticked with insect noises. I watched the stars for a time, closed my eyes and saw similar constellations of retinal sparks, microcosmic Milky Ways. I began to drowse then but a fragment of my mind remained alert, monitoring the fugitive night sounds. There, a rustle in the junipers—only the breeze. A remote sibilance. And later the eerie babble of some coyotes.

The coyotes tuned up with frenzied yelps and squeals that sounded as though a dozen puppies were being stepped on; and then their voices rose in both pitch and volume, and some of the notes were lengthened into siren whines. It was not a mournful sound like the howling of big wolves; this was quick and sharp, comical, a vocal competition. Two coyotes, probably. Two coyotes could sound like a dozen.

The concert lasted only a few minutes and then they silently moved away. No doubt they had observed me walking across the desert, penetrating their territory, and had curiously followed me to where I now lay. Waited and watched. And then performed for me the same kind of mocking serenade they periodically gave the Ranch's treasonous canines.

I stiffly got up and brushed soil off my trousers. Dawn was approaching. The moon was down and a thin aura of pale violet light traced the jagged mountain ridges to the east. The stars along the horizon had started to fade.

And then I was aware of a sudden stillness. The insect noises, so faint and familiar, ceased, and the air seemed to thicken in the ensuing hush.

There was a flare of light to the northeast, toward the Trinity Site. It rippled through the sky like the Aurora or sheet lightning, and then swiftly brightened. An arc of white fire lifted above the mountains. The seething globe of light expanded, brightened, and in the center was a pure incandescent whiteness, a pulsing seed. My eyes hurt but I did not close them. Hallucinations do not blind.

The fire storm carried with it a great cloud of dust which gathered into the famous mushroom shape. It ballooned bigger and bigger as the light correspondingly dimmed.

The earth seemed to shift slightly underfoot. A gust of wind, hissing through the trees, rushed toward the explosion. Air hurrying to fill the vacuum created by the blast.

The noise was reduced by distance and the intervening terrain, and sounded like a single prolonged stroke of thunder, a deep *crump* followed by a series of diminishing echoes.

Awed and frightened, incredulous, I turned and started down the slope. I resolved not to mention the atomic blast to anyone, not even Dr. Whillans. Either the blast had actually occurred or I was an hallucinator of sublime genius. Either way, it was a phenomenon to be dreaded in private.

The sun, the true sun, rose to the south of its imitator. I kept walking. I did not look back. By the time I reached the cottage I was exhausted and so thirsty that my tongue cleaved to my palate.

Billy, Lopez's son, and two other boys, were waiting for me outside the cottage. I drank two cans of beer and three glasses of water, got my glove and a couple of base-balls, and went back outside.

"You kids been up long?"

"Yeah. A while."

"Did you see anything funny over there? That way?"

No.

"No strange lights or anything like that?"

No. Uh-huh.

"Okay. Shall we play catch?"

Yes sir. You bet. If you don't mind.

20

〰

The telephone rang while I was sleeping. I didn't know if there were several separate calls or one long series of rings. The sound was absorbed into my dreams. In the last dream I was walking down the tree-tunneled side street of a familiar city. It was night, the streetlights were not burning, and there were no lights behind the house windows. No people, no sounds, no motion. I paused in front of an old frame house. Where had they—we—gone? A front window was broken; the door was crooked on its hinges; weeds grew knee-high in the yard. A telephone was ringing inside the house. Suddenly it was daylight and a swollen white sun siphoned all color from the land and sky.

At one-thirty I got up, showered, shaved, dressed in tennis shorts and shirt, and went out into the dry furnace heat. The thermometer outside my door read 109 degrees. The ground deflected the sun's rays in waves that glazed the air. I was still possessed by the mood of my dream and this actual desolation, following the dream one, frightened me a little. Here too there was a sinister quiet. No thing moved. The heat, the vertiginous sense of void, were crushing. I felt that I hardly existed, was little more than a possibility, and that my essence might evaporate like last night's dew.

I slowly crossed the quadrangle, accompanied by my shrunken shadow. Near the main building's front door, in the shade of a cottonwood, lay three panting dogs. They looked flattened and broken-spined, as if they had been hurled there from a great height. One of them, his tongue lolling, lifted his head and gave me a shamefaced grin.

It was dim and cool in the enormous entrance hall. That must have been a fine room when it had been the hotel reception lobby; now it was just an oddly proportioned cavern that collected sounds from other areas of the building. I could hear, like faint audio hallucinations, the whining of a violin, a radio or television, footfalls, murmuring voices. In the old days the carpeting and furnishings must have absorbed such remote sounds.

Hallways angled off to the left and right, and a broad, curving stairway ascended to a landing which debouched into other halls.

A middle-aged woman in a white smock and practical white shoes, her hair done up in a tight bun, emerged from the downstairs east hall, proceeded fifty feet into the room, noticed me and abruptly halted. I did not know her.

"What are you doing here?" she sternly asked.

"I'm a visitor."

"You're supposed to be in class."

"I'm here to measure for the carpeting and drapes," I said.

"Yes, well, we'll see about that," and she turned briskly and returned down the same hallway.

I assumed that she was a nurse or some kind of assistant, although she might have been a patient. Many psychotics came to believe that they were staff members; some were quite convincing.

The office doors were situated on the far wall where the registration center had once stood. Mrs. McGregor, Whillans's hatchet-faced bookkeeper, greeted me with cordial scorn. She was one of those competent elderly women who continually attempt to seize her employer's authority and perquisites. Insurrection kept her lean.

"Is Whillans in his office?"

"*Doc-tor* Whillans is not in his office."

"Where is he?"

"About his duties, Mr. Moon, about his duties."

"My phone rang while I was asleep."

"Indeed it did!" She wore rimless octagonal glasses that reduced her eyes to blue lasers. Long yellow pencils had been thrust into her dyed black hair.

"Well?" I said.

She exhaled wearily, instilling guilt, and passed me several scraps of paper. My lawyer had phoned, and Blas Cintron, Buckley, Patsy, and—I could hardly believe it—the FBI. Scoot, Moon, the Feds have your scent.

"Did anything strange happen this morning?" I asked her.

"Strange, Mr. Moon?"

"At about six o'clock."

She stared at my mouth.

"Out on the desert. Toward the mountains. I just wondered."

She sighed and reverently bowed her head over the
ledger. "There are many strange occurrences around this
place, Mr. Moon," she said, making it clear that she considered me among them.

I went up the stairway and down a long, dimly lighted
hall that smelled of wood rot. The old silk wallpaper was
water-stained and tattered, and chalky pieces of plaster
littered the floor. The eight-foot-high double doors were
mahogany, the hinges and doorknobs had been cast of
bronze. Most of the rooms up here were empty; all but a
few of the patients and staff members were quartered in
the better-maintained east wing. But Dewey Yankhe, the
political prisoner, had his suite of rooms down this corridor, opposite a fire exit ("They'll try to fry my fat one
night").

His door was ajar but I knocked loudly and called
"Dewey!" before entering. He had scrounged old furniture from the Ranch complex, all that had been
overlooked by the lawful looters and scavengers:
rich wine-red carpeting, Tiffany lamps, velvet drapes,
silk-upholstered furniture, gilded porcelain vases and
figurines, nineteenth-century landscapes, and enameled
chamber pots.

"Dewey!" I called again.

In one of his rooms he had a bed that looked like a
maharanee's palanquin.

Dewey reputedly received a small monthly stipend
from his wealthy family. He could live cheaper and better
here than on the outside.

A door to my left opened and Dewey appeared in the
frame. "Moon," he said. "Did you bring any good
hootch?"

"No, but I have some beer in the cottage."

"Never mind. We'll drink my rotgut vodka."

I followed him into the "operations center," once a sitting room and now lined with filing cabinets and workbenches, everything cluttered with as yet unclipped and unfiled "documentation"—newspapers and magazines, books, spools of film. On one of the benches were glue pot and scissors, manila file folders, stacks of index cards, a bottle of contraband vodka and some crystal glasses.

"I heard you were back."

"Not for long," I said.

He poured several ounces of vodka into each of the glasses and handed me one.

"I think I may have the bastards soon," he said.

He was a skinny old man who now, as usual, wore espadrilles, baggy khaki trousers, and an armless undershirt.

"Capitalism is a house of cards, my friend. Locate the key card, remove it, and the whole rotten structure collapses. The Chase Manhattan Bank is the key card. The structure will soon come down. You'll come down with it, Moon. Sorry."

"What the hell," I said. I never knew how much of Dewey's madness was pure humbug. He was serious about his socialist mission, he often talked in linked non sequiturs, but there was always a dry vein of satire in his craziness.

"I'll educate you yet, Moon."

"I'm a dull student." In another room there were bookcases filled with radical literature. Dewey, hoping to convert me to the Marxist cause, had loaned me several books, but I had become lost in Hegel and was not sure that I would ever find my way out.

"You house niggers think you got more to lose than the field niggers."

"We do," I said.

"And that's why injustice prevails. Because everyone's trying to make a separate deal. The ruling class knows that. Divide and piss upon, that's their motto."

"Communism isn't doing very well these days," I said.

"That's exactly what we want you to think. Keep thinking that way, Boyo. We're going back underground. We're descending once again into the catacombs. We'll rise again, purified."

I glanced at the newspapers on his workbench. There was a copy of *L'Humanité,* another of the *London Daily Worker,* and yesterday's *Albuquerque Journal.* A *Journal* headline read: "Simulated A-bomb at Trinity."

"I read about your most recent escapade," Dewey said. "You hit the wrong man. You hit a man who's got calluses on his hands. A worker. Wake up, boob, and start hitting the people with soft hands."

"Women and children?" I asked, skimming the article.

"Yeah," he said in disgust. "Widows and orphans. Old invalids."

The article stated that at six A.M. tomorrow (today) six hundred tons of ammonium-nitrate fuel oil would be detonated near the old Trinity Site. The blast and "shock environment" were expected to equal that of a one-kiloton nuclear device. The test was being conducted by the Defense Nuclear Agency, and among the one hundred and five separate experiments was one to determine the effects on "anthropomorphic dummies."

"You are essentially a fascist," Dewey said.

"You are essentially an anthropomorphic dummy," I replied.

A headline in the sports section caught my attention:

MOON SLAMS GATES

The article stated that I had left the team after an altercation with the manager, Jim "Fungo" Gates. Gates was in the hospital with a broken jaw. No one knew the whereabouts of Theodore Moon. The implication was that I had cracked up once again. "Moon has a history of bizarre behavior and has twice been hospitalized . . ." Blas Cintron was quoted as saying that the abusive Fungo had received exactly what he deserved. Then he spoiled it by adding that Fungo and Moon were both dementos. An unidentified teammate said, "Until today, it appeared that Moon had been expanding the parameters of his maturity-factor mode." That would be Buckley, of course, gallantly trying for a sentence of pure Negative Meaning.

"I'm what?" Dewey said.

"An anthropomorphic dummy."

"I am what History made me," he said, pretty well satisfied with History's will and craft.

"Dewey, I don't want you to scare Lily anymore with your horror stories about concentration camps and mass exterminations."

"I didn't invent those things."

"I know. History did."

"But I suppose I might have made my point a little too vividly. The twentieth-century mass mind is so deadened by lies and entertainment that you have to shock it awake. Stir up the viscera and the brain ignites."

"Yeah, well, Lily doesn't want anything to do with the twentieth century."

"All right. Now you do me a favor."

"What?"

"Loan me twenty dollars. I don't own a shirt."

I gave Dewey twenty dollars—which he'd spend on newspapers and magazines—and turned to leave.

"Moon?"

"Yes?"

"I understand the symbolism. Transsexuals are the perfect symbol of the decadent capitalist society. But those poor, poor souls—did you have to kill them?"

"I didn't."

"I want to believe you. But, comrade, read between the lines in the fascist establishment press and you'll find that you're already halfway up the gallows' steps. Take my advice, leave the country. Go to Cuba."

"I'm innocent," I said, and I learned at that instant that there was something degrading about asserting one's innocence. I felt and sounded guilty. I could see my guilt reflected in Dewey's eyes.

"Go to hell," I told him.

I returned to the cottage and sprawled on the bed for twenty minutes, listening to the labored respiration of the air conditioner, waiting for the telephone to ring. I let it ring several times before picking up the receiver.

"Asshole."

"Blas, you're supposed to be playing baseball."

"I'm calling from the clubhouse. Are you crazy again?"

"No. I'm just another anthropomorphic dummy."

"Yeah, you're crazy."

"What do you want?"

"Are you coming back to the team?"

"No one has asked me to."

"I'm asking you."

"But you aren't the manager or GM."

"Fungo is in a hospital here with a broken jaw. Haugen appointed Grosbeck to finish the season as manager. Grosbeck wants you to rejoin the team in L.A. So does Mr. Haugen."

"The choice of Grosbeck is logical. Grosbeck is the second most stupid man in baseball, just behind Fungo."

"We'll be flying out to Los Angeles after the game today."

"Do they really want me back?"

"What have I been saying? There'll be a fine, Moon, a big one."

"That's okay."

"They'll pin your ass to the outhouse wall after the season."

"What do the guys think?"

"We think you're a jerk, but it sorely tries our hearts to see Prosper start to warm up in the eighth inning."

"All right."

"Call Mr. Haugen."

"No, I'll just head out to Los Angeles."

"When?"

"Twenty minutes, half an hour."

"How is your hand?"

"Hand?"

"Your pitching hand, the one you hit Fungo with."

"It's not my hand I'm worried about, Blas, it's my root. My root is oozing stigmatozoa."

"Aw, Christ," he said, and he hung up.

I telephoned the bookstore in Iowa City. "Patsy?"

"Moon? Hi."

"I'm at the Ranch."

"I phoned earlier because I was worried. I know how you drive."

"I'm leaving for the West Coast. Do you want to come out to L.A. for a few days?"

"I can't, Moon—the business."

"One of your college kids can run the shop. You really ought to get away."

"Moon, thanks, but I can't leave right now. I'd really like to, but . . ."

"Well, I'm sorry."

"I'm sorry too."

"Oh, Patsy, by the way, have you seen your gynecologist lately?"

"What?"

"I just wondered."

"Moon . . ."

"I've got the clap."

A long silence.

"You are accusing me of giving you—you son of a bitch!"

"No, no, don't hang up. I probably gave it to you. The night before last."

"Oh, God."

"I'm sorry, kid. Really sorry."

"You're *always* sorry."

"I didn't know I had it when I saw you. There were no signs then. I think I might have picked it up in Pittsburgh. Or maybe Cincinnati. I don't know what the incubation period is."

Her laugh was operatic, the shriek of a dying diva, and then the line went dead.

21

Dr. Whillans was in his room, lying in an old four-poster bed. The pouches beneath his eyes looked like prunes. An old air conditioner hummed and drizzled water on the tiles.

"Are you sick, Doc?"

"Hung over."

"I'm sorry. I shouldn't have dragged you out last night."

"I enjoyed it. Aren't you hung over?"

"No. A little tired is all. I haven't slept much during the last few days."

"You have a Promethean liver."

"I'm heading out to the Coast."

"Are you?"

"Doc, why don't you come out to Los Angeles tomorrow or the next day? I'll put you up at the hotel, and you can eat a couple of good meals, see some ballgames, visit a classy whorehouse or something."

"Are you inviting me as friend or physician?"

"Friend."

"I'll think about it."

"Good. I'll phone you tomorrow." I got out my check-book, wrote a check for three thousand dollars and gave it to him.

"Thank you. You're a generous man, Theodore."

"Doc, I think I've got the clap."

He stared at me. "You aren't going to ask me to examine your male member, are you?"

"Could you let me have some penicillin?"

"I'll phone downstairs. See Nurse Stetner. Follow the dosage exactly, and see a physician when you reach Los Angeles."

"Thanks, Doc."

His voice stopped me when I reached the door.

"Theodore—maybe you shouldn't leave here right now."

"I'm fine, Doc. Really. It's not as though I'm hal-lucinating atomic blasts or anything."

I picked up the penicillin downstairs, walked to the cottage and packed my bags. I decided to wear my os-trich cowboy boots, with faded jeans tucked inside and bloused a little, and my big pearl-gray Stetson.

"Howdy," I said to the mirror. "Hot, ain't it?"

"Shit yeah, Bo," the mirror replied.

I took a six-pack of cold beer from the refrigerator and placed it on the car's front seat. "We crossin' the *Jornada del Muerto,* Bo."

I drove west to the Interstate and turned south. The desert didn't appear quite so deadly when viewed through the tinted windshield of a Mercedes Benz. I opened a beer and placed it between my thighs. "Just th'ow the can out the window when you finish, Bo."

On an El Paso radio station two women, their voices rich and melodious with compassion, were discussing "home-support systems" for working women. Astronaut chitchat. (Baby sitter and cleaning lady in place, all home-support systems are *go,* Mission Control.) A little later they began talking about "female bonding." Old Behaviorist jargon. I rejected science in favor of art, spinning the dial until I picked up a country western station.

> *Honeytonk angel,*
> *Dancin' all night,*
> *Barroom butterfly,*
> *Makin' men fight.*
>
> *Gonna buy a jukebox*
> *For our little room.*
> *Lock you in it,*
> *Call it your tomb.*

A terrific song, a peek into the psyche of a hillbilly at three A.M. on Sunday morning. Big Adam's apples on scrawny necks, flick knives.

A dyslexic read five minutes of news and then Little Miss Gingham sang about the dark side of love.

> *Honey, I got my country's flag,*
> *You can head out that door.*
> *I got my old family Bible,*
> *I don't need you anymore.*

I stopped for gasoline in Hatch, New Mexico. The attendant, a fat man in a stained green jumpsuit, wiped the insects off the windshield with a rag that left oily rainbows. The heat seemed to arrive in waves, each blast heavier than the preceding.

"Howdy!" I said. "Sure is hot."

"Sure is."

"Damn hot."

"Heat killed my poor old dog," he said.

I took State Route 26 down to Interstate 10 and stopped at a cafe in Deming. There was a long counter with stools, a few Formica tables, dirty plate-glass windows, and twisted strips of flypaper black with corpses. A wiry old lady—maître d', chef, dishwasher, waitress—cooked my hamburger on a grill behind the counter.

"Ain't it hot, though," I said.

"I've seen hotter."

"Maybe so, but this is *hot.*"

"Hotter when you complain."

"The heat killed my poor old dog," I said.

The hamburger was so greasy that it made the lettuce and raw onions transparent; the French fries were thick and cut with many odd facets, like crystals, and they smelled of fish. I ate everything and ordered two more hamburgers for the road. I could eat them cold with beer. I hadn't had a hamburger for years that tasted as good. Squeamish notions about health and sanitation were ruining our native American cuisine.

I returned to 10 and ran the speedometer needle up to ninety. There was not much traffic, some late-summer tourists, dented pickup trucks, eighteen-wheelers, and old couples hauling aluminum trailers.

> *I didn't mean*
> *To kill that boy.*
> *Mama, don't you sigh.*

Guess I'll go back to 'Nam,
Finish what I started.
Just go back and die.
Mama, turn away
While I cry.

America did not lack sentiment, by God. You could still buy a botulburger on rural back streets and cry when things went wrong. We were still a great people.

I stopped for gas in Lordsburg. Vultures circled over corrugated steel roofs. A thin Mexican came out and filled the tank.

"Howdy," I said. "Sure is hot."

He nodded.

"Heat killed my poor old dog."

He nodded again. "Yesterday my horse died between my legs. I was practicing for a rodeo up in Silver City. I guess she was sick."

I went into the station. There was a very old woman sleeping in a rocking chair next to the Coke machine. A fly swatter crossed her thighs. Her hair was pulled back tightly in braids and her face was webbed with wrinkles. She snored.

Inside the bathroom there were machines that dispensed condoms and combs and pornographic playing cards. I bought a deck of cards.

I went back outside. The attendant was wiping the windshield with an oily rag.

"Was she a good horse?" I asked him.

"My only horse."

I got back into my frisky steel steed and headed west.

Darlin', I ain't a man to sit,
I just got to ramble.

I ain't a man to sharecrop
While I know how to gamble.

I opened a can of beer, warm now, and drank it along
with one of the cold hamburgers. The playing cards were
the real thing, truly salacious.

I stopped again for gas in Benson, Arizona. A skinny
boy, sixteen or seventeen, came out to service the car. I
saw him admiring my ostrich cowboy boots.

"Howdy," I said. "Ain't it hot, though."

"Yes sir."

"Had a horse die atween my legs today, so hot."

The kid screwed up his face and said, "The river turned
to mist today at noon."

"I've had lots of beasts die under me, but that was my
favorite studhorse."

"White mist flowing along the riverbed."

"Lather was gushing out of my horse like shaving
cream from an aerosol can. I couldn't see my legs for
lather."

"You could watch the mist fish and mist turtles and
mist crawfish swimming through the mist river. It was
something, mister. My ma fried up some mist trout and
they turned to water in the pan."

"My horse turned into a centaur just afore he died."

The boy's lips twitched.

I tipped him five dollars. He showed promise.

Nearby there was a cinder-block building that adver-
tised "Anteeks & Soveneers." I went inside and rummaged through the piles of junk: wagon wheels and rusty
lanterns, plastic turquoise, milk cans and toy typewriters,
comic books, rifles held together by wire, saddles, potted
cacti, thirty-year-old black holes, stuffed birds, dented

hubcaps. A glass case contained half a dozen live rattlesnakes.

The proprietor, a husky Indian, slept in a rocking chair
while flies crawled over his face. The muscles around his
eyes twitched but the flies did not take offense. His left
hand was a scarred lump with three stiff fingoids.

I found a pair of Mexican silver spurs hanging from a
nail. They had big jingly rowels and were heavy enough
to be sterling.

"Howdy," I said. "I like these spurs. How much?"

One eye opened and then the other, and then his
mouth. Most of the flies crawled up into his hair. The Indian looked at my expensive hat and boots and said,
"Five hundred dollars."

We bargained and I succeeded in paying only fifty or
sixty dollars more than the spurs were worth. Then he
tried to sell me a stuffed armadillo but I told him that I
already owned more armadillos than a man could properly use. "I got one for a watchdog, and one to eat the
snails on my lawn, and another for a weathervane. I
don't need no more armadillos, live or stuffed."

He got two cans of beer from a little ice cooler and we
drank them in the furnace heat of the shop.

I said, "Did you know that flies graze on your face
while you sleep?"

He nodded. "They drink from the corners of my eyes."

"Flies are dirty. They come directly from dogshit to
the little water holes in your head."

"What's your name, cowboy?"

"Don Coyote," I said.

He caught me looking at his maimed hand.

"Vietnam," he said.

"You were over there, huh? You ever have flashbacks?
Ever hit the concrete when a car backfires?"

He laughed. "Not yet."

"Did college punks call you baby-killer when you got back home?"

"No."

"Well, did hippies spit on you when you returned to the States?"

"No, nothing like that."

He was the sole exception to the rule.

"They did me," I said. "Buncha long-haired, dirty, barefoot, pregnant hippies calling me baby-killer and spitting all over my medals."

He smiled. "Take a cold beer with you, Don."

"Thanks."

"Take the armadillo too. Free."

"What the hell," I said. "A man can always find employment for one more armadillo."

I drove all night. I was exhausted but I could not persuade myself to stop at a motel. Wasn't I a man with a destiny, or at least a destination? Tucson, Phoenix, Buckeye, Blythe. I drank coffee with jittery, red-eyed truck drivers while Mexican aliens mopped the floors.

"Howdy," I said to one driver. "Big country, ain't it?"

He stared sullenly into his coffee cup for a time and then, without looking up, said, "Too big. Too fucking long, too fucking wide, too fucking wrinkled."

It was almost a poem. This Dex-crazed truck driver, smelling of diesel fuel and sour clothing, had struck a true chord: he had plumbed the depths of the American psyche with a few adroit twists of the idiom.

PART THREE

Be yourself, up to a point.

—*Carole*

22

Newport Beach, an enclave of the militant rich, resolutely faced away from proletarian junkyard California.

Carole owned a small redwood cottage which she had cutely named Shangri-la-di-da. The garage doors were open and so I drove the car inside and parked it next to her red Porsche.

A door led from the garage to the kitchen. I got my armadillo, knocked on the door, rang the bell, knocked again, and finally the door opened as far as the safety chain would allow. Carole looked puzzled, and then a little frightened.

"Howdy," I said. "You ordered a roasted armadillo, ma'am?"

"Moon?"

I removed my Stetson and held it over my heart. "Don Coyote, ma'am, idiot savant, stud, midnight marauder on the side of good."

She smiled tentatively, then unchained and opened the door. The kitchen smelled like an Indian restaurant. We embraced once, twice, thrice, and then walked down the hallway past the bedrooms and bathroom to the big living room.

"Are you okay?" she asked.

Through the sliding glass doors I could see one hundred yards of beach, ruffled lines of surf, and an infinity of blues—an ultramarine sea that extended west until it finally converged with the turquoise sky. Japan was out there somewhere. A few white sails punctuated the blueness, and a freighter—filled with Toyotas?—angled in toward Long Beach harbor.

"You look tired, Moon."

"I am."

"Are you hungry?"

"Are you Hindus eating eggs these days?"

"Don't make fun of me. I like the Hindu culture, and you would too, if you knew anything about it."

"The only thing I like about Hindu culture is the practice of suttee."

"Your spurs are damaging my beautiful dhurrie rug," she said, and she turned east and headed back down the hallway.

I removed the spurs and placed them on a shelf next to a statuette of the many-armed goddess Durga—West meets East. Howdy, ma'am. The armadillo found pasture among a herd of porcelain unicorns.

Carole had lived the first twenty years of her life in Indianapolis and the last nine in Southern California. California had gilded rather than polished her. She now could undress for the cameras; call two hundred million-plus Americans the "fly-over people"; laugh when she felt like crying; be cordial to persons she despised; describe fellatio as a religious experience (there was a stone lingam, representing Shiva's phallus, in her bedroom). Carole knew couples who named their children "Kali" and "Sea-of-Tranquility" and "Ganges." She believed in spiritual experiences, pyramid power, channeling, the magic of crystals, astrology, auras, reincarnation, sorcery, the ecology, the rights of gays and mutes, vulnerable men, lifestyles, and personal growth. She believed in just about everything.

Carole, Indianapolis bred, born, and raised, had chosen to flee to these savage western provinces. I liked her without being absolutely certain she existed. Was there a latent soul beneath the layers of acquired ignorance? It didn't matter: I was attracted by her insubstantiality, which in many ways corresponded to my own. Ghosts we mated, ghosts we disengaged.

She brought my food into the living room on a silver tray: a pair of poached eggs that looked like diaphanous mollusks, flat unleavened bread smeared with chutney, a mound of brown rice, and a pot of tea.

I punctured one of the mollusks with my fork and watched the yellow viscera ooze across the plate.

"Don't play with your food," Carole said.

I said, "Patsy, I hope in your next incarnation you come back as a blood-lapping Christian."

"My name isn't Patsy," she said lightly. She was sitting on the sofa with her long legs folded beneath her.

"I'm sorry. Pamela."

"My name is Carole."

"Of course it is! I'm sorry, I'm exhausted, women's names are coming at me from every direction."

"Well, at least you didn't call me Mom."

"Hell, you are all women to me, Carole. You are Womoon."

I punctured the abdomen of another mollusk and watched its sticky yellow juices seep out and infiltrate the mound of rice. The food was vividly colored and slimily textured, disgusting. I was ravenous but I could not eat. I was afraid. Was this the prelude to a psychotic episode? Some kind of existential nausea? A disharmony had seized the world: the wall clock ticked off beat; the room compressed and tilted; the seascape beyond the glass doors was two-dimensional, a forgery; and it seemed to me that Carole was my enemy, cunning and merciless.

"Moon, are you all right?"

"I'm tired. Very tired."

"Poor baby." She smiled and everything was fine; she was good, a friend, and I was reassured by her concern.

The bedroom was dark, dark and warm, safe, and I slept like the guiltless dead. Carole resurrected me.

"Moon, the phone. Do you want to talk?"

"Who?"

"Oliver Buckley."

"Jesus."

"I'll tell him that you'll call back."

"No. Buckley? Jesus, tell him . . ." I got out of bed and staggered down the hallway, ricocheting from wall to wall, and I was surprised to see that it was storming now. The glass doors were rain-blurred and vibrating in the wind gusts. Gray, a smoky gray, with pellets of rain bouncing off the patio flagstones and rain smoking the twilight. Foaming combers advanced halfway up the beach.

I picked up the telephone. "What?"

"Do you know where we are, Moonman?"

I pictured Buckley's bland, quizzical stare; one eyelid lowered in a perpetual half wink, one corner of his mouth dimpled in a goofy half smile.

"Well. Do you know where we are?"

"I'm in Newport Beach. You're probably at the ball-park."

"Do you know where we *are?*"

"Where?"

"We are close to the Source, Moon. The Source."

"Ah."

"The mystic wellspring of Negative Meaning."

"You're right. I can feel it."

"What is it that you feel?"

"I feel good about myself."

"Yes. And what is it that you know?"

"I know that you must love yourself before you are capable of loving another."

The cottage was like a drum, resonating beneath the blows of wind and rain. Carole, smiling faintly, watched me from the sofa.

"And what is in your heart?" Buckley asked.

"Love."

"Concentrate."

"Self-esteem."

"Concentrate."

"Compassion."

"Compassion, yes. And it is beautiful. Beautiful. Do we stop here?"

"No. We go on. We complete our pilgrimage."

"Our what?"

"Our quest. That's the bottom line—our quest."

"And what shall we slake?"

"We shall slake our spiritual thirsts at the mystic wellspring of Negative Meaning."

"And the riffraff call you mad," Buckley said tenderly.

"I love. I pity. I communicate."

"God bless you."

"I'm warm. I'm open. I'm caring. I've paid my dues."

"Indeed," he crooned softly.

"I'm creative. I'm supportive. I relate."

"Moon, we're almost there, we're entering the vortex now. Don't lose your nerve, not after we've come so far."

"I'm not afraid," I said. "I won't flinch. Negative Meaning is good."

"The serpent has become the dove. The acolyte has become the master." He hung up the telephone.

"What was that all about?"

"Carole, I don't know, I'm sleeping."

"I don't like Buckley."

"No one does. What time is it?"

"Six-thirty."

"Six-thirty, my God! I'm supposed to be at the ball-park."

"Moon, look out the window."

"It doesn't matter, I'm supposed to report."

"Report, then."

The house thrummed with the echoes of booming surf, and through the window I could see a breaking wave advance to within thirty feet of the patio and then claw backward down the sloping sand. Storm winds and high tides were combining to scour the beach. The cottage seemed threatened. I was exhilarated by the display of nature's anarchic power. Roar, howl, flood, inundate this tacky Babylon. Aye, let the wrathful winds blow and the mounting seas obliterate—Moon didn't have any dough invested in California real estate.

It was dry, warm, cozy in the house. The black hole in the corner was pleading to be illuminated. Somewhere in town there was a fat-marbled prime porterhouse steak, fresh mushrooms, an Idaho potato, and the exactly right bottle of Bordeaux wine. Let the vegetarian lament and beat her silicone-augmented breasts. Carnivorism is the only ism left for the twentieth-century anthropomorphic dummy.

"Carole."

"Hmmm." Her body was coiled, flesh warming flesh, and she was tightly coiled within herself.

"I'm going to run out to a market and buy some bloody Christian chow."

"You're going out in this?"

"Aye."

"Get some popcorn."

I cooked the steak (Carole refused complicity in the desecration of cow) and ate it with a bottle of St. Emil-ion.

We spent the evening watching tapes of Carole's television performances: Carole as a savvy undercover cop, in-viting rape and mutilation; Carole as the weepy mother of a child afflicted by cerebral palsy; Carole as a business-woman suffering sexual harassment at and by the hands of her swinish male colleagues; Carole as the mother of a leukemic child; Carole as the ebullient guest on a TV talk show ("I'm a very private person"); Carole as a glitzy broad announcing candidates for an Emmy award. She had more faces than the goddess Durga had arms.

The corporeal Carole was enchanted by her various spectral personas. She had viewed these videotapes many times, and now she caressed her white throat, or smiled, or looked incomparably grave, in synchrony with her di-minutive screen image; and her lips silently formed the same words that were being uttered by the cop, the griev-ing mothers, the business executive. The contrived situa-tions and banal dialogue moved her now as they must have previously moved the huge television audience.

"Isn't she pretty?" Carole said in a detached way, as

once my ghost writer and I had discussed the "bozo" Moon. Your public personality, like a tumor, gradually becomes an integral part of you and yet remains alien.

Carole frequently glanced across the room, inviting me to share the pleasure implicit in her beauty, her craft, her generous hack-scripted heart. And I did. She was pathetic and endearing, my Carole.

At midnight she switched off the black hole and stretched luxuriously, like a cat, well pleased with herself and not unwilling to please me.

"Baby," I said. "They claim that you can't pick it up from toilet seats, but I swear . . ."

23

---◆◆◆---

I awakened on the sofa at a little after seven. It was still
raining. The surf was huge, gray-green combers that
cracked like thunder and sent fizzing avalanches of foam
to within a few yards of Shangri-la-di-da. Half a dozen
morose seagulls were huddled behind the low patio wall.

I went into the kitchen, made coffee and toast, returned to the living room and switched on the black hole.
I like to play TV like a slot machine and this morning I
hit the jackpot with the early-morning newsy-chatty network shows: CBS was interviewing a man who was
slowly dying of myasthenia gravis and had written a
book about it; a guest on ABC, his face in shadow, was
blandly confessing to committing incest with his two
daughters, one a preteen; and NBC had a shocking report about the heretofore unmentionable practice of
necrophilia among morticians. (It was "America's unreported crime.")

I was intrigued by the latter exposé. Necrophilia might be the coming hot pop-topic: it had everything, death, rape, male chauvinism, perversion, and an exotic ambience. Media gold. With just a little ingenuity you could add incest and child molestation. Celebrities. Infectious disease. Religion. Abject and titillating public confessions: How I caught AIDS from my late daughter the child film star lesbian, God forgive me.

I started to go nuclear.

The psychologist who attempted to explain the dynamics of that strange midnight depravity referred to those who employed the services of morticians as "consumers." Indeed, this was an outrageous example of consumer abuse. And the consumer, bowing to necessity, must remain mute. No wonder this was America's unreported crime.

I was approaching critical mass.

I didn't want to disturb Carole and so I took my guffaws out onto the patio. The seagulls erupted and planed away on the wind. Laughing, I lifted my face to the cold rain. I was glad that no one could see me here, standing in the rain and laughing like a loon. Looney Moon. And glad too that the roar of the surf smothered my howls. Was this madness? What a square peg I was! How much happier I would have been as a criminal or circus clown. Or mortuary attendant.

I returned to the house and began searching for my lithium tablets. There was a ringing in my ears, a chill at the base of my spine. Here comes the werewolf.

The lithium was not in my jacket or pants pockets, not on any of the tables or shelves.

On the black hole a sincere man in a laboratory coat was peddling "personal cleansing wipes."

Perhaps I had left the lithium in the glove compartment of the car.

When had I last taken a dose of lithium? Yesterday? The day before? My mind was jumping from topic to topic without transition, unraveling, running out of synch with the slow, dreary world. How slow people seemed, how full of *merde*. I knew that they could never catch up with me and so I had to tranquilize myself down to their torpid pace. I must live like them, as if there were no urgency, no limit to time, no mortality. Otherwise I would spin faster and faster, hotter and hotter, until I was ignited by their friction—their resistance—and immolated.

I switched TV channels, searched for my lithium beneath the sofa and chairs, gazed out the rain-smeared window at a smoking comber. A kid in a sou'wester was trudging along the beach.

My coffee and toast, untouched, were cold now. I lit a cigarette, put it down somewhere and could not find it, lit another. The room appeared to be tilted. I ascended to the high side. My weight overcompensated for the imbalance and so the room slowly levered in the opposite direction. I found that I could restore equilibrium by standing with a foot on either side of the room's centerline.

I did not actually believe in this tilt; I regarded it as a temporary perceptual anomaly; but it seemed prudent to behave as if it really existed.

The telephone, leaking smoke, buzzed like a rattlesnake, and I glissaded downslope and snatched the receiver off the hook.

"Yo."

"Who is this?" Buckley's voice.

"A concerned consumer," I said.

"Right. Listen, this morning in a background deep briefing for nonattribution, a high unofficial unsource declined to either confirm or deny that the president said what everyone heard him say yesterday."

"Ah, disinformation."

"No, a normalization, a finalization, a renewed emphasis on heretofore neglected priorities."

"Disingenuous," I said. "Who was the unidentified unspokesman?"

"Not an unspokesman, a high unofficial unsource who alluded to unspecified cabals."

"Are we uninfluenced?"

"Negative, an anonymous whistle-blower at State hinted that an unnamed potential adversary might be behind this new disincentive to renegotiate."

"Good work," I said. "We'll put you on the air at exactly five-forty, just after Valerie completes her feature on necrophilia."

"I respect your methodology," Buckley said.

"You'll find our methodology incorporated and explicated in an information-retrieval system shelved at your local learning resource center. It's titled 'Skeins of Conceptualizations.'"

"Right. A word to the wise—the Thought Police are on our spoor, sniffing at our droppings." He hung up.

I ascended to the room's center of balance. Weird Oliver. Still vainly attempting to penetrate the intricate metaphysics of Negative Meaning. A pioneer. How many solipsisms could dance on the head of a pin? Could language be so deprived of meaning that it became pure sound, primordial utterance, syllabic static like the jungly twittering of insects? More, could it pass completely through the sense-warp and come out the other side? That might, for all we now understood, destroy life on this planet, expose God as a befuddled civil servant, a G-9, implode the immutable. It was exhilarating, but terrifying too. We were venturing into the cosmic *terra incognita*. Hold my hand, Oliver!

Oh, where was my lithium?

On the black hole there were pictures of the storm-assaulted California coast. A voice said that this was an unseasonable storm. Sure, all of the weather was unseasonable these days.

I slalomed down to the telephone and tried to call Pamela in Oregon, but my index finger was too big for the tiny dial buttons and I made several mistakes.

The phone bleeped in my ear, next time twittered like bats, and then I was scolded by a cold, remote, tape-recorded voice. My brain was operating too swiftly for my fingers; I wanted to condense the digits, combine them as I sometimes combined words. Woe, what a complex world.

I sat on a chair for five minutes and pumped myself full of lethargy, and then I dialed the number in slow motion. Very good. The phone was ringing now. Still ringing. Wake up, Pammy.

"Hello. Who is this?" she said, painfully exhaling the vowels and swallowing the consonants. I had awakened her. Her body, when she slept, smelled like a clean, furry animal. Exhalations bubbled and burst softly on her lips.

"Hi, baby," I said.

"Oh," she said. "Shit," she said.

"Listen, Pammy, I've got a great idea, terrific. Why don't you and my little hostages to fortune come down here for a few days? I'll put you all up at a hotel near Disneyland. I can see the kids, the kids can see the mouse. At my expense, of course. Hell, bring along your dentist."

"Moon, damn it, Moon, here we go again. Do you know what time it is?"

"Seven-forty. It's late, Pam, peasants have been cutting sugar cane and harvesting rice for hours."

"I'm not a peasant."

"Will you come down with the kids? Or just insert the kids into an airplane and I'll pick them up at the airport."

"They can't fly alone, they're babies."

"Will you do it, Pam?"

"Certainly not."

"Pam, you have no right to obstruct me when I'm to see my kids. Didn't you hear the judge? If you won't cooperate I'll cut you off. You'll have to go to work in a drugstore or beauty parlor. You'll have to *work.*"

"Tell it to my lawyer."

"I'll run away. I'll play baseball in Japan. You'll have to hire a Japanese lawyer who thinks women are vermin. God damn it, Pam, I'll go away, I'll vanish forever into the heart of darkness. Do you hear me? You'll have to become a charwoman. Your knees and elbows will become flaky and red. You'll smell of ammonia."

I heard laughter, Pam and a male voice in the background. Her dentist was awake and listening. Was this funny? Maybe it was.

"You'll have big red knuckles," I cried. "Your teeth will rot. No one will want to kiss you, not even a dentist."

They were still laughing. Did I hear children's laughter too? Had the kids rushed little-footed and pajama-clad into the room to assist in the mockery of their procreator?

This is how murder is incubated. The telephone turned into a hatchet with a smooth haft and a wickedly honed blade. I neatly cleaved Pamela's skull, split her open from crown to chin, and then went to work on her dentist. Oh, boy! I performed a surgically precise craniotomy with the hatchet, a primitive tool but effective when expertly wielded. Ah, there, the exposed brain sack, a plastic baggy stuffed with squirming offal. Yuck. What a jerk— dwarf lobes, atrophied cerebrum, syphilitic cerebellum, a disgusting medulla oblongata, fatty deposits on every synapse. *Adieu,* DDS. No more lingering brushes across an adolescent's breast as you sadistically probe a cavity with your little steel hook. You'll never sneak another feel from a high school cheerleader. I just severed your sleazy libido.

"Don't call here anymore, Moon," Pamela said. "Call my lawyer in the future. What kind of mother would send her children off to a crazy man?"

I put down the hatchet. There were three cigarettes fuming in the room, and one of them had burned a crater in Carole's sofa.

Maybe I should kidnap the kids this winter. Maybe not, though; they were awfully boring. The tiny Moon wasn't even housebroken yet. The girl Moon whined and bitched a lot, like her mother. I probably should wait five or six years before kidnapping the children, snatch them after the feces and the whining were out of the way but before Pamela had molded them into good citizens.

I wrote a note to Carole, got my spurs and Stetson, and went out to the car. The lithium was not in the glove compartment.

It was rush hour and the freeway was a swift steel river. A million lemmings blindly hurtled toward their individual and collective fates. The air was brown and stank of chemicals. Tires hissed loudly on the pavement; engine noises blended into an infernal hum; and in the distance I could hear the keening threnody of a Klaxon (two or three or a half dozen permanently out of the race).

I was going eighty-five miles per hour and cars in the hero's lane passed with ease. Soft bodies encapsulated by hard shells. One million anthropomorphic dummies encysted in carapaces of steel and glass.

24

Jonah Hardy was the only player in the hotel lobby when I entered. He smiled at my spurs and cowboy hat and said, "Been poking cows? Been punching cows, kid?"

"I got the clap," I said.

"You got the cops too."

I received Blas's room key from the desk clerk and was whisked upward in an elevator whose operator, an old Chicano, asked me if I was going to the party. Party?

I could hear voices and music halfway down the hall. The room door was open and what earlier must have been a marvelous party was expiring inside. Two serving carts contained the remains of caviar and onions and toast, and a dozen ice buckets contained bottles—most empty now—of French champagnes. There were liquor bottles and setups on top of the dresser. It was nine-thirty.

Blas, fully clothed, was sleeping on one of the beds. One side of his gunfighter's moustache had been shaved off. There were flecks of lather around his open mouth.

Kopfhammer slept on the other bed. A thin snail-track of saliva trickled down from the corner of his mouth. Hammer drooled daintily for such a gross swine. The mad midnight shaver (Oliver Buckley?) had removed his sideburns and Kopfhammer looked like the ideal yokel.

I found a half-full bottle of Taittinger in one of the buckets. It was good wine, though a little flat and not very cold.

A young blond girl, her eyes dilated to nearly the full circumference of the irises, precariously leaned toward me.

"I know you, cowboy," she said. "Bastard."

"It was business," I said.

"Bastard."

"I did it for your own good."

Blas's father, Esteban, wearing a well-cut though pink-ish-hued tropical suit, was looking out of the window. With him was a sinuous black-haired girl who had the profile of a figure in a Mayan fresco. Esteban, disheveled and fatigued, was droning at three-quarter speed in his lisping Spanish.

Two Latino thugs were playing cards at a round table.

A slender young man had a girl pinned against the wall, and he was alternately whispering and nibbling at her neck and ear. She stared blankly at me over his shoulder.

An old bellman was sitting on the end of Blas's bed, watching the flashing but silent TV.

"My boyfriend's gonna cut out your heart and eat it," the hostile blonde told me. And then her face crumpled and she began crying. "I can't get a break," she sobbed.

"Alls I need is one break. No one knows how to relate anymore."

I retreated to the bathroom. A naked girl, tanned all over, was sleeping in the bathtub. Someone had shaved off most of her pubic hair. She was small but well formed, a tall midget, and fit comfortably into the tub. She looked dead. Maybe the same stuff that had dilated the blonde's eyes had snuffed this poor girl.

I washed my hands, lathering the soap, and then I gently smeared some froth over her nostrils. An iridescent bubble expanded and burst. I wiped away the soap. Alive.

I returned to the room and covertly watched Esteban Cintron, bureaucrat, drug smuggler, whoremaster, fascist, father of my best friend. A plump, jolly fellow at times, not without charm. Esteban could be good company. Fat before, Esteban had gained more weight, and the contours of his pendulous belly had achieved a noble, sculptured aspect. It was the right belly on the right man at the right time.

The girl with him was Indian, with lank black hair and skin the color of a new penny. She was about fifteen years old. No doubt Esteban had found her out in some bush village and become her patron. He had tarted her up in a tight glittery dress and spike-heeled shoes. The girl was ugly, placid, probably stupid, and so sensuous-looking that she made my fingertips tingle.

Esteban sensed my stare and turned. His expression was cold; he looked like a wood carving of some fierce minor jungle deity. But then he recognized me, his face came alive, and he cried, "Teodoro! *Como estás, hombre?*" And he advanced belly foremost, spreading his arms. "How are you being, my friend?" He embraced me in a crushing *abrazo*, thumping my back with his palms.

His belly was as firm as pork flesh. His cologne smelled like rotting fruit.

I pulled away. "Howdy, Esteban."

He smiled fondly, his face cracking like dried mud, and he announced, "This here Teodoro is like my very own son," but his eyes were calculating. He knew that I despised him; and knew that now we were playing in my backyard. This is Amurica, pal. "Ah, Teodoro, it is so much—*como se dice?*—it is so much good to be where you again. How long, eh, *joven?* Long times."

"Welcome," I said. "Welcome to my *patria.*"

"Thank you. Ah, thank you, it's good, my old friend. It make my heart hot. Yes, that is true. I tell you the very true without lies. Ah, my old friend, hello."

He introduced me to the girl, whose name sounded like "Zenda," to the pair of gorillas playing cards, and the suave young lover who was an official at his country's embassy. He did not introduce me to the weeping blonde, the old bellman, two men who might have been cops, or the sleeping Kopfhammer.

And then: "*Mira! Mira,* Teodoro. This Blas. Look. A sleeping dronk, one lip hair only. Why? This is my tired jazz. You say, this here is Esteban's own son. Yes. Maybe yes, but the jazz was tired that night, I think. Hey, Blas, wake up, you focking piss-jazz." He grinned at me, flashing gold and silver and pink. "You know jazz?"

"Jism?" I asked.

"Okay, but he is sure one good boy. My boy. He love me. Hey, Blas, get up, you bad jazz."

Blas groaned softly and turned away from his father.

"I fock too much," Esteban confided. "Blas come out piss, you know. My macho is soft." He stared down at his son. "Hey, wake it up, piss-jazz," he said affectionately.

"Piss-jazz is comatose," I said.

"Yes. Okay. Poor boy. Hey, Teodoro, you want the wine? You want the fish egg? You want a little fock? My Zenda fock you one time, my friend. Two time, I kill you. One time you are my very good friend. Kiss her, fock her, use you spurs."

"I'll take a rain check," I said.

He informed me that the war was going very well in his country; the rebels had made a fatal strategic error by occupying so much terrain, all but two provinces. They were spread too thin and would soon be extirpated. The government counteroffensive was certain to triumph. In fact, the war was proceeding so well that he, Esteban, could be spared from his official duties while he attended to business interests in the United States. He did not know precisely how long he would remain here; it had been years since he'd enjoyed a real vacation.

I inferred from this that the war was lost and all the high government rats were abandoning the sinking ship of state. No doubt other politicians, policemen, and generals were packing for long-deferred vacations in Miami and Madrid and Paris. Esteban had stuffed the diplomatic pouch full of dope and U.S. aid dollars and gone into honorable, prosperous exile.

"This war is almost finish," he said. "It make me so happy for my good land, my good people. My poor suffer, oppress people," he said emotionally. "Ah, I am one man of the people, Teodoro. One great patriot."

Esteban was finished with me. A transparent membrane, like the secondary lid of sharks and reptiles, descended over his eyes. I was dismissed.

Fossey was standing at a window, half concealed by the velvety drapes: I saw one foot and leg, a vertical strip of torso, one arm and hand (the hand holding an empty wine glass), and one eye. The eye tracked my approach.

"What are you doing?" I asked.

"Pretending I'm white. I've been pretending I'm white for about five hours."

"What's it like being white?"

"Strange man, very strange."

I eased him out from behind the drape. His muscles were rigid, his joints frozen.

"You look the same," I said. "Black."

"Sure. But inside I'm white. I see everything through the mind and blue eyes of a young, energetic white businessman. Married but no kids yet. Kristen and I are waiting. The babies'll be born underwater. I don't know why that is, Moon, it's goofy, but about two hours ago I just knew that our babies will be born underwater, in a tank. Right now we've got two golden retrievers. We live in a house on a hillside. Kristen works too. She's blond, I've got this thin brown hair that's falling out. You know? Every time I comb my hair I look at the comb's teeth and see all these fine sandy hairs that just pulled out of my scalp. I drive a Blazer and Kristen got a BMW. We own a sailboat. We plan to go trekking in the Himalayas next vacation."

"Do you enjoy being a white man, Fossey?"

"It's got its up side and its down side. It's okay. But it's so real, Moon. I worry if my soul's been taken over by this white guy. His name is Blake. His first name. You see the problem. Will I ever be able to get back my Negritude?"

I said, "I hope Blake can play shortstop."

"You see those guys over by the door?"

I had noticed them earlier. The white man was stocky, with an oversize head and a myopic squint as he surveyed the far reaches of the room. His lank hair was peroxided and he had the perfect, even tan that comes from using reflectors on the beach. He probably had a garage stacked with old surfboards. His partner was bigger, a beefy coal-black man with a shaved skull and belligerent jaw. Both men wore sport jackets and faded jeans and loafers without socks.

"What about them?"

"I look at the black guy, Moon, I've been studying him, and I wonder—is he a good coon or a bad coon? Is he our kind of coon, mine and Kristen's? I don't think so. I worry. She's at her dance class now, but when she gets here—will that dangerous-looking coon walk over to her, you know, hit on her, smile at her with his big teeth? My pretty blue-eyed blond wife. And I think, Moon, will she laugh at his crude ghetto sexual innuendo? Is she gonna wonder what it's like to . . . you understand. My stomach hurts. I can feel more hair falling out of my head. What if one of the babies born underwater turns out to be black?"

"Just get out of here," I said. "Get some sleep."

"I can't leave. Kristen will be joining me here soon."

I was getting jittery. I was seized by a familiar, claustral feeling, a sense of impending panic, imminent doom. Déjà vu: I am lost, trapped again among the Undead in the dismal purgatory of the Incorrigible's Ward.

"Just who are those guys?"

"Cops."

"What do they want?"

"I don't know. I guess they just want to party."

"Jesus, doesn't anybody care? There's dope in the room, underaged girls, fugitives, psychopaths . . ."

"The coon worries me. The other one's okay."

"Who are they after?"

"I don't know, Moon. They showed up yesterday afternoon and have been here ever since."

"They want me," I said.

The two cops saw me coming and shifted to block the doorway. No exit. They were half paralyzed by drugs and alcohol and exhaustion. Their eyes were dark burning holes, the apertures open to about f/4. Even so they retained a certain stoned cop dignity, cop arrogance.

"Theodore Moon," the aged surfer said. "Old Moony. It's time you showed up." He sniffed delicately. There was a patina of white powder rimming his inflamed nostrils.

"Who are you?" I asked.

"Think of me as Detective Sturm, L.A. County Sheriff's Office."

"And I," his black partner said. "I am . . ." He lost the thought. "Tell him, Warren."

"Think of Charlie as Detective Drang."

"Do you want to talk to me?"

"Do we want to talk to Moony, Detective Drang?"

"That's why we're here."

"That's why we're here," Sturm told me.

"Tell him not to leave town."

"Don't leave town, Moony."

"Tell him . . . tell him that wherever he goes, whatever he's doing, no matter how far he runs or how hard he tries to hide, tell him . . . tell him that if he looks over his shoulder, he'll see us. No matter how long it takes."

"You heard," Sturm said to me.

"Tell him he's on our turf now."

"You heard."

"Now give it to him."

Sturm reached inside his jacket (I recoiled) and withdrew a thick, ragged sheaf of papers folded lengthwise. A subpoena? A transcript of my confession ready for my signature?

"Tell him," Drang said.

"Give this to Joseph Horvath pronto." He gave me the papers. "You got that, Moony?"

"Now tell him to beat it."

"Beat it, scumbag," Sturm said.

25

I obtained Buckley's room number from the desk clerk, rode the elevator up two more floors, and walked down the hallway. Why hadn't I stayed at the Ranch? I knocked, and when there was no response I began kicking the door.

"Who is it?"

"It's me."

"How do I know it's you, Me?"

"Open the focking door."

Buckley opened the door and followed me into the room.

"Esteban's here," I said. "One man of the people."

"I know."

"Were you at the party?"

"For a while."

"Who are the thugs?"

"Esteban's bodyguards."

"Esteban offered me Zenda. Fossey's turning white. There are two berserko cops down there. Someone's been skulking around and shaving body hair. Was it you? Moustaches, sideburns, pubic thatches."

"You're overwrought," Buckley said gently.

"There's a naked girl in the bathtub."

"You're dizzy," he said sympathetically. "You've lost touch."

"I've been on the edge of cracking up for days," I said. "But people seem dangerous, I'm afraid to let go."

"Poor fellow."

"Honest to God, Buck, sometimes I have a hard time believing that I'm crazy. Why me and not Blas or Esteban or Fossey or Red Girt or Fungo or Kopfhammer? Why me and not you?"

"You are blind and I have eyes," he said in an oily tone. "You are deaf and I possess ears. You are mute but I am blessed with tongue. My limbs are clean and straight while yours . . . alas, there is little in the way of justice."

I watched him.

"Were my limitless pity balm, your wounds would swiftly heal."

"You're a dark figure, Oliver. Sinister."

"When love fails only mercy suffices."

"And God? What about God, Oliver?"

"Everything was good when God was a philosopher. But then God became a merchant and now we are alone."

"And Man, Oliver?"

"Alone. Man lives and dies alone. He is redeemed by love, by pity."

"And what about death, Oliver?"

"There is no such thing as death, my son. Death is

change, death is rebirth, death is resurrection. Your molecules are immortal, your atoms prevail. We are composed of the stars and to the stars we return. No one dies, he merely reenters the eternal flux of the oceanic One-in-All. It's vain to mourn the loss of consciousness, of self. For it is better, I tell you, to be one crippled cell in the corpus of the universe than to endure as a human animal."

"Thanks," I said. "I feel okay now."

"Good. Take off your spurs, relax. Light up. Are you in the mood for some saturated fats?"

"You bet. Pepperoni, Italian sausage, extra cheese. Olives, green peppers, mushrooms, onions. Thick crust."

"There's a place down the street. Me fetch."

When Buckley left I unfolded the stained, dog-eared sheaf of papers. It was a screenplay titled *Sturm and Drang.* The authors were Warren P. Stirmel and Charles M. Drangel. The story was about a pair of tough, wise-cracking cops, one white—Sturm—and the other black, who investigate a series of brutal Tong murders in Chinatown. There were rooftop gunfights, duels in dirty alleys, car chases and wrecks, scenes of torture, tender sexual interludes, men thrown off the roofs of tall buildings, devastating explosions. The climax took place in a waterfront warehouse stacked with wooden packing crates. "This is the nexus," Sturm tells his partner as they stalk warily across the room. "This is where all the parameters converge." Suddenly hundreds of screaming Orientals swarm out of the packing crates and engage Sturm and Drang in a frenzied martial-arts melee that eventually spills out of the warehouse and onto the wharf. Shrieks, bone-shattering chops and kicks, balletic whirls and leaps, a furious hurricane of death and maiming. Finally the Orientals are vanquished. Sturm lights a cheroot and deliberately drops the match into a thin trickle of liquid that zigzags up the wharf and through the warehouse doors. "Let's go see Mr. Big," Drang says. They walk away down the silent, empty street. A foghorn mournfully wails. The end credits begin to roll. Behind them we see a flash of light, and then there is a secondary explosion and the wharf, warehouse, and the city of Long Beach rise flaming into the night sky.

Fini

It was incredibly cheap and vulgar, a stupidity-virus, a vile cerebral pollutant. I phoned the desk and asked them to send a typewriter up to the room. When it arrived I typed a new title page.

STURM AND DRANG
BY
THEODORE MOON

26

Blas was awake and prowling when I returned to our room. He told me that the party had moved to Esteban's suite of rooms. We were left with the debris, the casualties. Blas looked like a dangerously unstable man with his mutilated moustache and booze-raw eyes.

"Who's the girl?" he asked me.

"I don't know."

"Is she one of your transsexuals?"

"I don't think so."

"What is she doing in our bathtub?"

"I don't know, Blas."

"Some pervert shaved her crotch." His voice was hoarse.

"Is she still alive?" I asked.

"What?"

"I asked you if the girl in the bathtub is still alive."

"My God."

"Is she?"

"Are you going to drop her down the laundry chute?"

"Maybe. Go see if she's alive, Blas."

"How?"

"Touch her, see if she's warm."

"I never touch dead girls, never."

"It's the coming thing."

"My God, she looks dead. What will we do if she's dead?"

"Take her up to Esteban's rooms."

"Moon, please, you go. I don't like dead people."

I went into the bathroom, lifted the girl's wrist and found a pulse. She opened her eyes and stared ferociously at me—a disturbed vampire—and then her eyelids slowly descended over the gluey eyeballs.

When I returned to the room Blas was intently staring at his reflection in an oval wall mirror.

"She isn't dead yet," I told him.

"Someone shaved off half of my moustache," he said in a strangled voice.

"I noticed."

"Was it you?"

"No."

"Who?"

"I don't know. Someone shaved off Kopfhammer's sideburns and that girl's pubic hair."

"Buckley."

"Probably."

"Dozens of people in the room and no one stopped him. My father was here, my father's bodyguards, my friends," he said bitterly.

"Buckley's sneaky," I said.

"I look like a wimpy kid without my moustache. My

mouth is funny, thin and gullible. I don't have credibility with women without my moustache."

"It will grow back."

He started pacing. "I got to shower," he said. "I got to shave. Is that girl alive?"

"Yes."

"How am I going to shower?"

"Don't step on her, don't drown her."

"Okay."

"Blas, go back to sleep. You're still drunk, you're tired."

"No, I've got to go to Mass. And confession."

"Isn't it too late for Mass?"

"It's never too late. Communion, I need it."

"Blas, you eat your god four or five times a week. Let it go for now."

"Fuck you!" he said furiously. "Just fuck you, mister. It makes me feel good and pure to eat Jesus. Stick it, you crazed atheist! What do you know about beauty?"

And he turned and stalked away, slamming the door so hard that the room trembled on its frame.

Indeed, what did I know about beauty? Almost nothing. Perhaps only that, contrary to nearly unanimous opinion, it is to be discovered not in mystery but in the subversive thrill of demystification.

I hunted through the room and found a nearly full bottle of flat, warm Mumm's *sec*. I then smeared drying—perhaps toxic—caviar on squares of stale, hard toast. There are Communions and communions.

What the hell, I was crazy. Life didn't always hurt, though. People were a problem. Still, some of the happiest moments of my life had been spent in human company.

I interrupted my reflections to check on the girl: she

breathed, she existed, though not on an exalted level. I did not stare at her body. Voyeurism is okay as long as it doesn't become too leisurely or clinical. I didn't want to think of her as a plastic dolly. If you perceived women as too real or too unreal, you might get a soft macho. The balance was delicate. Women were most appealing when they were only slightly more or slightly less than human. Strange creatures, star-crossed, flesh-in-flux, gloriously banal. But how kind they are! They throw out food for birds and feral killer dogs. They warm the body, enrich the blood, ennoble the timid heart, provide succor.

I turned on the black hole and circumnavigated the dial. What was this? An ebullient emcee was holding aloft what appeared to be a six-inch-long scorpion. It had the same glossy transluscent beige color, the long tail (though not curved), and possessed a tense scorpial menace. But this was no venomous arachnid: it was, the emcee informed us, a "prosthetic penis implant." I sat on the edge of the bed, fascinated and terrified, staring into the blackest of black holes. The prosthetic device was the "last alternative for the impotent man." It was connected to a long tube with an oil-filled bulb at the end, and when a chap got in the mood for a little sexual self-expression he could pump himself up. Pump pump and once again sex rears its ugly head.

With the emcee were two men, a pioneering proctologist and a Ph.D. in psychology. The audience was typical of such shows, mostly middle-aged women with narrowed eyes—lewd puritans, unyielding Valkyries.

Coitus could last, the proctologist told us, for as long as the parties desired. The penis could be deflated afterward. Deflated!

Technology had gone too far. This was virility beyond man's—or woman's—wildest fantasy. You could see that this device was going to be far more popular than the vibrator, which buzzed unpleasantly and ran up the electric bill. How long before men of ordinary potency surrendered to the science of hydraulics and sprawled supine under the knife. "Gimme about thirty-two pounds pressure per square inch, Doc." And how long before wives and girlfriends began to murmur over the morning coffee: "Darling, it doesn't have to be that way. Here's a telephone number . . ."

I went into the bathroom and rummaged through the cabinet behind the mirror—Blas's pharmacy—and removed two chloral hydrate capsules from the bottle. A double Mickey Finn. Enough to stun the werewolf without excessively numbing the Moonman.

The girl in the bathtub was sleeping peacefully, modestly, with one hand cupped over her mons. Thou shalt not pass.

Back in the bedroom I picked up the telephone and punched out the digits for Dial-A-Prayer. "We are an exhausted civilization," I said. "Do something."

I decided to stay here in the room, never emerge. What was out there anyway? All that I required was right here in this compact cubicle: a telephone, the black hole, my checkbook and credit cards, maid and room service, a window through which I could periodically observe the evolution of machines, a bathroom for the efficient disposal of body wastes and for showers, although I suspected that cleanliness was not going to be crucial to my future. I'd let my hair and beard grow into verminous nests. My finger and toenails would curve into yellow claws. And like some of the old religious ascetics, I would cultivate maggots and tenderly replace them when they fell out of my wounds. I'd expose myself to spinsters who appeared on the TV screen, howl imprecations into the air-conditioning vent, stick pins into dolls molded out of dung, burn candles to Our Lady of the San Andreas Fault. Teddy Moon, sole prophet of the Scorpion God.

I was becoming drowsy. Perhaps one Mickey Finn would have been sufficient to pacify the werewolf.

The little bathtub girl, still naked, walked out, turned off the television, closed the drapes, and crawled into Blas's bed.

My sleep was deep, my dreams demented. When I awakened the girl was gone and Blas and Oliver Buckley were standing at the foot of my bed, staring down at me.

"Why, lookit there, Hirum, that feller is sleeping in his boots and spurs."

"He don't look real smart," Blas said.

"No sir. Lookit them eyes. A crazy man."

"Could be you are right, Dr. Smood. Chronic schizophrenia, undifferentiated type, I reckon."

"No sir, that's a manic-depressive psychotic if I ever seen one."

Oliver had taught Blas the jargon with which they frequently persecuted me.

"Primary narcissism," Blas-Hirum said.

"Delusions of persecution."

"And grandeur."

"Alienated."

"Depersonalized."

"A sick copulator."

"Anal sadistic, you think, Dr. Smood?"

"I got to say no, Hirum. This here is one of them oral-fixated snivelers."

"Depressed," Blas said.

"Sublimated."

"Inhibited."

"Repressed and disoriented."

"Gawd," Blas-Hirum said. "Impoverished ego."

"Tyrannical superego."

"That feller's got an id that'd make any decent man's blood turn to ice."

"He is a mean-looking cornholer, Hirum."

"Don't invite him to the dance."

"It's just when he were a tyke he got confused by that Oedipus thing."

"Gawd, Mr. Smood. You mean he kinda fantasized killing his paw and bedding his maw?"

"That weren't no fantasy, Hirum, not with this here degenerate geezer."

With that he cracked up and howled with laughter. Blas, holding his stomach, leaned over and wheezed helplessly. My friends.

It was late afternoon. They told me that Dodger Stadium was a swamp and so tonight's game had been postponed. Carole had been unable to reach me, I hadn't answered the telephone, and so she had called Buckley and told him that we were invited to a very important cocktail party this evening. She would pick me up.

"Who is Joseph Horvath?" Buckley asked.

"He runs a big independant production company. His outfit made *Safe at Home.*"

"A powerful character?"

"Very."

"Could he get us into the movies?" Blas asked.

"If he wanted to. He wouldn't want to."

Buckley turned a fond, loopy stare on me. "Carole said that this Joseph Horvath has his finger on the pulse of the American public."

I said, "He's got his finger up the anus of the American public."

"I'd like to meet him," Blas said.

Buckley smiled and thrust forward his little potbelly. "Me too."

27

⚉

Carole was pleased that I had not chosen to wear my cowboy hat and boots, and the spurs, to the cocktail party. She demonstrated her pleasure by giving me what she probably regarded as negative reinforcement.

"You're such a show-off, Moon. You demand constant attention. You're such a prima donna."

I was still hung over from the double Mickey Finn I'd consumed earlier, and I stared gloomily through the insect-splattered windshield while Carole deftly avoided the accidents she had almost caused. The Porsche engine whined in agony: Carole seldom remembered fourth and fifth gears and so now as usual the tachometer needle hovered above the red line. She was beautiful tonight, and she loved me.

"I love you, Moon, very much, really I do. We have a

good bonding. But I hate to see you make a fool out of yourself because then you're making a fool out of me. So please behave yourself this evening, all right? I love you."

I was constrained by my seat belt and by Carole's words. Her love was contingent upon my good behavior. That was not unfair, it was the standard contract, but even so I was resentful. It was not that I childishly demanded to be loved "for myself," that is, as a soul divorced from his acts and their consequences. I was resentful because Carole, knowing me well, presumed that I would misbehave tonight; she believed that she could predict my future on the basis of my past. And it was so. It didn't help me to realize that she was right, that others were right; it only made me rebellious. There are times when the most elegant form of revolt is to do exactly what is expected of you.

"Joe Horvath is a very important man," Carole was saying. "And his guests will be important people too. Very important, the movers and shakers, extremely powerful, and it means so much to me that they like me, like us."

"Don't worry," I said. "I'll be good."

"I mean it, Moon."

"I'll be dignified, Carole. I'll be sincere."

"Well, not *too* dignified and sincere," she said with a nervous laugh. "Be yourself, up to a point."

Joseph Horvath lived deep in the rich man's ghetto of Bel Air. Most of the houses were concealed behind brick walls and jungles of flowering trees and shrubs. I was able to imagine what I could not see: big houses with swimming pools, tennis courts, bonsai gardens, lavender pools containing rare neon carp, caged nightingales, statuary looted from Roman *Palazzi*. At night slavering Doberman pinschers, the moon duplicated in their eyes, patrolled the boundaries of each fief, as much to keep the servants in as intruders out.

"God, isn't it beautiful here?" Carole said. "Wouldn't you just love to live here, Moon?"

"No. These people are corrupt."

"Nonsense."

"All of the women who live here are having affairs with bisexual astrologers."

"Dumb."

"The men are impotent unless they play torture games."

"God, Moon, you can really be insensitive."

"I tolerate them only because they have the power to make me great."

There were unicorns cavorting on an arch above the Horvath driveway, an iron fence, a gatehouse whose guard made us produce identification, and then a road that looped through tropical foliage and lawns as smooth as putting greens. On the lawn a marble shepherdess attended to a flock of marble sheep. A fountain spewed, flags snapped in the breeze (a U.S. flag, a California flag, and the Horvaths' personal flag), a security guard saluted.

The house, sprawling over a gentle hillside, looked like a small Mediterranean village. White stucco walls, ceramic tile roofs, balconies and bell towers, red-painted gates, dovecotes, shuttered windows, courtyards, and detached peasant cottages—the guest houses.

"This place is worth eleven million dollars," Carole said.

"I'd rather live on Skid Row."

"You lie."

"Hollywood Versailles. Sheer excess."

"You're envious."

One of the Horvath family's adopted sons, a Cambodian refugee, was parking the cars. Carole was furious when I tipped him five dollars. "You don't tip members of the household, Moon."

We were admitted by a butler who for many years had played butlers in the movies, and directed into the "Great Hall." The Great Hall was indeed great, a vast space three stories high and maybe fifty yards in width and length. Birds fluttered about the rafters and stained-glass dome. Had they accidentally been trapped in the house or were they a part of the ambience? Somewhere between seventy and a hundred persons milled around among the space-dwarfed furniture and potted rain forest.

Joseph Horvath approached and briefly embraced Carole, then me. I was not used to being embraced by men other than Latinos, who generally have a piquant odor—Joe Horvath smelled like oil of cloves. Joe was a lean, sharp-featured man of about fifty, with wary eyes behind thick-lensed glasses, doughy skin, and a wonderful smile. The smile was a reflex now, a social tic, and did not always correspond to the stimulus. You're a thief, Joe. Smile. He had started as the lowest of the low, a freelance television plagiarist, and now was approaching the top of the dungheap.

Joe's wife smiled hideously. She had been the victim of a botched face-lift and now looked like a deceased Mongolian.

"Moon," Joe said, "if you're going to hit someone, why not hit some sonofabitch who counts?"

I said, "A friend of mine, Dewey Yankhe, said something similar recently. He thought I should hit men with soft hands. Show me your hands, Joe."

He held out his small, girlish hands.

I was sorely tempted to hit him. I said, "Dewey tells me that during both the French and the Russian revolutions, men were executed for no other reason than they had soft hands. That was evidence enough. The odd thing is, Dewey has palms as soft as a baby's, like yours."

"Listen, guys, right now I'm over my ass in festive trivia. You two circulate, I'll talk to you later."

The radiant smile, and Joe and his late wife drifted away.

"That wasn't necessary," Carole hissed at me.

"I'm sorry."

"Joe's a brilliant man, a genius. How dare you talk to him like that?"

I sent her off to mingle with the other geniuses and angled off toward a horseshoe-shaped bar. Joe's adopted son, Manuel, a refugee from El Salvador, was tending bar. I wanted to become as crazy as possible as swiftly as possible and so I ordered a double Myers's 151 proof rum on the rocks.

A few stools away an attractive redhead was drinking champagne and eating tortilla chips with guacamole dip. The dip was a bright neon-green.

She noticed me watching her and said, "God, I can't help it, I just love guacamole."

"Made with avocado, isn't it?"

"Mm-mmm."

"Did you know that the word 'avocado' stems from *ahuacatl,* the Aztec word for 'testicle'?"

She smiled. "No, I didn't know that."

"It is."

She laughed. "I've got to tell Barney."

"Foods with testicular associations are commonly assumed to be aphrodisiacal."

"Really?"

"You bet."

She smirked at me with her guacamole-green lips. "Say, are you trying to turn me on?"

"Sure."

"I'm faithful to Barney so far."

"There's got to be a hundred vacant bedrooms in this place."

"You come on too fast."

"Do you know what I've got? I've got agriothymia hydrophobica."

"Jesus, what's that?"

"It's an irresistible impulse to bite."

"Yes. Well. I'm full. I guess I'll go find Barney."

I signaled Manuel to bring me another drink. Not every woman was receptive to my approach.

I took the fresh double and slowly strolled around the huge room, eavesdropping on conversations. The distinctive thing about these people was their hair: the men and the women had gleaming, puffy, beautifully coiffed hair. Hair, perhaps, fabricated out of some new miracle fiber. I saw a few Dodger players; familiar actors and actresses; elderly men with cleft chins and noble bearing; urbane and witty faggots, still hours away from the time when they would weep about their *affaires de coeur* with schoolboys. And half a dozen of the bloody English—a serious logistical error. One Englishman or woman at a party could be amusing; he or she might even sparkle; but put two or more together in a room and the Collective English Soul became operative. They fired subliminal arrows of guilt and shame at each other, murderous fusillades that exsanguinated any American caught in the crossfire. The arrows were poison-tipped with Decency, Modesty, Conduct. *Don't you dare act the fool in front of these horrid Americans.*

I hove-to near a group and heard a man say, "It looks like George is going to pull it off."

"George is going to jerk it off," I said, and I glided away.

My glass was empty—so soon!—and I stopped a Filipino girl whose immigration had been sponsored by the Horvaths, and took a scotch and water from her tray. Give *me* your tired, your poor, your huddled masses yearning to breathe free . . .

Behind the house, through huge oak doors, I found a tiled patio and, on a lower level, a cobalt swimming pool that reeked of chlorine. There were a few swimmers, strutting young peacocks and peahens. At the end of the patio a group was gathered covenlike around a bearded man. I approached. The man, speaking diffidently, was a songwriter-singer whose lyrics had been compared to the poetry of Blake and Baudelaire. (Down lowdown and dirty / Uptown downtown blues / Sleepin' in tomcat alleys / A wino stole my shoes.) Nicky Puma, reputed to be half American Indian, though his hair and beard were blondish and his eyes were blue.

His voice was booze- and smoke-husky. He had the contrived humility of pop-messiahs and of a particular type of criminal psychopath. (The blood that purifies / The knife that heals / The victim prays / The killer kneels.) I hated Puma for his celebrity, for his wealth, for the reverence he inspired in the rabble, for his sad eyes and romantically ravaged face. I wished that I could be exactly like him, a secular Christ.

"I don't know," he was saying softly, almost whispering. "But we believe—my people believe—that everything contains spirits. There is life in all things. And beauty. And love. Nature is a sacred circle of love. Only white people are outside that circle. Not because white people can't express love, because you can. But you don't know how to *receive* love. From the rock, the tree, the serpent, the sky, the mean dog down the street. You can love God but you won't permit God to love you. That's the tragedy of white people, I think. That's what I learned from my people." His voice, full of static, faded out.

My people. Oliver Buckley was better at this sort of thing. Buckley wasn't afraid of sentimentality.

I said, too loudly, "Brother Tortoise is blind to all but the ground before him. Walk-on-two-legs-honky is blind to spirituality of rocks." I was surprised to hear Buckley's voice issue from my mouth. It was an eerie kind of psychological ventriloquism.

The crowd shifted to glare at me. Nicky Puma smiled knowingly; he had been heckled before.

I said, "Brother Fish eat Brother Worm. Man eat Brother Fish. Brother Worm eat Man. Sacred circle of love."

A few of the faces were merely curious; the others hostile. Let's get the hell out of here, Oliver. I turned and fled into the house. A close call. Another minute or two and the jackals might have torn me to pieces. Cannibal love, that was our game.

Inside I was collared by a trembling white-haired man in his anecdotage, and it was fifteen minutes before he suffered a fugue and I was able to escape.

I wandered over to the buffet. Joseph Horvath did not stint; these were prime-quality cocktail-party snacks. Escargots, oysters on the half shell, sushi, smoked salmon, caviar, marinated herring, ripe Brie and Camembert cheeses, Greek olives, Portuguese anchovies, steak tartare—get thee behind me, Colonel.

Someone ambushed me from behind. Carole.

"Isn't this a wonderful spread, Moon?"

"You bet. My palate is being educated lately."

"It's about time."

"I'm learning what to chew and what to eschew. Look at this, sturgeon spawn, snails, raw mollusks, raw fish, rotten cheeses, rare fungoidal growths—no more junk food for the Moonman."

28

I retreated to a long refectory table, sat down and stared at my plate. Nausea. I was hungry and yet incapable of eating. Anyway, food would only thwart my burgeoning manic flight. I took my fork and stirred the victuals into a bright, pointillist mound of fishy-smelling garbage. I yearned for release. Any man must go crazy every now and then in order to justify his past and enrich his future.

I got another double rum from Manuel and then glided ghostlike among the anthropomorphic dummies. Perhaps I would elect to confer a great philanthropy on one of them. I persuaded myself that I could neither be seen nor heard, and might be sensed only by a cool draft on the back of the neck or the faint odor of wet fur. Omniscient, omnipotent, Übermensch. I briefly joined a group whose members, alerted that some ineffable spiritual force had arrived on the scene, responded with signs of anxiety. Conversation stalled. Men touched their wallet pockets; women patted their hair and laughed nervously. Most stared toward the space that my corporeal self would have occupied were I not a celestial personage.

"God bless," I murmured. "Ciao."

This was a good time to explore the joint. I ascended a helical wrought-iron stairway and passed from cube to cube, found more stairs which led to the ultimate cube. The master bedroom. A disappointment: no Third World refugees chained to a wall, no captive starlets, no dwarfs in harlequin attire. Just a skylight, damask drapes, a white grand piano, an enormous bed, and five big oil paintings representing what looked like cancerous tumors: fleshy gourds and vines, bleeding pears, sprouting sweetbreads, clumps of glandular grapes, maggoty excrescences. Polyp art. Clearly, I was not the only savage in town.

I found Joe's study and left the *Sturm and Drang* script on his desk—a mahogany-and-leather construction only a little smaller than an aircraft carrier.

I returned to the main floor and explored some of the rooms off the Great Hall. In one a short, pudgy man of about forty was watching television from a grand leather chair. He wore a white linen suit, black horn-rimmed glasses with a hearing aid in one temple, and a pair of tasseled loafers. His tiny feet failed to reach the floor.

The black hole was showing a drama about the agony and ecstacy of child abuse in middle-class families. Sadism and remorse, sadism and soul-searching, sadism and psychiatric redemption. The erotic rewards of beating up children were nicely understated. I was surprised to see Carole, my Carole, appear on the screen. She played a brilliant lady psychologist.

I laughed, and the little man turned and glared furiously at me, his brown eyes magnified to the size of plums by his eyeglasses. After a moment his expression changed and he said:

"Hey. How's it going, Jocko?"

"Pretty good," I said. I tried to recall his name. "Pretty good, Aristotle." Aristotle something-or-other. Aristotle Kalamirus. An agent.

"Do you want a tax problem, Jocko?"

"I guess so. Sure."

"What kind of dough do you make?"

"Eight hundred thou per."

"Peanuts. Not even peanuts—ratnuts. They're robbing you blind, Jocko. How much did Joe Horvath pay for the rights to your book?"

"Ask Joe."

"I know Joe. Joe paid you ratnuts. Listen, I'm taking a few athletes into my select show-business clientele—prime beef only—and I'll give some consideration to taking you into my stable."

"I already have an agent."

"He's killing you. He's taking food out of your mouth."

"What would you do?"

"I'll increase your baseball salary by four hundred thou per and gradually break you into the entertainment industry. An actor. Maybe a star. You've already had lots of good publicity. You can have your own TV series—a former major-league pitcher who becomes a private eye. Or maybe you'd prefer to become a network sports announcer."

"I'd like to host a late-night talk show," I said.

"Tough. That's tough." He directed his attention toward the black hole.

"Well," I said. "A private eye—that sounds pretty good, really. For a start."

"Phone me, Jocko. Do you eat lunch?"

"Aristotle? I'm thinking of the Senate. Do you handle political candidates?"

"Fuck politicians, Jocko. You have to live under the table to collect your percentage."

"Maybe I will phone you."

"Do you like Greek food? I know a great place."

"Do I have to play a private eye? Couldn't I be a doctor?"

"Some of my beef is in the other room. Do you know Ugly Munch of the Rams? He's in my stable. Eddie Praeger with the Dodgers?"

"I know Praeger."

"Ask him what he thinks of Aristotle Kalamirus."

I found Eddie Praeger standing by a large aquarium: brightly colored tropical fish swarmed behind his head in a frenzy, and linked rings of light trembled on his cheeks. It was a dramatic backdrop—an aura of fish. Apparently they had just been fed, perhaps from the empty plate that Praeger held before him as a modest church usher might proffer the collection tray. I had seen Eddie, an average athlete, in a few TV commercials, on a game show, on a Special Olympics fund-raiser, at a celebrity roast, and he'd even had a part in *Safe at Home*.

I moved close and caressed the lapels of his sport coat between my thumbs and index fingers.

"Nice," I said. "Oh, nice. So soft."

"Let go, for Christ's sake."

"Oh, so soft. Is it baby's skin, Eddie?"

"Get away, asshole."

"Is it the skin of unborn babies? Fetus leather? You can tell me, Eddie."

He began pressing the edge of his plate against my abdomen. I released his lapels and stepped back.

"Jesus," he said.

"Nice jacket."

"Twenty-five hundred bucks." Then: "Christ, Moon, you can be scary. I really thought you'd gone amok again."

"That's a misconception I like to cultivate. It sows confusion and respect."

"I heard you broke Fungo's jaw. That's why I was a little concerned just now. Aristotle says I have a million-dollar jaw."

"Eddie, that punch has given me a new social confidence. Call it savoir faire."

"Are you okay?"

"What do you know about Aristotle Kalamirus?"

"He represents me."

"Did he get you all of your TV work?"

"Yeah, and he jacked up my baseball salary by six hundred grand. He threatened to take the Dodgers into arbitration."

"What else?"

"I'll be doing four, five guest shots on TV in the fall, a couple of game shows, and a tic douloureux charity telethon."

"I'm better looking than you."

"No you're not. Anyway, I'm a pretty good actor. I've been taking acting lessons, and dancing and singing lessons too."

"Dancing and singing? What for?"

"Some of Aristotle's contacts are putting together a Broadway musical comedy with a baseball theme. It's about Lou Gehrig's death from amyotrophic lateral sclerosis, and—"

"What! Broadway? Jesus, why didn't I think of that? *Safe at Home* would make a superior musical comedy."

Praeger smiled. "Moon, I doubt if you'll be able to milk any more dollars or pity out of the story of your life."

"You killed some of those expensive tropical fish, Eddie. They're floating belly-up. That's piscicide as far as I'm concerned."

"I didn't think sushi would hurt them. Fish are cannibals, aren't they?"

"I want to be in the Broadway show," I said.

"No way. This is going to be a quality production."

"I'm going to stick a fastball in your ear, Eddie. Maybe tomorrow night, maybe the day after. Sometime during this series, Eddie-boy, I'll drill you with my best smoke."

I hurried back to the TV cube. Aristotle was still there.

"Can you get me into the Broadway show?" I asked.

He cocked his head. "What's that, Jocko?"

"Praeger told me about the Broadway show, the one about Lou Gehrig. Can you get me a part in it?"

He raised his hand, palm down, and tilted it from side to side. "Sure. Something small, a useful credit."

"*Safe at Home* would make a great musical comedy."

"Hey, I thought about that, Jocko. But I know about Joe Horvath's contracts."

"What about them?"

"Have you ever read the contract you signed with Joe?"

"No."

"Joseph Horvath owns all of the literary, dramatic, and musical rights to your life in perpetuity."

"My God."

"You bet," Aristotle Kalamirus said.

On the black hole a hysterical battered wife was screaming at her husband; and he, sobbing and groaning, curled into a crouch while staring at his hands. The hands of a brute.

"Your pal was on the tube a moment ago, Jocko."

"My pal?"

"On a special news break."

"Who?"

"The Cintron kid."

"Blas? What happened? Is he all right?"

"The cops were taking him away in handcuffs."

"What?"

"He confessed to the murders of those transsexual persons. All four of them. They found another body. In Chicago."

"Blas? No. What are you telling me?"

"A serial killer. There's big bucks in that, Jocko."

"This is crazy. I don't believe it."

"That Cintron kid's got poise," Aristotle said. "And he's good-looking in a sullen, broody way. A young Geraldo Rivera. But his accent would limit the kind of parts he can play."

"Can't act, can't sing, can't dance," I chanted. "And he's got an accent."

"Yeah, sure, but the kid's got something special. Style. Menace. He has the potential to become another Geraldo, a Fernando Lamas, a Ricardo Montalban, a Tony Quinn. But bigger. Gigantic, now that he's a confessed serial killer."

Abruptly, without transition, I was sober. My carefully cultivated mania expired without a whimper.

"Yeah, within a few hours the kid's face is going to be on the front page of every newspaper and every TV tube in the world. I worry about the kid. The offers are going to come pouring in. He can't discriminate. What does he know? He needs a great agent."

I tasted bile. My mind and heart were torn in halves: I pitied Blas, I sorrowed for my friend; and I bitterly envied him. By morning he would be world famous. No, better than that, he would be notorious. And I remained a second-rate celebrity, a clown, a garrulous fool, a harmless nut. In one stroke—in four strokes—Blas had insured that the world would take him seriously.

"Now see here, Jocko—Cintron's your pal. He'll talk to you. Tell him that Aristotle is available. Aristotle has room for the kid in his stable. Aristotle will seriously consider representing him in the difficult times ahead."

I leaped out of my chair. "Fuck you, Aristotle! You're *my* agent."

29

Carole dropped me off in front of the hotel. "I never trusted that Blas," she said. "I didn't like the way he looked at me."

I went directly to the room and turned on the black hole. Electronic solace. Instant community.

The Los Angeles area had about forty channels, free and cable, programming in English and Spanish and Japanese and Vietnamese and Esperanto. One channel did nothing but provide today's astrological forecast for the twelve signs of the zodiac. Another showed stock-market quotations; another programmed European sissy sports like bocce and curling; another flashed the time, temperature, and the numbers of the Rape Hot Line and the Child Molester Hot Line. Child Molester? "Hewwo, my name is Walphy and I yust . . ." Child molestation was really popular this season. It was beginning to push incest and rape and battered wives and infants-in-need-of-liver-transplants off the tube.

I flicked the remote control so swiftly that the images blurred into retinal and cerebral chaos: a car crash, karate blows, a kiss, a shootout, mating gray whales, talking heads, war, a dancing tube of hemorrhoid ointment, a car going off a cliff, a woman screaming, a baby in diapers, a foamy glass of beer, a rock singer in drag, war, a dog licking a kitten, a man wielding a bloody hatchet, a bucket of fried chicken, a spectacular flaming head-on crash, a gesticulating evangelist, two men wrestling high on a fire escape, a racing police car, another woman screaming, a panda (I paused; the panda had been artificially inseminated and everyone hoped . . .), a man suffering some kind of paroxysm, a singing quiche—and there, Nicky Puma!

Nicky Puma again, the bastard. It was one of those surrealistic video numbers: Nicky Puma with five white women in blackface and five black men in whiteface. All were lurking among the shadows and trash cans of a stylized nighttime alley. And all were dressed like chic bums, with patched swallowtail tuxedos and battered top hats. And Nicky Puma, the bastard, was singing—or rather half singing and half talking his new song hit.

> *My song disgusts,*
> *So you say, ain't it so,*
> *Mrs. Smith, General Jones.*
> *My song corrupts the little ones.*
> *Ain't it so, so you say.*
> *I live in your gutter*
> *And sing of the beauty I see there,*
> *Wrinkled cakes of mud,*
> *Trickles of blood,*

Condoms that in the flood
Bloom like Easter lilies.

Nicky Puma, poet and saint. He had co-opted my natural constituency.

The phone rang. "Moon here," I said. "Poet and saint."

"Moon? It's me."

"Blas?"

"I'm sorry."

"Blas, say it ain't so."

"It's true. I killed them."

"Jesus. Why?"

"I wanted to."

"But why!"

"I was in the mood."

"No, no, *why*! For God's sake, man, why did you kill those people?"

"I enjoyed it."

"I'm not interested in your sicko emotions, Blas. I want to know the reason."

"It was fun."

The man was out of touch, out of reach, a galaxy away.

"Each time I got this delicious little frisson, you know?"

"Blas . . ."

"What do you want me to say?"

"I want you to tell me the truth."

He paused. "Is it because I'm only hitting .220?"

"Don't ask me, tell me."

"I was bored."

"You stupid jerk."

"Stupid, huh? That's what you think. Book publishers

have already offered some huge advances, Moon. A million-five's the best so far. A major motion picture is in the works. A TV miniseries. My autographed baseball cards at this moment are worth ninety-five hundred and going through the roof. I'm not even going to mention foreign rights, endorsements, an album, personal appearances."

"Blas. Christ. What can I say?" I could not order my thoughts. It was monstrous. It was diabolical. "Blas, you didn't kill those four transsexuals because of the commercial and celebrity advantages, did you?"

"Won't say yes, won't say no."

"You did!"

"Who can untangle my dark, twisted motives?"

"Yeah, well, they're going to kill *you* now. Ohio or New York or Pennsylvania or Illinois. It may take them five years, or ten, but they're going to kill you."

"It's worth it."

"You're sick."

"Sticks and stones. Pots calling kettles black."

"All right," I said. "Can I do anything for you? Do you want me to get you a lawyer?"

"I need a good agent. Will you have Aristotle Kalamirus come around to the jail?"

"Fat chance," I said, and I hung up.

At around midnight I was awakened by noises at the room's door, panel-crushing fistblows and ghastly, sobbing moans. I switched on the bedside lamp. The television was still glowing. A gunfighter was stalking down the center of a dusty street. There was more pounding and more throaty, bestial moans. The hair on my neck and arms bristled. I could hardly breathe. It was happening as I'd always feared it would—the Undead had come for me.

"Sleazy scummy shit slime."

No, it was only Kopfhammer. I crept forward; the door was securely locked and chained.

"Dick?" I said. "Where do you want to go out for dinner tomorrow night?"

"Rotty yellow stinking shitty slime scum piss snot."

"You'd better go away," I said. "I hope for your sake you go away because I feel a homicidal rage coming on. I fear for you, Kopfhammer. My medicine is wearing off. When the cops get here they'll say, 'Mother of Mercy, only a werewolf is strong enough to dismember a man that way.'"

"Scum come piss spit tumor slime bowel scab puke."

"That's a dismal litany, Kopfhammer."

A prolonged groan. The man was insensate with booze and fury.

"Hammer? I don't hate you. I pity you."

Silence.

"Pity not hate. Sadness not contempt. Compassion. Oh, it's sad, it's tragic. Kopfhammer?"

I went back into the room, lifted the phone and dialed the desk, and when the clerk answered I said, "Sir, this is appalling. What kind of hotel do you people operate? Genocide is going on up here. A primal brute is assaulting women and children on the tenth floor. My own maiden wife has been compromised. Hurry!"

I returned to the door. It was quiet outside in the hall for a few minutes and then I heard voices. Dick Kopfhammer. Two other men. Hotel security, probably. Maybe the cops. Beat him up! The Hammer was eventually persuaded to return to his own room.

I sat down in my urine-stinking pajamas and watched the black hole. Just like old times.

The late news. "Police have released from custody star second baseman Blas Cintron after determining that he could not have been the assailant responsible for the murders of four transsexual persons during an eight-day murder spree known as the Pantyhose Slayings. Cintron's confession was one of forty-three false confessions received by local police during the last twenty-four hours.

"We have Dr. Emma Pathan-Shote with us now. Dr. Pathan-Shote is a psychologist in private practice, and she will tell us why men confess to crimes they have not committed. Nice to have you with us, Doctor."

"Thank you for inviting me, John."

"Now tell us. It seems incredible. Why do some men confess to crimes they have not committed? Confess to—I might add—the most heinous, brutal crimes imaginable."

"It's a fascinating phenomenon," Dr. Pathan-Shote said.

I turned off the television and the bedside lamp. Darkness now, except for the dim glow of slanty yellow eyes; and silence, excluding the hushed flutter of bats' wings and, from the hallway, the pneumonic respiration of Bezareth the Soul Collector. I lay there and wondered what death is like for the type-A personality.

Bezareth was the creation of a paranoid schizophrenic who had become my mentor at the snakepit. A dim memory of him survives my amnesia of the period. Very few persons, he told me, kept their souls throughout a lifetime. Most died soulless. Souls weren't lost or stolen, they were abandoned. That is, at a certain point a person decided that his soul was an intolerable burden, cargo that must be jettisoned in order to save the imperiled ship. That's when Bezareth arrived. He collected the derelict soul and conducted it to the recycling plant. Then the body had to carry on alone—a ship without a compass, an ambulant corpse without a pilot.

Toward morning I was awakened by more sobs and groans and nail scrabblings from the door, and crooning evocations of my name. "Moooon, oh please, Moooon. . . ." Bezareth, or Kopfhammer again, or maybe Blas, released from jail and unable to enter the room we shared.

PART FOUR

‹‹‹•••›››

You have killed
the woman within you.

—*Terri*

30

~∞~

The club management, disturbed by our losing ways, hired a Human Potential Consultant to lecture us before the twilight-night doubleheader with the Dodgers. (Red Girt, wearing an iguana-green plaid suit, sat in a corner of the clubhouse and glared furiously at this secular humanist usurper. Red had come to see himself as a team member, a team leader, in fact.)

The HPC, a bearded psychologist of about forty-five, confidently, messianically, asserted that we were stifling our deepest and truest loving natures by conforming too rigidly to outmoded concepts of masculinity. Our athlete's pose of machismo, a vestige remaining from the obsolete Paleolithic hunter-gatherer societies, was harming us as individuals, as a team, and as productive members of "tomorrow's tradition."

"Perhaps we are still hunters in a way. But now we

must be gatherers too. Just as women are now both hunters and gatherers."

The problem was that by maintaining allegiance to old reality we were maiming our potential for citizenship in the new reality. We thought that displaying affection was weak, feminine. No! We were foolishly denying the female side of our natures, the women within us. We were unable to enjoy the loving-caring-sharing orientation. We were stunting our personal growth potential. But wait, it was still possible to liberate our most powerful energies through the simplest and most human of acts—touching. Did we know that monkeys became cross and sometimes even genocidal when they were denied the touching concept? Were we aware that macho laboratory rats had a shorter life expectancy than rats free to become ambivalent about their sexual roles? True. It was true of the rat environment and true of the human environment.

"We can all see that athletes are instinctively, unconsciously alert to the libidinous energies released by touching. The touching of hands, the high five after scoring a basket or touchdown. The slap on the back, the playful cuff, the infinitely gentle pat of encouragement. And yes, the reciprocal flow of erotic power when your palm palpitates the other fellow's buttocks."

I could hear the vestigial hairs of thirty ruffs—an inheritance from our Paleolithic ancestors—bristle all over the room. It sounded like wind in dry reeds. It sounded like murder.

"Come on, all of you, come to the center of the room. Come together and touch each other, touch, hug, embrace. Kiss. Yes, kiss each other. Relax, it really isn't so difficult. Laugh while you touch, cry if you want to. Love."

Jonah Hardy abruptly stood up and in his dual authority as team captain and six-feet-six-inch, two-hundred-and-thirty-pound badass, ordered the HPC from the room. His voice was husky and throbbing with old-reality rage.

Then Bob Brieschke screamed, a howl of laughter it was, but to the retreating HPC it must have sounded like a primal, totemic dawn-of-man caterwaul of blood-thirst and blood guilt, and we all simultaneously arose in a lynching fever—don't touch!—but by then the terrified man was gone, and we vented our fury by symbolically crucifying Red Girt.

Red, for a moment, was ecstatic. We had routed that man-kissing emissary from Sodom, that secular humanist espouser of paradise here on earth, paradise without God.

"Boys, I am so proud of you I could dance. I could take a drink, I could smoke a cigar, I could fondle a woman not my wife. Boys, whooee, whooee boys, let's all kneel to the Lord and pray."

We dragged him off to the showers and baptized his new suit. (*"Ego te baptizo,"* Buckley intoned.)

The Dodgers beat us both games, eight to one and five to three. ("Touch me," Buckley whispered after striking out while pinch-hitting for Fossey in the first game. "Hug me.")

I was selected to apologize to Red Girt after the game. ("Just go ahead and talk to the asshole, Moon. He likes you for some reason.")

Red was devastated, inconsolable. He sat hunched on a clubhouse bench, facing the wall.

"Howdy, Red."

His shoulders moved slightly, no more than if a fly had alighted on the still-damp iguana-green suit.

"Red, we feel bad about what we done. Did, Red."

"Sokay," he muttered. "Sallright."

"Red, we done a bad thing and I wud picked to apologize." I couldn't understand what had happened to my speech: did I deep down believe that there could be no real understanding between us unless I spoke Oklahomese? "It wudn't right, Red." Some of the guys behind me were sniggering. I was not doing this on purpose: my genii had popped out of the bottle. "I know it dudn't do no good to"—I inhaled my laughter and then exhaled it in a long, low hum. Just go ahead and talk to the asshole, Moon.

"Red, I like that there suit. But I doubt it's a suit Jesus'd wear even if they'd sold iguana suits in old Jerusalem."

His ears were red and flaky. I was getting tired of this. Why did he think he could make us suffer?

"You're a sorry old dawg, Red. I wouldn't take you on a rattlesnake hunt the way you are now. Stiffen up. Shuck them wet skins. Cheer up. Laugh once in a while, what the hell."

He sourly stared at me for a time and then said: " 'Sorrow is better than laughter: for by the sadness of the countenance the heart is made better.' Ecclesiastes, chapter seven, verse three."

I had nothing to say.

The corners of his lips twitched; his eyebrows were elevated. " 'The heart of the wise is in the house of mourning: but the heart of fools is in the house of mirth.' Ecclesiastes, chapter seven, verse four."

Was I the fool he had in mind? The son of a bitch.

Buckley followed me onto the team bus. "I don't know, Moon, I like Red's suit. We wear suits like that in my part of Texas."

I walked directly to the rear of the bus and sat down on the last seat. Buckley settled in next to me. He was silent until we approached the hotel and then he quietly said: "I don't know, I'm not a tailor, not a metaphysician—even so, I did like that suit. What I don't like, Moon—I don't like the red hair."

He followed me up to the hotel room, pushed in behind me and sat on one of the beds. He produced an empty pipe and sucked on it for a time, then he said: "Let's consider that suit. First, we must *a priori* suppose that the suit exists independent of your senses. The suit exists as an hypothesis. The red hair exists as an hypothesis. I believe that may be ontologically sound. Now the suit and the hair, which we have posited as existing, seem to collaborate in disharmony—unless you refute that as philologically absurd. Do you?"

"Do I what?"

"So far so good. Now you understand that we are not talking about the suitability of the suit, but its essence as suit, its suit*ness,* if you will."

I yawned.

"The suit. Your first impression was . . . what?"

"Reptilian green."

"Ah. Is the suit in fact a reptile?"

"Probably not."

"The suit *a priori* and *a posteriori* is probably not a reptile. What else did you visually observe?"

"Some yellow, some nonreptilian greens, a few crimson threads."

"Excellent. Was the suit perceived by your other senses? Aurally? That is, did you hear the suit?"

"I heard a kind of insect whine. Mosquitoes, gnats, flies. And I heard coon dogs baying."

"Yes, that suit would be loud even if there were no one

present to hear it. Tactile impressions?"

"Oliver, I'm tired."

"Of course." He put the pipe in his pocket and stood up. "But let us quickly conclude our ontological odyssey. So, in all probability the suit and the hair exist, although at this point we cannot demonstrate that you, the perceiver of the suit and the hair, exist."

"Go away, Oliver."

"I pity you," he said, and he went away.

I snatched open the top desk drawer and removed the Gideon Bible. Ecclesiastes. I punched out Red's extension number and when he answered I said: " 'Then I commended mirth, because a man hath no better thing under the sun, than to eat, and to drink, and to be merry: for that shall abide with him the labor of his life, which God giveth him under the sun.' "

He was making a sound that can be described as snorfling when I hung up the phone.

31

~~~

Early the next morning there was a knock on my door.
The Legion of Fear? No, Oliver Buckley and a girl whom
I did not at first recognize, but then she smiled and I noticed her little milk teeth: Terri, from Chicago. Diminu-
tive, squirmy Terri.

"Hi, big guy," she said.

They rudely pushed past me into the room. Buckley sat
on a bed and regarded me with sadistic glee.

"You told me you were Oliver Buckley," Terri pouted.

"I am," I said.

"You're not, you're Theodore Moon."

"He means," Buckley said, "that in our profoundest
depths we are all Oliver Buckley."

"I decided to accept your invitation," she said. "I
asked the desk for Oliver Buckley's room number and
this funny man answered the door."

She said that in Chicago I had asked her to join me in Los Angeles for the Dodger series, all expenses paid. I could not recall that particular folly but it undoubtedly was true: I was always issuing invitations to people who had the ill grace to accept. Terri thought that she would eventually move out here and initiate the process of becoming an actress. Show business was, hopefully, going to become her new career choice. She had set realistic goals. She hopefully would define herself by structuring a new career concept.

"Fine, Terri," I said, "but you'll have to fuck a lot of nasty swine along the way."

She considered that. She sucked her index finger and held it aloft, as if testing the wind direction. "That is not wholly inconsistent with my goals and value system," she said.

Buckley smiled at me. "You old fox," he said. "You found our priestess of Negative Meaning and didn't tell me."

"I like him," she said, hooking a thumb toward Oliver.

"You're the only one," I said.

"I like you too, Terri," Buckley said.

"God," she said with a happy smile, her perfect little teeth moistly gleaming, her eyes crinkling at the corners. "I know that I'm going to love California."

"And California will love you," Buckley said.

She wriggled ecstatically.

"I'll get a room for you down the hall, Terri," I said. "We'll have dinner. I'll show you the town. I'll introduce you to some very influential men, movers and shakers in the industry."

Buckley sprawled back on the bed and covered his face with a pillow.

They were not gone ten minutes when the phone rang.

"Moon, hello."

"Patsy?"

"I'm calling you from the airport."

"What airport?"

"Des Moines."

"Where are you going?"

"Well, I'm thinking about flying out there. Remember, you invited me."

"You said you couldn't come."

"I changed my mind. You're always saying that women always change their minds. Well, okay, I changed my mind."

"Good, come on out."

"I don't know now. Maybe it isn't a good idea. Do you really want to see me?"

"Absolutely. Please come."

"I don't know. Honestly, Moon, I shouldn't get involved with you again. My parents don't think so either. They're very much opposed."

"I cause nothing but heartbreak."

"Daddy promised to buy me a car if I stayed away from you."

"There's a lot to be said in favor of machines. In a thousand years we'll all be hybrids—machumans, techumans, enginoids. What kind of car did he promise you?"

"I don't know the name. It's made in Korea."

I laughed. "Cheapapa. I'll buy you a Mercedes. No, I'll buy you a . . . horse." Patsy loved horses but had never owned one.

"Yes, a horse!" I said grandly. "An Arabian mare with long eyelashes and dainty hooves. Creamy mane and tail, fast as the wind. She'll have blood in her, not oil. You'll name her . . . Moonbeam."

"No I won't."

"She'll nicker when she sees you coming. You'll let her drink honey out of your palm."

"No I won't."

"I'll book a room for you down the hall. I can't pick you up at the airport, we play a day game today, but you can take a taxi to the ballpark. I'll leave a ticket for you at the main entrance."

"Never mind that, baseball is boring. I'll take a taxi to the hotel. Moon, listen, do you really want me to come out there?"

"We'll have a first-rate dinner tonight."

"All right. I guess. Moon—will you really buy me a horse?"

"It's done."

I replaced the receiver and stood transfixed as a crackpot fantasy insinuated itself. It was like drawing three cards to a straight flush, like making ten straight passes with the dice. It was like eavesdropping on faint, garbled communications from another world. "Three of them . . . can he last? . . . despicable . . . can't allow it . . . quartet? . . . wouldn't dare . . ."

It seemed to me—I chose to believe—that circumstance was providing me with one last chance for a manic flight. Buzz around up there for six hours, seven, and then home. The planet would be home to me then. I'd clip my own wings, finally. Moon? He's been grounded. Not a kid anymore, you know. Last I heard he was selling insurance down in Tampa.

I really did want—even if only for a few hours—to become again the renegade Moon, prodigious drinker, prodigious eater, prodigious spender, prodigious liar, prodigal Moon. It would be a kind of farewell performance. A small manic tour de force. Modest in conception and execution but possessing in miniature all the qualities of a three-month debauch.

It had to happen soon. Next month, next week, might be too late. I awakened bored most mornings, bored! Get up, scratch, spit, piss, turn on the black hole—hey, look, there's a guy with Alzheimer's disease. So normal, so low, and once I had been a sort of squalid god. My highs had been loftier than those of ordinary men; my lows lower; my mediums—I hadn't any mediums. Soon I would become just another guy, and there is no cure for that, and only the one dismal acquittal.

Carole, Terri, and Patsy would be in town at the same time. Two of them staying in the same hotel . . . in neighboring rooms. Hell, three of them. I would rent a room for Carole too.

Yes, take all three to dinner tonight at the same time. The logistics might be a problem, though not unsolvable. A limousine and driver were essential. Three restaurants in the same general vicinity. Indian food for Carole; seafood for Patsy; Mexican food for Terri. Carole liked the Soul of India restaurant. I'd select two other restaurants from the Yellow Pages. The thing was to look for key phrases like "cuisine" and "gracious dining" and "Mr. Tommy playing nightly at the piano bar." Cocktails, excuse me, hors d'oeuvres, excuse me, entrées, excuse me, desserts, excuse me. It was brilliant.

I would be three men (in my prime I'd been half a dozen); I would drink as three, eat as three, be as potent as three, burn as hot and bright as three, and before the earth completed its revolution I would perform as three and show up that plastic prosthetic dildo as a comically childish implement, another sad example of technology's reach exceeding its rasp. Yes, up and down the hotel hallway, slapstick entrances and exits, moaning womoons—"Hurry back, darling."

32

⚬⚬

The stretch limousine was a marvel, long and low and black, with a glass partition between classes (I communicated with the driver via telephone), a compact bar, a tiny black hole, and tinted windows that thwarted the servile stares of the street rabble. The driver, resplendent in gray livery, was an Iranian whose name sounded like "Jimmyjamjohnny."

I explained my perilous mission over the car telephone and asked for volunteers: "Some of us may not return, Jimmyjamjohnny." But he was game: these fanatical Moslems have not yet beat their swords into Cuisinarts; their guts do not turn to water at the thought of the female whordes massed on the horizon. Wasn't Allah a He? Wasn't Allah on our side? As yet no Moslem female had dared to suggest that Allah was a woman. Allah and his prophet, Mohammed, were still warriors. Hunters, not gatherers.

"We advance, Jimmyjamjohnny. We return victorious or supine on our shields."

I sent him back to the hotel to pick up Patsy. "May Allah guide you safely across the desolate Empty Quarter."

The Fin and Pincher was a big redwood joint cantilevered out over the surf. Some Eastern lobsters were crawling across the bottom of a glass tank in the foyer. Fools, tonight you die. My advance was halted by a braided purple rope and a sign: WAIT TO BE SEATED! Another threatening bulletin from the Legion of Fear. Beyond was the dining room, with a rich wine-red carpet, many white-clothed tables, and all around banks of windows looking out over the foaming surf.

The hostess, tottery on her high heels, approached me with a commercial smile. She was a big, deeply tanned blonde in a long dress, perhaps an actress awaiting the precise constellar conjunctions that would propel her into the hearts of the dreary multitude.

I shot my left cuff, flashed my Patek Philippe. "Table for two."

"Name?" she asked, consulting the reservations book.

"Vlad the Impaler."

She ran her forefinger down the page.

"Just kidding. Moon, Theodore Moon."

A cold smile. "Yes, but you are early." She started to unhook the rope.

"Wait. Would you seat the courtesan when she arrives, and then come fetch me in the lounge?"

"Of course."

"I need a drink or five. The Dodgers beat us again today. I'm a baseball player."

"Oh."

"Theodore Moon. You probably heard about me. A

television docudrama about my heartbreak and hope, my laughter and my tears, is going to appear on network TV this October."

"Oh."

"It was produced by Joseph Horvath. Have you ever heard of him?"

She appeared bored, eager to get on with whatever tedious things hostesses did. I felt anxious. Was this becoming a test of my charm?

"Listen, would you like tickets for tomorrow night's game? No obligation. Just pick them up at the ticket office."

"I have to work tomorrow night."

"Well, maybe the next time I'm in town."

A genuine smile, finally. "Yes, okay, I think I'd like that, Vlad."

"I'll get in touch."

"Do you really know Joe Horvath?"

"I do indeed."

"What is he like?"

"Joe? He's a teddy bear. Joe would give you the shirt off his mother's back."

She wriggled her fingers bye-bye. Bye, Brunhilde. One of those legendary California blondes, wide shoulders and hips, bounteous breasts, nipped-in waist, thighs of laminated steel. I hurried into the lounge. Down, root. I thought it odd that while I—ego, psyche, soul—was able to realistically evaluate the potential for swift gratification, my root was not. We're in a nice restaurant, root, there are people everywhere, she's working. Dumb root. What if, say, my right arm autonomously saluted every time a flag appeared?

I sat down on a stool at the piano bar. "Double scotch on the rocks," I told the cocktail waitress, a debauched adolescent who, in the murk, looked no more than fifteen. Sure, it was still going on. They were compelled to work in waterfront joints like this for a month or two, until the freighter arrived, and then they were shanghaied off to Yemen or Saudi Arabia or God knows where. Swarthy princes who smelled of camels and figs used them and discarded them. One day they were roller-skating on the beachfront promenade and a week later they were fetching bowls of couscous and being addressed as "Christian pigdog."

Sitting at one end of the piano bar, sipping chardonnay, was a young couple who had been attired by Banana Republic, shod by Nike, and coiffed by nervous homosexuals. The world amused them. The piano player and I were temporarily a peripheral part of that world.

"Howdy," I said. "I'm in textiles. What're you in?"

They smirked and turned toward each other. Mirror profiles.

The pianist, who was black, wore a raspberry blazer, a ruffled shirt, and a cummerbund, and had a hoarse three A.M. voice that had been half ruined by too many cigarettes and too much whiskey and too many demoralizing experiences with women.

I scribbled a few of my favorite song titles on the green side of a fifty-dollar bill and slid it across the bar. He glanced at it, folded it lengthwise, and dropped it into his brandy-snifter tip jar. The fifty elicited a three-second smile.

He started out at the top with "Moonglow," played about half of it before neatly bridging into "Moon Over Miami," and then, with a virtuoso's ease, segued into "Full Moon and Empty Arms."

The couple at the end of the piano bar looked at each other. The girl laughed.

"You like moon songs?" she said to me.

"Yes. It's my name. Theodore Moon."

The name meant nothing to them; evidently they weren't baseball fans or serial-killer groupies.

"Theodore," I told them, "means beloved of God."

"That so," the man said, sounding bored and contemptuous.

I said, "The moon—the celestial orb, not yours truly—has for thousands of years been regarded with awe and reverence. Yes, worshiped. Astarte, Diana, Selene, were all moon goddesses."

The pianist, halfway through my fifty now, was beginning to get in the mood as he commenced a bebop jazz version of "Blue Moon."

The couple was restless. How'd we get involved with this freak?

"Of course," I continued, "the moon is not all romance and lovely, naked goddesses. It has a dark side, so to speak, a devilish aspect, an aura of mystical madness. Your lunatic—of which I am an example. Werewolves, vampires, ghouls, all have a symbiotic, not to say synergistic, connection to the waxing and waning of the moon."

The man seemed to be looking for a place to spit. The woman picked up her change off the bar and put it into her purse.

The pianist performed a tricky four-chord riffle that led directly into "Moonlight in Vermont."

I said, "Police claim that crime and generally weird behavior increase with a full moon, but that hasn't been established. And then you have the silly notion that a woman's menstrual cycle is somehow determined by the phases of the moon. Personally I prefer sensual moon goddesses to the sanguinary minutiae of menstrual cycles."

The couple, a dull duo, sun-fun philistines, slipped away just as the pianist began playing the first magical notes of Beethoven's "Moonlight Sonata." It moved him. He frowned and bit his lip. This was a freebee, an encore, perhaps, since I had neglected to scribble "Moonlight Sonata" on the back of the fifty. It sounded fine to me. He wasn't Rubenstein but he wasn't merely Tommy-at-the-piano either.

The hostess appeared and said, "Vlad, your courtesan has arrived."

"This way," she said, and she led me through the sacred velvet barrier.

Patsy, her hair up and her décolleté down, was seated by one of the big windows. Her dress subtly harmonized with the blue sea beyond. Her eyes too

I kissed her cheek, murmured "Whore," and went around to my chair.

She smiled cynically.

"I was chatting with some folks in the lounge," I said.

"And I suppose you invited them to join us for dinner."

"What? No, of course not. Anyway, I amused them. No, I amused myself. I let the genii out of the bottle, but not too much."

"I could smell the genii when you kissed me." Then she smiled again and said, "Moon, it's so good to get away. I didn't realize how much I need a holiday. Thank you."

A sneering waiter arrived with the menus, and before he could scuttle off and hide in a storeroom, I ordered a dozen oysters on the half shell, some cold smoked salmon, two martinis, a bottle of white burgundy and bottle of bordeaux. It was ten minutes after eight: I had only twenty minutes before cocktails with Carole, fifty minutes before aperitifs with Terri.

"What's new with that Fun Ghoul person?"

Fun Ghoul? Fungo. "He's going to sue me."

"Well, you shouldn't have hit him."

"I like to think of myself as an agent provocateur."

"Provoking whom?"

"The Legion of Fear."

"And serving whom?"

"Obscure forces, arcane influences. They telepathically issue me commands. I obey."

She giggled.

"Regard me as point man for the addled."

She gazed speculatively at her menu. "What is abalone?"

"A shellfish."

"What is it like?"

"Like . . . conch. Sort of."

"I'm from Iowa. What is conch like?"

"Fishy-tasting gristle."

"Agent provocateur, point man for the addled—your trouble, Moon, is that you can't accept being ordinary."

"They beat it with a mallet to tenderize it."

"You aren't exactly ordinary, dear, but you aren't all that extraordinary either."

"They cook it."

"If you would only quiet down."

"You squeeze lemon juice on it."

"I mean—how old are you now?"

"And then you chew it up small and swallow it."

She laughed. "Old Moon. The last Stoic."

The waiter arrived with our martinis, took our orders, and soon after returned with a wine bucket and stand.

"This is fun," Patsy said.

The waiter came back with the dishes of oysters and salmon, lemons, a basket of crackers, and hot sauce. And then a man with the aspect of a mortician showed up and ceremoniously opened the wine.

Patsy leaned over the table and watched as I squeezed lemon juice and Tabasco sauce over an oyster.

"It moved," she said.

"Don't worry, they aren't very fast."

I chewed and swallowed the slippery little chap and drained the shell juices. I prepared another.

"That one moved too! Moon, you're eating those animals alive!"

"They'd eat me alive if they could."

Patsy prodded the salmon slices with a fork, and when it seemed certain that they were deceased, she ate them greedily. People had more taboos about food than they did sex. More gusto too, generally.

"Excuse me, Patsy, I've got to make an important telephone call."

Across the dining room, over the rope, past the lounge and foyer and out into the heat.

No limousine, no Jimmyjamjohnny. No matter, a taxi was unloading beneath the portico. Fortune kneels before the bold.

"To the Soul of India, driver. Don't spare the horses."

33

The Soul of India was a hokey place, cinematic Hydera-
bad or something: five or six little dining alcoves, sitar
music, yellow elephant tusks on the wall, beaded curtains
and painted bamboo screens. A Brahman maiden intercepted me as I was climbing over the velvet rope. She had
a caste mark on her forehead and a tiny jewel piercing the
flare of her left nostril.

"Good evening, sar."

"Howdy. I have a reservation. My guest has probably
already arrived."

"Very good, sar. Your name, please, sar?"

"Gilles de Rais. Wait, just kidding. Teddy Moon."

She led me through the maze of rooms, down a final
corridor, and through a final beaded curtain into a final
room. There were half a dozen tables scattered around
and, in the corner, wearing a white sari and a vermilion

caste mark, the memsahib. Carole was relaxed and chatting with a threesome at a nearby table—members of her ashram, no doubt.

I apologized for being late. Carole coolly introduced me to the three; the names meant nothing but the faces seemed familiar from old dreams. One man and the woman nodded, smiled mechanically, and then ignored me; the other man rose and shook my hand. He was tall with glorious white hair and eyebrows.

I sat down across from Carole. "I'd like a drink."

She gazed at me with superior Oriental resignation. "They don't serve alcohol here, Moon. And you can't smoke. But they have wonderful fruits and juices."

"What kind of fruits? Do they have fruits of our toil? By their fruits ye shall know them? The tree of evil bears bitter fruit? Fruit of the Loom?"

And then: "I'm hungry. Where's the waitress, out in back genuflecting to heathen idols? I'm hungry, not all of us have the patience of Hindus. I've only got one life, you have scores."

Carole's friends concentrated on their chow. Do not engage the stare of a madman or he'll interpret it as an opportunity to palaver. But Carole was serene, Carole was fatalistic. Her little smile informed me that she was not responsible for my filthy karma.

"Excuse me for a minute," I said. "I've got to phone Aristotle Kalamirus. He's hounding me to star in a big Broadway musical."

I had shrewdly told the taxi driver to wait. "Restaurant Zacatecas," I told him. "And step on it."

"Restaurant Zacatecas? Are you sure?"

"Sure I'm sure."

"Okay, pal, but it's a real dump."

"It can't be a dump. They've got a full-page ad in the

Yellow Pages. They serve the best Mexican food in the world. *En todo el mundo.*"

I had been betrayed by the Yellow Pages. It was a dingy cafe with filthy windows and a huge plastic taco hanging above the door. Worse, much worse, there were about thirty motorcycles parked along the mean street, the bad bikes, Harley-Davidson hawgs, and no doubt inside the cafe thirty brutish motorcycle thugs and thirty sluttish, slouching female auxiliaries. Leather, chains, boots, dirt, slaver. Poor Terri. I'm sorry. Can you forgive me? Gang rape is bad but worse still is the sacrifice of innocent bystanders—the Moon, for instance. This is going to play hell with your personal growth process and individual human ecology. The thing, Terri, is to survive; don't let these animals drive a permanent wedge between your body and your psyche.

I'd decided to return to the taxi but instead I found myself opening the cafe's door. What would happen? Nothing much: some baleful stares, gap-toothed grins, a sneer or ten. The jukebox was howling a Mexican *corrido.* The place smelled of hot animal fats and hot motor oil and hot blood. I had overestimated the bikers' numbers though not their humanity. There were about twenty men and six or seven pouty-mouthed sluts. I had heard about the sluts: they were fiendish when the men condescended to give them a victim, they delighted in torture and could inflict a prolonged and excruciating death. They could keep you alive for three days.

Terri, overdressed, gussied up for some Hollywood-type nightclub, was sitting at a booth. She was spooning in some orangy fluid from a bowl. Even from the doorway I could see wet streaks of tears on her cheeks. Had she been insulted by these stinking swine?

I approached, slinking past the barbarians, and

slipped into the booth across from her.

"Hi, baby. Hope you haven't been waiting long. I got held up by a big show-business deal."

Sniffling and weeping, she lowered her spoon.

"What are you eating?" I asked.

"Soup, gazpacho, I think it is."

I lifted the bowl and smelled it. "Terri, this isn't soup, it's salsa."

"Salsa?"

"It's a sauce made out of peppers and tomato and onions and napalm. A hot sauce, you pour it over your food if it's too bland."

"Oh. It was on the table."

"It always is. So the flies can refresh themselves."

"Mother-fucker!" one of the gang-rapers roared good-naturedly.

Terri wiped away her salsa tears, leaned forward over the table and hissed, "What kind of place is this?"

"Look, I know it doesn't seem like much at first look, but they serve the best Mexican food in the world here."

"But the people!"

"They're movie extras. Jesus, I get disappointed in you sometimes, Terri. Don't be misled by the superficial squalor, this is the chic eatery with the *in* movie crowd."

"Movie extras?"

"Sure. They're shooting a Harley hawg epic down the road. Sylvester Stallone is in it. Marlon. Jane Fonda. Nicky Puma. Come on now, are you kidding me?"

"What? No, honest, I'm not kidding. I just wondered, that's all."

I had mistakenly intercepted the glare of a hairy walrus in black leotards and leather, and was entranced, hypnotized, as his white-fuzzed tongue emerged, elongated, lifted, stretched beyond anatomical limits, until the wormy tip explored first his left nostril and then his right. Then the tongue rolled up like a paper dragon, vanished, and he smirked at me. It was a hell of a good trick.

I didn't have much time to spend with Terri right now. Mexican food was quickly prepared, in fact it had been ready since February, and only needed scooping out onto the plates.

"Look, kid, order us a plate of nachos and two margaritas. No, four margaritas. I'll be back in a few minutes."

"You're going to leave me here?" she hissed.

I smiled. "Don't be a hayseed. These people are pussycats. Don't be surprised if I return with Sylvester Stallone. Old Sly wants to meet you."

"Don't leave me alone here. Please."

"Stiffen your spine, Terri. I hate whining."

I managed to pass safely through the gauntlet of eyes and boots. The sluts were most to be dreaded. The men merely stomped on you until you rather dreamily expired.

Jimmyjamjohnny had the limousine parked outside. I paid off the taxi driver.

"Soul of India," I commanded.

Nothing had changed in the restaurant. Carole was still chatting with her friends. I sat down.

"I'm starving," I said. "When are we going to order?"

"I ordered for you, Moon."

"You ordered for me? What did you order for me?"

"Biriani."

"Biriani? I hate biriani. I've always hated biriani. I've hated biriani for thousands of years, ever since I can remember. How about cow? They got cow in this temple? I want a cow, a whole cow, barbecued in an open pit, with lots of cole slaw on the side."

"You don't want to make a fuss, do you?" the tall white-haired man said. "There's a good chap."

An Englishman!

"I'm tired of fighting your wars," I said.

There were glasses of water on the table. I lifted mine, took a mouthful, then coughed violently and sprayed it against the wall. It was just average city water, the sewage taste masked by dangerous chemicals.

"Oh shit, oh damn, where did they get that sludge? The Ganges? They throw corpses into the Ganges. Oh God, oh Kali! I swallowed some of it."

Other diners stared at me, but the trio—the quartet including Carole—ignored me. They must have heard about the Moon; prepared themselves to encounter the savage. Just ignore him when he behaves like that. If you don't give him attention he'll settle down. Don't encourage him. He's really a dear but he's been, you know . . . well, sick. But you'll love him when you get to know him.

I fled to the men's bathroom. A skinny Dravidian was trying to resuscitate the toilet with a plunger. He was an Untouchable, no doubt; that was the kind of work assigned to the caste. He was sweating. Pump pump—the toilet was clearly a goner.

I confronted myself in the mirror. See here, fellow, are you doing the right thing? One more manic episode might scorch your brain to cinder. You'll end up on a back ward with the drooling Undead. You'll sit for days, rocking back and forth. You'll sulk: Me dunt lahk kerts, me lahk peas. You'll beg: No, please, my shit, dunt take away. You'll reflect: I was, now I wunt.

I went outside and jumped into the rear seat of the limo.

"Fin and Pincher, Jimmyjamjohnny. And don't worry. Everything is working exactly as I'd planned."

34

"You're just in time, Vlad," the hostess said. I could see that the food was on our table, and Patsy, herself always punctual and responsible, was anxiously looking for me. Behind her the sea glowed a radioactive indigo. Smog had been incandesced by the nuclear sunset. I boldly strode across the room—busy man, busy man, busy man. Sat down, snapped open my napkin and spread it over my lap.

"Sorry, baby," I said. "That was Nicky Puma on the horn. I just couldn't shake loose."

She gazed levelly at me. Patsy knew that I was a creator of timely myths—a liar—but she also knew that I really did now and then rub shoulders with celebrats and celebeauts.

"It's all right," she said. "The food just arrived."

On my plate was a two-inch-thick charbroiled steak;

on Patsy's an enormous mutant lobster.

"Did you know, Patsy, that 'lobster' comes from the Latin *'locusta,'* or 'locust.' But that lobster looks fine, they did a splendid job of boiling it alive."

"That will be enough, Moon."

The bottle of bordeaux stood open on the table, breathing quietly and deeply. I poured myself a glass, then fished the white burgundy out of the ice bucket and filled Patsy's glass.

I lifted my wine. "To Patsy," I said. "Simple in a time of complexity, true in a time of perfidy, direct in a time of humbug, and always pretty."

I expected her eyes to mist, but she just lowered her gaze and began to skillfully autopsy the lobster.

These days my appetite, while still sharp, was no longer heroic. I knew that I could consume the steak without difficulty, but the potato, the artichoke, and the rolls and butter must be sacrificed so that I might ensure a respectable showing on the Mexican food and the biriani—whatever that was. There were three desserts marching toward my bowels as well.

"You know, Patsy, it's inevitable, don't argue, we shall remarry someday and live happily ever after."

She laughed. "I'll reply to that after you've paid the check."

"But first I must marry and divorce a member of the European aristocracy. A princess, a duchess, a viscountess."

"Sure," she said. "Go for it."

"When I was twelve I made out a list of the one hundred things I wanted to do in my lifetime. Pitch a World Series game, climb the Matterhorn, ride my bicycle no-hands for ten miles, fly an airplane, marry a member of the European aristocracy . . ."

I had just invented the list but it immediately became true; and it would remain true until ultimately it became factual. It was the sort of detail biographers seized upon: one sultry summer day little Teddy Moon climbed up into his tree house, opened the cheap spiral notebook to which he confided his dreams, licked the tip of the pencil, and in a childish scrawl wrote, *#73—marry princess.*

I annihilated my steak. Patsy ate too slowly; she was putting my schedule in jeopardy. I ordered desserts and cognacs from the waiter and excused myself.

"Where are you going?"

"Don't ask."

"Where?"

"I have a touch of dysentery," I said.

JJJ drove me across town to the Soul of India. No Carole. The Brahman maiden informed me that Carole had finished dinner and left with the tall "sar." She had defected to the enemy. My small masterpiece seemed to be collapsing. Manic fantasies, so brilliant in conception, so mathematically elegant, always seemed to founder on the shoals of reality. Time and space were resisting me again. This development would force me to improvise during the hours put aside for erotic marvels. No Carole, no Hindu smut.

JJJ drove me to the Restaurant Zacatecas. Good old Jimmyjamjohnny. Don't cut *my* throat if this proves to be the night of the long knives.

Terri was still waiting; the morotcycle gang was waiting. The bikers seemed strangely subdued. Thank God for deadly drugs.

I sat across from Terri. "Sorry, baby, but Sly couldn't break away from his meeting with Arnold. We'll all get together later."

There were four margaritas on the table. I drained the

first and toyed carelessly with the second for ten or fifteen seconds.

A fat waitress arrived and hurled menus at us. *"Menudo está especial,"* she said. *"Posole está especial. Chalupa está muy especial.* What you want?"

I said, "We'll take two combination plates. And four more margaritas."

The waitress vanished into a steamy place and soon after reappeared with two big combination platters. *Gracias.* The food on my plate looked like a cross section of some squat, smelly beast, a road kill, but it tasted great. Lord, this *was* the best Mexican food in all the world. One flavor, one odor, but a diversity of colors and textures and consequences. I showed Terri how to mold all the various foods into a single viscid mass, a volcano, and then hollow out a crater and fill it with hot lava—the salsa.

"Good, eh, Terri?"

"Look at them assholes!" one of the bikers shouted, and he doubled up in laughter that abruptly ended in apoplexy. The walrus tried his tongue-nose trick again but it didn't work now, he'd abused his gift and lost it. A pair of blank-eyed sluts attired in leather and grease came over and watched us eat. A biker in the corner suddenly began sobbing. The Undead seemed to be slipping back into their temporary, terrible slumbers.

I left two fifty-dollar bills on the table, one for the house and one for the bikers.

"Jimmyjamjohnny," I said, "drop me off at the Fin and Pincher, and then take the missy back to the hotel."

I turned to Terri. "Sorry, baby, I'll join you later. Crawl beneath the covers and keep your taco warm for me. Right now I have an important meeting with Ted and Jane. But I shouldn't be delayed long."

She refused to talk to me. I tried to cuddle but she was cold and unyielding. She recoiled when I touched her. It was that recoil they all learn; as if your fingers were five reptiles that had crawled up out of the drain.

When the limousine was parked beneath the Fin and Pincher's portico she said, "I was wrong about you. I believed that you were a vulnerable man."

"But I am vulnerable, Terri. Jesus. I'm a wreck, a nut. You can't find a more vulnerable man than me."

"No," she said with a sad, cool hauteur. "No, Teddy Moon. You have denied the female side of your nature. You have killed the woman within you."

I watched the funereal limousine cruise as silently as death down the driveway and out onto the boulevard. Was it true that I had killed the woman inside me? Maybe so, maybe so. Yes. But hey, the bitch had it coming.

I smoked a big Jamaican cigar with my Martell cognac. The smoke, thick and blue and prettily striated, drifted eastward and engulfed a table of antismoking fanatics. Petty functionaries of the Legion of Fear. I intercepted their stares and ran them back for touchdowns. *You're endangering the health of my unborn child!* a woman telepathically informed me. I replied, *Nonsense, it will do the little waterhead some good.* They made a theatrical display of their wrath. But I turned their stares, converted their sarcastic comments into mumbles.

"Maybe you shouldn't smoke, Moon."

"A cigar is a civilized thing, Patsy."

"I know, a good cigar is a smoke while a woman is only a woman."

"It's bean curd that will kill you," I said loudly. "Bean curd, yogurt, wheat germ, fibers, leafy green vegetables, fish. Jogging in this poisonous brown smog. Just living here is like sucking on an automobile exhaust pipe three hours a day. And they complain about tobacco smoke!"

"Moon, please don't make a scene."

"These people are terrified of eggs, Patsy, eggs, but they'll let their poor children drink Perrier. Cholesterolphobes. As for me, I eat six to eight eggs every day, without fail."

"That will be enough!" one of the men at the table growled. His face was as red as the lobster's carapace. He had bulging hyperthyroidal eyes. It was the praise of eggs that had driven him toward violence. I know these people: admire an egg or a piece of cheese or a greaseburger and they go berserk.

"Look at them," I said in a near shout. "They own chemical companies, they manufacture pesticides, they operate lumber mills. And they complain about the sweet, rich, comforting aroma of a cigar."

The waiter suddenly appeared. "Will there be anything else, sir?"

"Who wants to know?"

"Moon . . ."

"The check," I said. "And mind your arithmetic. Wait—and give my compliments to the menial who thaws the grub and pops it into the microwave. Now let me see your heels."

Outside, walking across the parking lot, waiting for JJJ, Patsy asked, "Why do you do it?"

"What, specifically?"

"To start—why humiliate that poor waiter? He's only earning his living."

"He was insolent all night."

"I didn't notice, but so what if he was? You were insolent all night too."

"I was?"

"Anyway, I thought the food was good."

So did I, but I said, "That's because your palate was ruined by Midwestern church suppers. Stewed chicken with dumplings. Corn on the cob. Jell-O."

Jimmyjamjohnny arrived, got out of the limousine and opened the door for us. I smelled alcohol on his breath. We slid into the rear compartment and I inventoried the liquor box. He had tapped the bourbon. Well, since the seal was already cracked . . . I poured myself a stiff shot. Leaned back. Picked up the telephone.

"*Avanti,* pal, and drive carefully. You don't want to plead your case to Allah with alcohol on your breath."

"Now there you go again," Patsy said. "You're teasing that man. Why do you always pick on powerless people?"

"Wake up, Patsy. Because they can't retaliate."

35

—∾—

I escorted Patsy to her room and then walked back down the hallway. Things were not working as I'd expected. I had managed to get off the ground a few times but lacked the madness to stay aloft, to soar. Caution intruded. No sooner was I airborne than I began to bore people. It is an awful responsibility to be the Moonman. The standards are too high.

There was a dainty pile of lingerie on the floor outside my room: bikini panties, a black lace bra, a slip. Silk and lace, filmy stuff, as light as air and scented with lavender. I imagined a delicate creature with wounded eyes and puffy lips.

It looked as though yet another transsexual ingenue had been snuffed and shuttled down to the basement via the laundry shaft, and the Moon was being framed for it.

I stuffed the incriminating undies inside my shirt, rode the elevator up two floors, and deposited the evidence outside Red Girt's door. Here's a little dynamic motivational catalysm for you, Leroy.

The party was still proceeding in Esteban's suite of rooms: there were at least sixty people inside, four tons of flesh pressed back to back and belly to belly. Music, loud voices, the air reeking of testosterone and estrogen. Kopfhammer's head bobbed above the crowd like a buoy on a stormy sea. His face was flushed and his eyes reflected a boozy glitter. But his Mr. Hyde had not yet snarlingly emerged: he saw me, grinned, and shouted, "Moon! Moon, do you want to have dinner tomorrow night?"

The two cops were there. Half of the people in the rooms looked like Undeads, but few were more convincingly Undead than Sturm and Drang—mobile cadavers. They stank of fleshly corruption and cheap embalming fluids.

I said, "Don't you guys have to report in at the morgue every two or three days?"

Sturm leaned precariously toward me, squinting. "Well, if it ain't. So it is, so it is. You got me there. Monkey."

"Moon."

"Moony, right."

"Ask him," Drang said.

"Did you deliver the property to Joseph Horvath?"

"What property is that?" I said.

"Ask him the other."

"How you gonna play baseball without kneecaps, Moony?"

"Joe's people will get in touch with your people."

"Tell him."

"We want six hundred thou for the property and one mil each to star in the vehicle."

"Plus," Drang said.

"Plus some points."

"Listen," I said, "aren't you two supposed to interrogate me about the murder spree, the reign of terror?"

"Interrogate the mutt, Warren."

"Moony, did you or did you not brutally slay those four trans . . . transaxials . . . transwhats . . . transsexuals?"

"I did."

"Yes or no."

"Yes."

"You're lying."

"Tiffany, LaMenta, Courtney, Michelle. I plucked those fair dewy roses one by one and crushed them."

"One thing I hate's a fucking liar. Get outta my face, scumbag."

The female underwear was back in front of my door. Touché, Red. I got a wire coat hanger and skulked down the stairway to the floor below. Kopfhammer roomed alone; not even a rookie could breathe the air polluted by his nightlong flatulence. I pushed the lingerie underneath the door with the coat hanger. A job worth doing and a job well done.

An observer, stationed behind the ice machine, say, would have seen a jaunty Theodore Moon enter his room. Silence, and then the observer would see a different man emerge.

A tall, slightly bowlegged man in faded Levi's and denim shirt, cowboy boots with three-inch heels, jingling spurs, and a high-crowned Stetson hat. A tall slow-moving bowlegged dangerous man with eyes squinched up against the sunlight and dust. A hard man with a soft voice. Broken knuckles and a definite limp. The observer, anxiously crouched behind the ice machine as the desperado passed, might have imagined certain sounds and smells: mesquite fires, sage, the outraged bawling of calves, the stink of burnt hide and hair, the ratchedy buzz of a rattlesnake, and the sharp odors of work-sweat and leather and red-hot iron and smoking Winchesters.

Don Coyote lurched bowlegged down the hall. He was more comfortable astride than afoot, and, too, the spurs' rowels kept catching in the nap of the carpet. So he shuffled down the hall, jingle jingle, entered an elevator, and pushed a button. Boxes going up and down. Why don't they build these danged places sideways so a man can stay close to the horizon?

Don Coyote paused in the door frame of Don Esteban's rowdy hacienda. The place was full up with greenhorns dancing and drinking and milling around like cows before a thunderstorm. Don Esteban was there, his degenerate face puffy with booze and noxious body wastes. Nearby stood the sensual Zenda, brown jungle goddess. Jonah Hardy and Fossey and Howard—blackamoors. Many strangers. And there, across the room, little Terri dancing with—Oliver Buckley! Dancing, she screwed herself into the floor, becoming tiny, and then unscrewed herself to full height. Showing her little milk teeth, wriggling, vibrating, shuddering, happily convulsed. Buckley, his jaw slack, thumped around awkwardly, no match for his partner.

Spurs jingling, Don Coyote entered. Stop the music.

"Howdy, pard," Jonah Hardy said.

"Never seen a nigger what could ride," Don Coyote said. "Never seen a nigger what could rope. But I seen lots of niggers what could shoot and cut." He passed on, half-expecting a sledgelike fistblow to crush his brainbox, but Jonah and the others just laughed.

"Howdy, Deputy Sturm. Howdy, Deputy Drang."

They stared at him.

"A word to the wise. An anonymous tip. Search the room of Richard Kopfhammer."

Don Coyote moved deep into the room.

"Howdy, Don Esteban."

Don Esteban was walleyed with dissipation and fatigue. White beard stubble speckled his cheeks. The flesh beneath his eyes was ringed and bruised. Now his eyes revolved crazily, tried to center, struggled to coordinate and focus, and finally he gazed at Don Coyote with only a slight cast in his left eye.

"Teodoro! *Dios!* Hey, okay my good friend, how are you being? Why I no see you?"

"Don Esteban, I want to borrow Zenda for ninety minutes."

"What is this I am hear?"

"You said you'd loan me Zenda. I want her now."

"What am I hear? I am sorry, my ears stink. What is wrong?" He stuck his little fingers into his ear holes and punished them.

"I'll give her back to you in an hour, ninety minutes, not much the worse for wear."

"What am I hear?" Esteban cried in an anguished voice. His left eye spun off into orbit, twitched horribly, and then returned to its home. The pupil of his left eye was dilated; the right was a pinpoint. Had the poor man suffered a stroke?

Zenda was standing nearby, brown and calm, waiting. She did not know English but Don Coyote imagined her saying, I go with you, Master. I lift my skirts, Master. I lie down as you bid, Master. I bathe your feet, Master.

"Don Esteban," Don Coyote said, "I'm calling you. You promised me Zenda one time. I want her now."

"What am I hear?" Esteban moaned. "My ears stink!" And he unbuttoned his suit jacket, pulled back the left flap to reveal a shoulder holster and the heavy butt of a revolver. "I hear wrong, Teodoro, help me!"

"You gotta study your English more, Esteban. I just wondered how you and Zenda were doing, that's all."

"Ah, my friend, it is good, it is grateful to hear you say."

Don Coyote wandered away and, when Esteban's back was turned, he stole two bottles of Piper Heidsieck champagne and a four-ounce can of Caspian Sea caviar. Tribute. Gonna come back and lump up your haid, Don Esteban.

He stored the booty in his room, got a sock from a drawer, and began filling it with sand from a big cylindrical ashtray in the hall. Gonna lump up your haid too, Oliver. Gonna lump up the haids of a couple of cops when I'm warmed up.

"Moon, just what are you doing?"

Miss Patsy. She moved as stealthily as an Injun. Don Coyote touched the brim of his cowboy hat, said "Howdy, ma'am," and finished filling the sock with sand and crumpled cigarette butts. He tied a knot at the top, hefted its springy weight, and then cracked it against the wall several times. Go to sleep, Don Esteban.

"This here's a blackjack, Miss Patsy. I'm gonna bust some haids in three minutes."

"Are you crazy?"

"That a rhetorical question, Miss Patsy?"

"Moon . . . Jesus!"

"I'll call them out of the room one by one. Knock them cold, maybe daid."

"You're going to hit people with that . . . that jackblack?"

"Blackjack. You bet, Miss Patsy. Right behind the ear holes. Give them subdural hematomas."

"Like hell you will," she said angrily.

"Women don't understand about honor. This is a matter of honor, Miss Patsy."

"What is this 'Miss Patsy' nonsense? Why are you wearing that dumb costume, Moon?"

"Not Moon, ma'am. Don Coyote."

"You aren't cute, Moon, not at all. Now just put that old jackblack away before you get into trouble. You'd better come down to my room where I can keep an eye on you."

"First get my booty," Don Coyote said, and he returned to his room for the champagne and caviar. They started down the hall.

"Why are you walking bowlegged?"

Don Coyote did not reply. He was beaten. Cowed, tamed, broken. Damn the womoons. They're fencing in the West, cowboy. Building schools and churches. Used to be a man could ride for days without seeing a fence or a school or church or honest woman.

"Take off those stupid spurs," Miss Patsy said when they were in her room.

Sure, take off your spurs. Stop scratching your things in public. Put out that smelly cigar. Don't come around here with whiskey on your breath.

"Do you want to make love, Miss Patsy? I'll leave my boots, spurs, and big hat on, just slide my Levi's down a little. You'd like that, wouldn't you?"

She laughed. "Sure. Do you want me to dress up like a heifer?"

"I sure am horny, honey."

"You're also diseased."

"*You're* also diseased."

"No. The tests were negative."

"They were? Well, then, how about it?"

"No. Settle down, Moon. Order some ice and toast and onions for your booty. We'll spend a quiet evening. I brought some books from the shop. We'll read."

They demolished the whorehouse and erected a gallows. They bred savage killer wolfdogs down into tiny yapping fuzzballs. They read books.

Don Coyote crawled onto the bed. "Did you bring a copy of my autobiography?"

"No, sorry, I didn't pack any trash."

He lay quietly beside her, staring up at the ceiling, and he said, "Nietzsche advises us to go to our women with a whip in hand."

Patsy giggled. "As I recall, Nietzsche never had a woman. He never even came close to having a woman."

"He owned a whip, though, damn it. Just in case."

Don Coyote stared at the ceiling. Miss Patsy, pretending to read, was sniffing repeatedly, trying to inhale her laughter. She was moving her legs and rocking gently from side to side. Suppressing laughter can be strenuous. Timing was very important now. She was approaching hysteria but Don Coyote still had to push her over the precipice. He waited until he thought she was ready and then delayed even more by counting slowly to fifty.

"Miss Patsy? Do you know what your problem is?"

"Oh God. Oh, please don't. Moon, don't. Come on. I don't want you to do this. Stop, please."

"You have denied the masculine side of your nature. You have killed the man inside of you."

She made a prolonged high-pitched whining sound at the frequency that causes dogs to bark and spin in circles, and then she commenced siren wails of laughter. She writhed, clutched her belly, howled.

Don Coyote knew that eventually she would develop a muscular cramp and beg him to massage it away.

PART FIVE

You're jeopardizing the entire fucking product!

—*Doppelgänger*

36

It was a nasty evening for baseball, wet, cool, and windy, and the ballpark was only about half full. The grass had a slick lacquered gloss and glowed emerald-green in the lights. It rained during the third inning and again in the fifth. I sat at my usual spot—the philosopher's perch—at the far end of the dugout. There I held court.

"Buckley," I said, "give me some tobacco."

"Are you high tech?"

"Sure I'm high tech. State of the art, floppy disk, software, micromacro, enhanced information retrieval system. Give me some tobacco."

"Computer language implemented?"

"Indo-European."

He clucked sympathetically. "Computer illiterate. Not your fault. It's a revolution."

"Wait," I said. "Concepts, modes, systems, networking, quality time."

"Sorry, no tobacco. Can't use you. You're obsolete. It's a revolution, you see." He walked to the other end of the bench and sat down.

Braverman, sitting nearby, laughed.

I said, "Braverman, fetch me my chewing tobacco from the clubhouse."

"Huh?" he said. "What? Fetch your own damned tobacco."

"You don't understand, Braverman. In 1205 Pope Innocent III stated that Jews are condemned to perpetual servitude as Christ-killers. Go get my Beechnut, Braverman."

"Christ is alive. He was resurrected. Everyone knows that."

Blas, sitting a few yards away, piously crossed himself.

"And," I continued, "Saint Thomas stated that since the Jews were the slaves of the Church, she could dispose of their possessions. Give me *your* tobacco, Braverman."

"Oh, well. I didn't know. If I had known . . ." He dug in his back pocket and handed me a crumpled pouch of Apache Chief. It was a peppery chew that dissolved the mucous membranes and cauterized the sinuses. I kept the package.

Braverman got up and moved to the other end of the bench. Blas slid toward me.

"I want you to stop insulting my religion," he said.

"I don't understand."

"You understand."

"Blas, when your church urges you to confess, it doesn't mean confess to the police. Falsely."

"Don't change the subject."

"I have great respect for your creed. In fact, my favorite saint is Saint Francis Borja, the great-grandson of Pope Alexander VI—Rodrigo Borgia—and the great-

great-grandson of Pope Calixtus III, Alfonso Borgia. Pope Alexander VI, you surely remember from parochial school, was the father of Cesare and Lucrezia Borgia."

Furious, cursing me in Spanish and English, Blas got up and moved to the far end of the bench. It was getting crowded down there.

I said to Dickie Brackett, "Pope Alexander VI died of poison when a servant mistakenly brought him a bottle of wine meant for guests rather than for His Holiness."

Brackett refused to reply or look at me.

"It's time I came clean, Dickie. I can't stand black music. Never could."

"Getting awful tired of you," he said. "Getting sick of your Afro-American genocide." He got up and walked down toward the others, where the lynch mob was forming.

Len Sharkey sat halfway down the bench. I crooked my index finger—come here, Lenny. He shook his head. Apparently my ravings about Pope Alexander VI had inspired him to try a few practice riffs of broadcast journalism. He nodded curtly, as if to an invisible producer, lifted the microphone—his fist—and excitedly but not loudly, said:

"This is a special announcement! The only pope is been killed! Lord, what is this world coming to? The pope of the world is just been blown to raspberry jelly by a swarthy Islamo demento what emerged from a mob of joyful pilgrims and throwed a bomb at the popemobile. What's that? This just in from our corresponder at the scene. What? We can't hear you, Nelson. Nelson? I'm sorry, folks, we have lost our emission at this point in time . . . Nelson?"

The Dodgers were beating us four to two after the sixth. Between the sixth and seventh innings I jogged out to the bullpen and sat next to Frank Prosper.

"He th'ow de baseball so hard it look little like a white pea when it come on you," Jules Hebert was saying. "Dat ball it *growl* at you, hey. Van Lingle Mungo the man name."

I waited half an inning, letting the tension build, and then I said, "Frank, I'm grateful for all the help you've given me in my attempt to understand Christianity."

He suspiciously stared at me.

"But something is puzzling. You always say that God is all-powerful."

"Almighty, yes."

"God is the creator of all?"

"All, yes, of course."

"Really—I mean, *all?*"

"Yes. Stop trying to qualify the Absolute, Moon."

I had no choice but to fall back on the famous Manichaean heresy.

"Then God created suffering, evil."

"What? No, no, you don't understand. God gave his only—"

"Either God can prevent evil and he won't; or God wants to prevent evil and he can't."

"You belong to Satan," Prosper said coldly. "Please don't speak to me again. Not ever. I don't like you and I abominate your master."

I had wounded his zeal; punctured his complacency.

"Si non caste tamen caute," I said.

Prosper was silent for a long time and then he surrendered to his curiosity.

"What did you say?"

" 'If you can't be good, be careful.' Saint Paul."

We scored four runs in the top of the eighth inning and now led six to four.

"Moon, hey!" Hebert said. "You don't get paid or what? Get you hot, Moon."

I went out to one of the bullpen mounds and started lobbing the ball down to Murphy. If our pitcher got into trouble, if he even looked less than confident, they would send for the saveman, the Moonman. I threw the ball easily a dozen times, lazy-armed, just flicking it off my fingertips, and then started using my full motion. Still easy, loose, concentrating on a coordinated motion and getting my full weight behind the ball. I was going to have good stuff tonight. Even throwing at half speed the ball moved a little; it seemed to accelerate two-thirds of the way to the plate, then jump and tail off to the right. The baseball came alive. It was only a ball and then somehow it became a bird with a will and velocity of its own. It was a matter of perfect coordination. Strong arms are for weight lifters. Strong arms are for guys who throw beer cases around. I wanted a flexible arm, loose-jointed, a whip, an arm that looked blurred and boneless in photographs. The power was in my legs and torso, in my stride, and my arm was a whip that worked both with and in opposition to my body. I was a human catapult.

Then I began twisting off some looping curve balls, making them with body motion and an easy wrist snap. Big high school curves. When I began throwing hard the ball would come in like smoke and then break sharply.

The first Dodger hitter of the ninth inning hit a four-hundred-foot home run.

"Moon!" Hebert screamed. "Don't no one sign you paycheck? They want you in there, Moon!"

37

I rubbed my palm over my moustache and eyebrows, frizzing them, removed my cap and plucked at the hair at the sides and back, then stuck wads of Apache Chief tobacco in both cheeks. When pitching I want to look like the kind of man that police automatically question when there has been a particularly heinous crime. I had the fever. Hate, hate, I thought, blood, hate, terror.

I grabbed my jacket, left the bullpen, and stalked across the wet grass. I liked the long dramatic walk, the bright banks of lights, the insults of the crowd, taking my time. Nothing happened until the Moonman made it happen. No quarter. No mercy. Sink the lifeboats and shoot the swimmers.

"Hate," I said, slouching toward the mound and staring homicidally toward the Dodgers' dugout. Talking to myself. Let them see my lips move. Let them review my awful history of mental illness. Let them imagine me hanging around hotel laundry chutes. "Smoke, smoke," I chanted, "stick the smoker in their ears. Kill. Eat."

Half a dozen men were waiting for me around the mound: players; the homeplate umpire; Bob Grosbeck, the interim manager. The mound was muddy and torn up. I stalked past them and began kicking dirt around, backward, like a dog covering his stool. Mad dog.

Grosbeck handed me the ball and then they all began drifting away. Alone at the center now. The three tiers of stands rose all around me; it was like standing at the bottom of a gigantic teacup.

During my warm-up I threw some fastballs that popped like gunshots in Rizzo's mitt, and some curves that buzzed like rattlesnakes—I hadn't had stuff like this in five years. Look out.

Their first hitter was a kid up from Albuquerque, a skinny spade, the kind of legman who hits for .080 and runs for .200. I despised him as all pitchers rightly despise the breed. The jerk should be earning six hundred dollars per month as manager of a slum tenement. I hated the way his helmet floated atop his bristling Afro. I hated his pathetic stick arms and legs. I hated his choppy snake-killing swing.

Brieschke was opening and closing his big first-baseman's mitt, calling, "Make him hit it to the lobster, Moon. The lobster is hungry."

I threw my best smoke high and tight and the kid swung without much conviction.

Then a curve that broke down over the outside corner, but he got his bat on the ball and tapped it back to me. I stood on the mound and watched him run. He was really fast. I waited, waited, and then threw him out by half a step. I like to let those fast men run all-out down to first;

it shortened their careers a little, and occasionally one pulled a hamstring.

I spat tobacco juice, kicked some dirt around, then turned and sneered at the TV camera in the stands behind third base. I gave them time for a good close-up, and time for the play-by-play announcer to say something like, "I guess you all know about this man's tragic difficulties, and his great courage in facing them." "The heart of a lion," the color man would agree. "Moon is a competitor, all right." I could feel a warm drool of tobacco on my chin. What the hell. I wiped it away with the back of my glove, adjusted my genitals, and returned to business.

The next hitter was also a man who had spent most of the season at Albuquerque. He'd made life miserable for pitchers in the PCL. Left-handed batter. Huge. His arms could well serve as a small man's legs. He had knuckles like walnuts, cruel eyes, hair growing well down his forehead, a chin cleft that would conceal a roll of quarters. Now he squeezed a few drops of sap from the bat handle and stepped up to the plate. Too cocky. Did he think he was still in Albuquerque?

I threw a good fastball at his chin and he went down. His bat flew one way and his helmet another.

Rizzo fired the ball back to me in case I should soon require a weapon.

The big guy bounced up and started out toward me, but Rizzo and the umpire grabbed him.

"Oh, my God!" I shouted. "Oh, Lord, I almost killed that poor boy!"

I threw him a good curve and watched him rock back on his heels. One and one. Another curve? Some smoke now? How about a slider that busted in at the last instant and broke the bat off two inches above his fists? How about a change-up so deceptive that he'd overswing and fall to the dirt writhing with back spasms?

I threw him smoke right down the middle of the plate and cock-high. He resentfully watched it pass.

It was drizzling again now, thin silvery streaks against the lights, cool sweet rain.

I missed with a fastball and then got another strike with a curve ball with so much spin that it probably sizzled like bacon frying as it swooped down and clipped the outside corner of the plate. Out. Go sit down. My God, tonight I was one of the Immortals. Kissed by my fickle Muse. Potential and actual had temporarily merged.

Next sucker. I squeezed the rosin bag, spat thrice, returned to the mound, and glared down toward home, and then something happened to me. I lost an inner harmony. Body and mind slipped out of synchrony. I staggered a couple of steps, regained my balance. Rizzo had risen out of his crouch and was staring at me. Rizzo, the umpire, and the hitter were all staring at me in an odd, expectant way. What was wrong? I felt sick and sad and lost. It was a little like being psychotic. All the clocks had stopped; I lived the same instant over and over again. The night was absolutely silent now. A textured fog veiled the lights and was beginning to blur my peripheral vision. I was sleepy and weak; my legs were hardly strong enough to bear my weight. Time resumed but in a viscous way, the seconds intolerably elongated. Now Rizzo and the umpire were walking toward me. Some players were leaving the dugouts. I looked down and saw an expanding splash of blood on my uniform shirt.

I collapsed, sprawled out supine on the mound. I remembered, as in a dream within a dream, my old delusion of the pitching mound as a grave. Now, though, it was my grave. I had been shot. Some crazy asshole had shot me. Assassinated!

I could see the moon almost directly overhead, and all around, tilting with perspective, the thousand fog-haloed lights—electric moons. Moons all around, Moon on the ground, Moon going down.

I was encircled by men whose moon-bright faces were turned down toward me. One of them kneeled—Buckley.

"Save yourself," I said. "Save the platoon." I was afraid. I was not ready to leave this world.

"You had good stuff tonight," Buckley said.

"Buck, am I going to die?"

"No." He winked at me. "You're going to live." He winked again.

Softly, in the background, half-lost in the excited vocal static, I heard the urgent whispers of Len Sharkey practicing broadcast journalism. "We interrupt this program to bring you a special report. Teddy Moon is been struck down in his virile youth on this dismal rainy night in Chavez Ravine. It don't make sense! All we know at this moment is the ace relief pitcher is been cruelly slayed by the Mafia chums what he allegedly betrayed with the kiss of death."

Nearby Buckley was loudly saying, "The old cock would have wanted us to finish the game."

Nausea swept me away on a powerful tide.

"He would have wanted us to be happy. Our triumph tonight is the only fitting memorial."

". . . just throwed a pitch," Len Sharkey was saying, "and proceeded to fall down and literally eat grass, blood spurting everywhichway . . ."

Someone kneeled at my side, a clean-shaven Santa Claus, a doctor. He opened my jersey, lifted my sweatshirt, looked and probed. His high-voltage fingertips brought pain and more nausea— I feared that I might vomit.

Sharkey: "I repeat for you tuner-inners, Teddy Moon is been shot cold pork dead out there—wait. Our reporter is going out onto the field. Be careful out there, Nelson, it's a fucking war zone, a minefield or something."

"This hurt?" the doctor said.

"Yes!"

"This?"

"Yes!"

". . . a sad, sad day for the game of baseball. Nelson, any last words from the Moon? Nelson? Please bear with us, folks."

"How about this?" the doctor said.

I screamed.

". . . okay, yes, hold a mirror close to his mouth-hole, Nelson. Nelson? I guess we've lost Nelson for the nonce."

A blur of white—an ambulance—emerged out of the fog and stopped a few yards away. Men swarmed around me, speaking fractured sentences, and then I was lifted onto a stretcher, raised, moved, shifted into the ambulance.

"Never mind, Nelson, we'll wrap it up here at the studio. Ladies and gentlemen, they're taking Moon away now. Alive or dead? We'll never know. And now we return you to our program in progress."

Buckley climbed into the ambulance with me. It was crowded; me, Buckley, the two paramedics. The doctor remained behind. Was that good or bad?

The vehicle began moving. Once outside the stadium the siren was switched on and my nausea seemed to exactly correspond to the desperate howling.

Buckley removed the Patek Philippe from my left wrist; then slid his hand beneath my hip and withdrew my wallet. I'd twice had valuables stolen from clubhouses and so I carried my money and watch onto the field.

"Moon would have wanted me to have these things," he told the paramedics.

He fondly gazed down at me.

"Oliver? Am I going to die?"

"Yes," he said.

The staff of the hospital's trauma center seemed to believe that my wound was insultingly trivial. Not worthy of their skill and dedication. They all were on speed. "I can feel the bullet with my fingertips, for Christ's sake. A .22 caliber, maybe .25. Shit. What'd they do, throw it at him? Get this malingerer out of here, we got a two-car on the way."

I was X-rayed, perforated with needles, sedated, someone tapped into my depleted bloodstream, I was wheeled down last-mile corridors and raised and lowered in elevators, and pushed into dirty rooms that had concealed God knows what agony, what Nazi atrocities. A flunky wheeled me through the maze.

"Am I going to be all right?"

"Oh, fuck, man, this elevator *still* don't work."

A Harpy bathed my torso with kerosene; a Fury stuck her thumb in my left eye; a Latino who looked and talked like Esteban Cintron excavated the bullet with an old garden trowel. They didn't even honor me enough to put me to sleep. The surgeon held the small bloody bullet up to the overhead lamp—"Ah, here she be"—and then tossed it into a bedpan. "Shit, man, you gonna be okay, don't worry, man."

They didn't put me into the intensive care unit, nor even the postoperative ward, but instead wheeled me into an expensive private room.

Buckley was permitted a brief visit. "How are you doing?"

"I'm dying."

"I've been on the phone. A kid shot you."

"A kid?"

"Twelve or thirteen years old. He had some kind of cheap gun—it's a miracle you got hit."

"A miracle," I said bitterly. "Why did he shoot me?"

Buckley pretended to be disgusted with me. Or perhaps he really was disgusted. "You, a prophet of Negative Meaning, you ask why?"

"Yes, goddamn it, why?"

"Because he loves you."

38

My dreams were hideous, the hallucinations of a mad dog. It was a long, tawdry *Walpurgisnacht,* and toward morning I began to have difficulty breathing. Delirious, seized by panic, I writhed and whimpered.

"Easy, Jocko, easy."

There was a little man sitting on my chest. He was about the size of a ventriloquist's dummy and at least as heavy as a bowling ball.

Who are you?

"I'm just a stray Doppelgänger, don't worry."

In the dimness of the room I could see that he had a long upper lip and hairy ears the size of saucers.

I can't breathe.

"Hey, don't worry about the little things, Jocko, that's my job. The nagging details, the vexations, the headaches, the asphyxiations—they're my province."

There was a sound like the rustling of dead leaves and the little man produced a sheaf of papers. "Sign on the dotted line, Jocko."

It's too dark, I can't read it.

"Don't you trust me?"

Of course, but . . .

"Sign the papers," he crooned. "Don't you want your own personal plaque embedded in the Hollywood Walk of Fame? Listen, I'm going to make you a big star. Movies, TV, books, concerts, albums, *People* magazine, White House dinners with Hillary, someday a seat in the U.S. Senate, maybe someday—why not?—the presidency." His voice was both coaxing and contemptuous.

President?

"You don't want to be a nobody, a mediocrity, a flyover person. Listen, Jocko, I already signed the kid who shot you. I'm sending him out on the road with his own rock band. He'll be top forty in a month, popgod in a year. The two of you can star together in the movie. He's going to be big, Jocko, and so are you."

I don't know.

And then, slyly wheedling, he said, "Look, whatever you want, it's yours. Another autobiography, a bestseller this time. You want to write diet books, exercise books, a volume of deep spiritual reflections? What else? Videos, that's easy. That mental health telethon you always wanted to host? Say no more about it. A cystic-fibrosithon on pay cable? Tell me, Jocko, that's why I'm here. A celebrithon, a supersalute to the superstars, any kind of spectravaganzacade you like. It's all yours, just sign here and here and here and here and here and here."

I don't know. Marcus Aurelius said, Neither a tragic actor nor a whore.

"Don't tell me nothing about Marcus Aurelius. His

kids go to school with my kids. Marc signed with me, he's in my stable. I'm grooming him for a sitcom."

I closed my eyes and lay passively. Maybe if he believed that I was dead he would go away.

The Doppelgänger leaned forward, gripped my ribs with his knees, and dug his heels like spurs into my flanks. His breath was a septic stink, an exhalation from some old fecal soup.

"I don't know why I bother with you!" he shrieked, and he stuck a finger into my wound.

I stifled my groans, my pleas.

"Outside agitator!" he yelled. "Lunatic. Heathen freak. You're jeopardizing the entire fucking product!"

What product?

"Words again, always the fucking twisty-turny words with you. The slippery slinky words, the dirty hate-America ten-dollar words as good as a whore's kiss. Do you know what words mean, Moon? Words don't mean nothin'."

I dared not speak.

"Words!" he howled. "Yit's yall yapples yan yo-ranges!"

I have no more words, honest.

"Shutup! My God! More words about words. Stop the words!"

And then his voice became rich and deep, mellow, with a theatrical lilt, and he said, "In the beginning was the Word, guy."

Logos, yes.

"Did you hear that, guy? Were you listening? I said, in the beginning was the Word."

Logos means 'word' in Greek.

His smile opened like a stiletto. "If the word 'Word' was good enough for the Lord Jesus-God it's plenty good enough for me. And it should be good enough for you too, guy. What is this *logos* crap? I can tell you something—Jesus-God wasn't a Greek. He wasn't a Hebrew neither. He was the first American. Think about that."

I'm sick. I'm very tired.

"Listen," he said, and he leaned close and I could smell woodsmoke and scorched flesh on his breath. "Listen, you're not crazy, you've never been crazy, you've just expelled the healing, compassionate Jesus from your heart. Ah, my poor friend, you've lived off the spiritual equivalent of barley gruel and greeny taters when you could have feasted on prime rib and brown gravy. You've provided your starving soul with junk food.

"Heal, listen to me, heal yourself, cry out for help and be healed, give yourself to Jesus and live, let Jesus's purity flow into you, be healed and hallelujah—thank God, thank you oh Lord! Be whole again, be a clean American boy again, get off welfare, stop chasing women, vote Republican. Relax, lean back and let Jesus fill your heart and your garage. Hallelujah!

"Oh thank you, Lord, thank you for being with us, oh we are healed, oh yes this poor sinner has returned to your flock, this degenerate rogue has accepted your hand, oh Lord, oh my, this is a very emotional moment, a soul has been redeemed, a life has been salvaged, oh my, yes, oh my yes, I can feel your healing energy flowing through me, Jesus, I can divine your will, I can—oh!—oh, this soul is saved! Put it on the scoreboard. Jesus one, the Devil zero. Do you feel it? This poor depraved wretch is healed, he is blessed. Yes, he is blessed and he will prosper. Oh, my! I'm out of breath. I have palpitations. I have nervous eczema. Thank you, Lord. Oh, I am worn out. Whoee! Look at the sweat on my brow.

"Look at the smile on this man's face, look at the

Moon beam. These people love you, Moon. Don't be timid. They love you and Jesus-God loves you. Jesus is the biggest celebrity in the world and you share his celebrity because Jesus lives in your heart. Get on up here, Moon. Come on, guy, get up here and testify to these good folk."

I was blinded by the lights, deafened by applause.

"Thank you," I said. "Thank you . . . Please sit down. What a great audience! Aren't they great? Beautiful people. Thank you, your reception makes me feel very humble, it really does. Wow! Aren't they something? Hey, I didn't know you had so much fun down here in Oklahoma. That's right. I didn't know you were so filled with Jesus-joy. I hope you don't mind if I think of myself as an honorary Okie. I know Jesus was an Okie, and Joseph and Mary, and the three Wise Men. Listen—what if Mary had had a court-approved abortion? Think about that. Write to your congressman.

"Thank you. Sit down, please. Don't throw things. My oh my, what a terrific audience. Love ya. Listen, I am saved. Saved. Yes indeed. Keep those cards and letters coming. I am happy now, oh I am truly joyous, but once I suffered—I suffered like sweet Jesus on the cross nailed.

"And now I'd like to sing and dance a number from my new Broadway show. It's all about the Iron Man, Lou Gehrig—who was a lot like Jesus, you know—and about his courage and humor when amyotrophic lateral sclerosis had him nailed to the cross. Thank you.

"Maestro, if you please, give me a middle G. Hey, feets, do yo stuff. Ha-cha-bop-bop-de-do-bop. Say it ain't so, Babe / Say it ain't so / Say I ain't gonna strike out / Against them bad ALS blues.

"Thank you, thank you. Love y'all, do indeed. Wowie!

Powie! And let's hear it for the band too. What a terrific crowd! Bye-bye, don't be shy, I'll be coming along to autograph your New Testaments after the show.

"God bless. Ciao."

PART SIX

~~~

Baseballman, *c'est moi.*

—*Baseballman*

39

In the morning I was awakened by a fat nurse.

"I almost died last night," I said.

"Foo!"

"I should have been in the intensive care unit."

She was carrying the Los Angeles area newspapers. "You're all over the front pages, honey."

"Of course."

"Good Morning, America phoned. They want to do a bedside interview with you tomorrow morning."

"I must consult Aristotle Kalamirus."

"A sick boy wants to see you. He wants you to hit a home run for him."

"I'm a pitcher," I said. "I'll surrender a home run for the kid. Listen, when are they gonna let me out of this charnel house?"

"The doctors will let you know. Maybe tomorrow."

"No, God no. Who will take the assassination seriously if I don't stay at least four or five days?"

"Well, you seem perky."

"There was a little man in the room last night—a crazed Doppelgänger."

"That might have been the pancreas in three-twelve."

I found an interesting paragraph in the entertainment section of the *Los Angeles Times*.

A spokesman for Joseph Horvath Productions announced today that work will soon commence on a major motion picture tentatively titled *Sturm and Drang*. The socially relevant crime thriller was penned by the award-winning writer and producer, Joseph Horvath.

Joe, the bastard, was stealing my script.

Physicians arrived to extend my pain threshold. The room filled with flowers and candy.

I slept for ninety minutes after breakfast and when I awakened the hospital began putting through my telephone calls. Everyone phoned, reporters, ex-wives and ex-girlfriends, ex-children, baseball people, Hollywood people, psychopathic strangers, werewolves, Doppelgängers, politicians. Ronald Reagan called and made some jokes about when he had been shot. He told me that I was a very great American.

I was popular. Strangers loved me. It was deeply moving. The attempted "assassination," no matter how absurd and botched, had conferred a special status on me—I had been recognized by my society. Validated. Authenticated. Exhumed. I was really somebody.

Blas called. "That bullet had my name on it," he said enviously.

Patsy was sweet and weepy; Carole solicitous; and Lily incoherent. Pamela was kind and friendly. She idly wondered if she and the kids were featured in my will. She put the children on the line; they giggled and shrieked, unable to find words suited to this emotional occasion.

Joe Horvath sent me a huge bouquet of flowers and a tape of the *Safe at Home* docudrama.

Aristotle Kalamirus called and suggested that tomorrow we take lunch in the hospital cafeteria. "Your price has gone way up, Jocko."

The thirteen-year-old boy who had shot me telephoned from the juvenile detention center. "I'm sorry, man. I'm really sorry."

"I know,"

"I never meant to hit you."

"I understand."

"You *moved,* man. How's I gonna know you'd *move?*"

"You couldn't know."

"It was *your* fault, man."

Esteban called. "You are one brave man," he said. "I like the way you die."

"I'm not going to die."

"I thought you was one coward, you know, I tell my son that—Teodoro Moon is one dirty stink coward, but it's okay. I like the way you die."

Dewey Yankhe phoned. He laughed hilariously and said, "I figured the oppressed masses would nail you sooner or later, Moon. You racist bourgeois exploiters can walk on the faces of the proletariat for only so long, and then they'll rise up in righteous, powerful phalanx and strike back. I like you, Moon, but I deplore your reactionary politics, and I approve of your symbolic extermination. Boyo, you learned that there's an iron fist inside the cotton work glove, and how does it feel?"

"Go to hell, Dewey."

"Moon, listen, I bought a used mimeograph machine, but I can't afford ink and paper and vodka. I want to publish a Stalinist newsletter."

"I'll send you a check."

"Get one thing straight, pal—I can't be bought."

Doc Whillans called. "How are you doing, Theodore?"

"Not good, Doc, not good. They're keeping a table ready for me down in the basement pathology lab."

I could hear his quiet emphesematous laughter.

I said, "I'm just a little soul bearing about a corpse."

"Epictetus," he said.

"The bullet nipped through a lung and penetrated half an inch into my heart."

"I talked to the surgical resident before phoning you. He told me that removing the bullet was about as serious as lancing a boil."

"Oh."

"But I enjoy your theater, you know that."

"All right, I exaggerated, but at the same time it was a horrible experience. I really thought I was going to die— that's almost the same as actually dying. Why do these things happen to me, Doc? Why can't I get a break? Am I beyond pity?"

"Pity is a vice," he said.

"Zeno."

"Bingo!" he said, and he wheezed with laughter.

"I'll be on the 'Good Morning, America' show tomorrow, Doc. Don't miss it."

"I won't, I won't," he said, laughing.

Oliver Buckley called. "Is it a window?" he asked.

"Yes and no."

"Tell me," he whispered urgently.

"Yes, it's a window."

"Is it a window in time?"

"No way."

"Is it a window of vulnerability?"

"Nope."

"Is it a window of opportunity?"

"No, no, no."

"Tell me. Please."

"It's a window of glass."

"You lie!"

I napped in the early afternoon and awakened to see a matronly woman leaning over me. Was she trying to sneak a smell of my breath? Kiss my fevered brow? She was plump, smiling, superior in the way mothers are superior to rascally children.

"Hi," she said.

"Hi," I replied. "How are you?"

"Oh, fine. How are *you?*"

"Better."

"That's good. I'm so pleased. Really." She straightened and gazed lovingly down at me. Was she going to give me ice cream and cookies? She was motherly. You looked at her and thought, Now there's a really nice mom, I wish I'd had a mom like her.

"Do I know you?" I asked.

"Mmmmm," she murmured.

"Do you work here in the hospital?"

"Oh, yes."

"What do you do?"

"I'm the Affect Control Officer."

"You are?"

"Yes."

"What is that? I mean, what do you do?"

Her eyes sparkled with humor. She was amused in a

condescending and comforting motherly way. "Can't you tell by my title?"

"You control affect?"

She laughed with matriarchal delight. "They told me you were a sly fox. Did you sleep well last night, old sly fox?"

"No. I had the sweats, ghastly dreams, visitors from the netherworld."

"Ah. I thought so."

"You thought what?"

"Post-traumatic stress syndrome, of course. It's the natural consequence of the event which violated the integrity of your body and dissolved your illusion of male potency, male autonomy. Being shot by a stranger, being penetrated by an alien object, is not unlike being brutally raped. There is the same sense of violation, a similar shame and outrage. But, listen to me, Mr. Moon—it was not your fault. Your sense of shame is irrational."

"Wait," I said. "Stop. Are you a psychologist?"

"Why yes, of course."

"Get out."

"I beg your pardon?"

"Get out of here. Right now. Go!"

She remained a mother but now she was the stern, punishing Mom, the one who, when no one was looking, pinched your ribskin hard and hissed, "Wait until I get you alone, buster." Her eyebrows merged; the tip of her pointy nose turned white. But her voice remained carelessly musical.

"Oh, my, paranoid ideation. Isn't that interesting? We'll have to think about that, won't we? You fit the profile, Mr. Moon. The police will be most interested in how exactly you fit the profile."

Not much later a skinny Chicano with a weedy moustache entered the room, closed the door, and began removing a complex apparatus from its sanitary wrapping. The thing looked like a mass of blood-suffused organs. They pulsed under the fluorescent lighting. There was a squarish rubber pouch, a fat maroon bulb, coils of arterial tubing.

"Hey, bro," the man said. "Shit, man, I'm sorry. I got to do this thing."

"What thing?"

"Roll over, *cuate,* I got to stick this tube up your *ano.*"

"What the hell's going on?"

"Time for your preop enema, man.."

"Get out of here before I stick that thing up *your* rosy *ano.*"

At four a new nurse came into the room and began arranging flowers in an earthenware pot.

"Hi, sleepyhead," she murmured. She was young and small, with frizzy red hair, green eyes, and a pixie face.

"Hi," I said.

"Bad old sleepyhead."

"Bad," I said.

"Do you have to micturate?"

"Will I get warts?"

She giggled. "Bad boy."

"Bad."

"Bad, bad boy. Punish. Shall I punish?"

"Please."

She closed the door, pulled down the bedsheet, and took my root in her hand. "Don't get fresh," she warned my root. "Oh, bad. Nasty thing. It doesn't want to micturate. I'll coax the poor thing. How is that? Does that feel better?"

"You bet."

She was a nurse and yet she had not noticed anything

pathological about my root. Perhaps I was cured of the clap. Perhaps I'd never had it.

"What an audacious frog," she said.

"I call him Caesar Augustus."

She addressed Caesar Augustus. "Oh, you ungrateful thing. You don't care. Bad red stick."

This kind of thing happened to celebrities all the time. It was something that must be endured. The anonymous public hopes to share our magic, to participate in our public joys and private griefs. They wish to manifest their love. We are loved and it is only that which gives us the strength to remain worthy. Such idolatry is neither a cross nor an albatross; it is, though, an enormous responsibility, and one that we repudiate at the risk of becoming just another mutt in the ravening *canaille*.

God bless. Ciao.

40

Sometime after dinner an elderly Undead shuffled into the room. He was about ninety-five years old and toothless; his mouth looked like a purse's opening with the strings drawn tight. He wore furry bear's-foot slippers and a wrinkled knee-length nightshirt assembled from crepe paper. His ears were big, purplish from poor circulation, and elfin; shocks of gray hairs sprouted from the dark center holes.

He was already stooped; he did not have to lean over far. So he just bent a little at the waist and drove his right fist into my belly. And then, before I could catch my breath and retaliate, he cackled and scuttled out of the room. I could hear his duck-quack chortling recede down the hallway.

The old bastard. He would not get the better of me in our next encounter.

At eight I turned on the ballgame. Nicky Puma was huskily sing-talking the national anthem. The two teams were solemnly lined up like delinquent urchins, their caps patriotically covering their hearts. A rippling flag was superimposed over the ceremonial sanctimony. I heard the remote thunder of artillery (or maybe kettle drums) when Nicky sang, ". . . the bombs bursting in air . . ." Nicky Puma again. This was no coincidence. I sensed the cool, cynical intervention of the Illuminati.

I punched the remote button. Talk show: a woman was telling the panel and audience that the habit of calling children's toys "toys" was terribly insensitive and emotionally devastating. "Toys." She spoke the word with loathing. Children who played with "toys" inevitably suffered serious psychological and social consequences. They abused their dolls and lead soldiers and little trucks, graduated to abusing their "pets"—another nasty word—and ultimately mistreated minorities and the environment and the mentally and physically challenged. "Inanimate playmates," was the correct term.

I switched to another channel. There was a commercial and then a trio of handsome young Undead appeared on the screen. They—a white male, a black male, and an Asian woman—sat behind a crescent-shaped desk, bleeding sincerity. The camera focused on the Undead in the center, Dan Quayle or one of his many simulacra.

He said, "There has been a startling new development in the Pantyhose Murders. Richard Kopfhammer, twenty-eight, an outfielder with—"

What? What! I quickly switched back to the ballgame. ". . . land of the free, and the home of—"

Back to the news.

". . . police, acting on a tip from an anonymous source, searched Mr. Kopfhammer's hotel room and discovered a secret cache of female undergarments and Polaroid snapshots of the transsexual victims, including that of Prudencia Jimenez, whose body was found this morning in the laundry room of the hotel—"

No! Quick, back to the game. Kopfhammer. The obvious candidate. I'd been hoping that when they nabbed the killer he would turn out to be Red Girt, or the Prosper-MacDonald pair.

The Dodgers were trotting out onto the field now.

The play-by-play announcer said, "Ah, there's nothing like fun at the old ballpark."

"You got that right," the color man, a former catcher, said. "This is fun, all right. I couldn't have said it any better myself, Charlie."

I pressed a button. Joseph Horvath was being interviewed by a blond fluff from "Entertainment Nightly." "With *Sturm and Drang,*" Joe was saying, "I returned to my first and best love, which is film writing—visual literature. I'll produce the movie too, to make sure the script's artistic integrity isn't violated. I can say this: the characters are significantly universal—everyone will relate to them. And the plot is derived from ancient lost Babylonian myths, so it's mythical in a preindustrial-society way. Associates have told me that this script—and the movie-to-be—combine *film noir,* expressionism, and existentialism in a totally new configuration. American existentialism, I mean, not the gloomy, intellectual European kind—"

I pushed a button. The anchor trio was now engaged in educational chitchat.

"What does this mean to American transsexuals?" the pretty Asian weatherwoman asked.

The Dan Quayle simulacrum pondered a moment, his frosty blue eyes seeking the horizon, and he said, "It may mean that the nightmare of transsexuality has ended."

The black man, probably the sports reporter, said, "But of course this Kopfellow hasn't been tried and convicted yet."

"That's true," the crypto-Quayle agreed. "Let's not forget that we are Americans in America. However, a police spokesman reported that Mr. Kopfhammer *has* confessed to killing the young transsexuals because, I quote, 'I didn't like the way they abused their bodies. You don't'—I'm still quoting—'you don't know what you're intercoursing with anymore. A body is a holy temple and you should keep the same body what God give you in the first place. It's a sin to change bodies.' "

"It's very uniquely tragic," the weatherwoman said. "It's just—I feel so painful for the mothers of those transsexuals. It makes you wonder about Mr. Kopfhammer's value system."

The sports reporter puffed up and shuffled some papers. "It's worth pointing out, Vance, Nan, that three of the six victims were minority people. One was Afro-American, one was Polish American, and another—L.A.'s own Prudencia Jimenez—was Mexican American. And of course all five, I guess, were women."

"That's really the sad part," quasi-Quayle said. "These are not merely crimes against humanity, they are crimes against minority people."

"Transsexuality is not prevalent among the Asian American community," Madame Butterfly said, "otherwise there might be grieving in the Asian-American community tonight."

Pseudo-Quayle's eyes wandered until he found the functioning camera. "We'll be taking you to the street soon, where our ace reporter, Guadalupe Escobar, is standing by."

I switched channels. Some men in knickers and tweed sport coats were tossing rings toward a stake. The Baltic States championship quoits match.

There were movies on adjacent channels: in one film a beautiful naked woman was savagely stabbing a man with a big kitchen knife; in the other a man was murdering a beautiful naked woman with a posthole digger.

Back to the ballgame.

"Well," the color man was saying, "even the mighty Casey struck out."

"A great poem," his partner said. "A part of our treasured Americana."

"Still, these guys make an awful lot of money these days."

"Chumley keeps licking his fingers. He might be developing a blister."

"Well, in my day, we just smeared blisters with cat—what do you call them?—cat faces. It worked. Now all the players got all these psycho—what?—psychostitions."

"Well, maybe yes, maybe no. I'm not criticizing. But I never seen Ted Williams lick a blister."

No, I couldn't stand it. Where did everyone obtain his moron tablets?

I pressed a button and a pretty, dark-haired woman appeared on the screen. She was barking excitedly into a microphone. Her earrings were tiny gold crosses, and she wore a gold Islamic crescent on a chain around her neck. Her voice was raspy, the kind of voice that has exhausted itself in domestic screaming contests.

"Vance, Nan, Roy, they're coming toward us now, the police and the alleged killer, the alleged killer's lawyer, and the alleged killer's mother, all surrounded by an unruly mob of media and curious bystanders and protest groups. We have protesting delegations from gay rights organizations, a transsexual support group, antiabortion activists, and other outraged citizens. And let me tell you, Vance, they are all angry at the alleged killer. Police here are quite concerned. Wait—here he comes now."

Through a gap in the mob I saw the handcuffed, bewildered Kopfhammer, escorted by two policemen—Sturm and Drang. The reporters shouted questions. Protesters screamed invective. Kopfhammer appeared blinded by the TV lights. Kopfhammer's mother was a big woman. His lawyer had snow-white hair and a vermilion potato nose.

"No statement now," he said. "No, later, please . . ."

Also nearby, almost lost in the crush of humanity, a dwarf scuttled—Aristotle Kalamirus?

Suddenly Kopfhammer stopped to address the media. His face, a hard mask of confusion and terror, vanished behind the bristling microphones. He said, "I know what I done impacted negatively."

The police were trying to hustle him along but he was a big man, a giant, and he successfully resisted. "My crimes were a cry for help. No one listened!"

More cops swarmed around to help. The Hammer was swept off his feet. You could see clubs rising and falling indiscriminately, hacking down Kopfhammers and reporters and animal rights activists. Kopfhammer vanished in the scrum but you could still hear his impassioned cry: "I never learned how to love!"

Cops were trying to pick him up, Lilliputians struggling with the fallen Gulliver.

This was grotesque. I turned off the TV and then, a minute later, switched it back on.

The scene was even more confused now, arms, legs, heads, and torsos scrambled together into a single writhing monster. Cops were dragging Kopfhammer up a flight of concrete steps. The camera jumped around, showing flashes of sky and gutter, then it steadied. I saw a slender woman enter the melee like a running back hitting off-tackle. She thrust her hand toward Kopfhammer and there were three popping sounds, not loud, and the crowd scattered shrieking.

The screen turned gray but I could still hear the screams and wails and the irregular crackle of small-arms fire.

I turned off the black hole and pressed the bedside buzzer. A few minutes later the redheaded nurse arrived bearing a bedpan.

"Do you have to micturate again?" she asked coyly.

"I'm checking out of this brothel," I said.

"Oh, no, you can't do that."

"Why not?"

"There are procedures, processes, papers. You can't just leave, you must be discharged. This isn't a motel, Mr. Moon."

"An old man came in here and thumped me in the gut," I said.

"Oh, my. Oh. Was it the pancreas in three-twelve?"

"I'm going to sue unless someone brings me my clothes fast. Cap, shirt, sweatshirt, trousers, shorts, jockstrap and cup, sanitary hose, stockings, glove, spikes. Do you hear me? A lawsuit."

She vanished and was replaced by a young physician, the resident, maybe, or an intern.

"Well," he said cheerfully, "let's see how you're doing."

"Malpractice, that's how. Reckless endangerment. I was assaulted by a senile psycho. Callous disregard. What's going on here, Doc? Am I a prisoner? Imperious neglect. Do I get my uniform or not?"

The doctor lifted my nightshirt and gazed at the wound. "What happened to the scab? It was scabbing nicely. Did you pick at the scab?"

"No," I lied. I had picked at the scab because I wanted an ugly scar, a glossy, twisted pit as big as a half dollar.

"Okay," he said, and he went away.

I punched the remote control's on button: riots were breaking out all over the metropolitan area. Random shootings had been reported on every freeway exiting the city. I closed my eyes and imagined a satellite view of nighttime America: a dusty sparkle of gun flashes centered in Los Angeles County but rapidly spreading north and south and east, tracing the Interstate highway system into the dark hinterlands. San Diego ignited, Santa Barbara, Portland, Seattle. The dense spray of flashing specks followed the highway system eastward, Phoenix, Salt Lake City, Denver; branched out over the concrete arterial byways to the South and Midwest—New Orleans, Miami, Chicago and St. Louis and Detroit. It was a conflagration. Now the bright little speckles reached the East Coast. There goes Boston, New York, Baltimore, Washington, DC. Hawaii and Alaska were still dark but the continental U.S. was glowing like the Milky Way. And the flickering pepper of lights was spreading into remote rural areas. Slaughter in the desert, the mountains, the swamps, the vast wheatfields. Everyone had pulled out his .357 magnum and was smoking his neighbor.

The nurse entered carrying a plastic basket containing my uniform and effects. I turned off the black hole; I turned off the grim satellite view in my brain.

The nurse sat on the edge of my bed while I dressed.

"Will you phone me?" she asked.

"Of course I will."

"No. I don't think so."

"I promise, I'll call you soon."

"I've heard that before."

"I'll phone. Write down your number. Please, I want to see you again."

"Use and abuse," she said. "Isn't that what women are for?"

"I love you," I said. "Write down your phone number."

"You don't love me. You're incapable of loving anyone but yourself."

My sweatshirt was crusted with blood. My cap had lost its crisp shape. My spikes dimpled the cheap carpet. The jockstrap and cup affirmed my masculinity. Perhaps busty women felt a similar relief when they cinched their bras. Except no one ever heard of men gathering in the streets to burn their jockstraps. It simply was not done.

"I do love you," I said. "Why can't you believe me when I say I love you."

I was transformed now, transmogrified. The mirror confirmed that I was indeed I, the Moonman, smoke and light, fight and flight, mental patient by day and protector of widows and orphans by night. *Baseballman!* A comic-book hero for our times. Stand aside, wretched widow, I'll teach them necrophiles a lesson.

"I love you too," the nurse said. "I wish I didn't."

There was a large rusty stain spread over the front of my jersey, dried blood, quarts of it, and a ridiculously tiny hole. I worked a finger into the hole and enlarged it. A .45 caliber hole now, evidence of a wound that people could respect. So. Evilman shoots Baseballman in the left auricle and the big slug hardly slows BB-man down. Hey! Get them grungy orphans outta my way—I'm mad, now.

I and my mirror image parted: it was as painful as the severing of Siamese twins.

"Honey," I said. "Honey? Could you loan me fifty bucks for cabfare?"

41

I considerately walked tippytoe down the halls, sparing the tiles spike pocks, and summoned an elevator. Come on, come on, I'm an important man. Eventually the elevator arrived, the door slid open, and I stepped aboard, joining a male nurse and a wheezing geezer in a wheelchair. Look out! He was not the pancreas in three-twelve but even so . . . Maybe I should neutralize the old bugger with a quick shot to the solar plexus. They scornfully surveyed me from spikes to cap—yokels, ain't you ever seen a comic-strip hero before?

The male nurse and the cranky methuselah got out at the second floor and the elevator carried me down past the street-level lobby into the sinister bowels of the hospital. Labyrinthine hallways, locked doors, a chemical odor, the lingering echoes of today's screams. This is where they cut up the bodies. This is where they grafted the calf's head onto the neck of the homeless person. This is where the snatched joggers were dissected and their vital organs removed for the bootleg transplant racket. Yeah, this was the nexus. This was where all of the parameters converged.

I found a cart filled with bags of laundry and extracted a dirty red polyester blanket. I knotted two corners of the blanket around my neck and so fashioned a respectable cape. All right. Let's go see Mr. Big.

A flight of stairs led me up to another hallway, windowless and doorless, where spatters of fresh blood spoor led me down the polished floor toward double swing doors and a neon: Trauma Center. Surely I would be welcome there.

I pushed through the doors and entered Chaos. The place was familiar. Here is where they had mistreated me last night. It was a big room divided into sections by movable screens. Groans, moans, whimpers, bloody men and women lying supine on wheeled carts; other scurrying men and women in hospital greens and whites, speaking tersely to each other, issuing commands and apologies—"Sorry, I thought you said sever." I rounded a screen and encountered Kopfhammer.

He was lying naked and supine on a padded table too small for his length and bulk. His eyes were closed. A nurse at his side was pumping up a blood-pressure belt. There was a chrome tree nearby with upside-down bottles hanging from the branches and clear plastic IV tubes running into Hammer's arms. He was getting a lube and oil change. His hairy chest was bloody and more blood was seeping through gauzy compresses that encircled his midsection and left thigh.

"Hammer," I said. "Can you hear me?"

His eyes fluttered.

The nurse glanced up at me, giggled, and returned her attention to the blood-pressure gauge.

"Hammer?"

He opened his eyes, focused them, and whispered, "Moon? Is that you, Moon?"

A doctor hurried around the screen and suddenly halted. "Just who the hell are you? What are you doing here?"

"Baseballman, *c'est moi.*"

Kopfhammer coughed weakly and said, "Moon? I still have much to give to the world."

"Get out of here fast, Baseballman," the doctor said.

Kopfhammer was getting an erection. Perhaps a short circuit, a lewd and inappropriate misfire, in his hypothalamus. Was an erection at this time a sign of imminent death or irrepressible life?

"Keep a stiff upper lip," I said, and I wandered off among the other casualties, all the prostrate and ambulant victims of urban pique. Here and there I dispensed a silent blessing.

A young woman was handcuffed to a bench in the waiting room. A cop dozed next to her. The girl looked familiar. She was dressed in sneakers and tight black toreador pants with tin conchas along the outer seams, and a buckskin jacket decorated with colored beads and tiny seashells and painted porcupine quills. She had a hard young face, pretty but tough, and the beauty salon had dried and crisped her hair to a material like the shavings you find packed in crates. There was a deep gash on her cheek and a bruised swelling on her forehead.

She lifted her eyes to meet my gaze. I could see the boy in the girl. She was the transsexual who had dashed through the crowd to shoot Kopfhammer. Now she clenched her free hand into a fist and defiantly raised it.

"I am Baseballman," I said. "I arrive and depart mysteriously. I go where I am needed."

"Get the fuck away from me, you freak," she said.

I scooted before the cop could fully awaken. Baseballman often found it necessary to work outside the rigid confines of the law.

So I pushed through a pair of big flapping doors and found myself alone in the dangerous night. My spikes clicked on the concrete. An ambulance, lights flashing, siren dying, was pulling into the dock with another poor bloody wretch. I inhaled the chemicals and exhausts and the cordite smell of violence that floated on the Pacific breeze.

A taxi stopped for me in front of the hospital. The driver, a Jamaican in dreadlocks, did not know English well and he insisted on taking me to Disneyland. Apparently that was where I belonged. We argued. Finally, with the promise of a big tip, he consented to driving on toward the bright glow above Dodger Stadium. I gave him the money he had extorted.

"Sank you, mon."

"Sank you."

The players' entrance was closed. I circled the ballpark but I couldn't find anyone who believed I was anything but a deranged dork in a torn, bloodstained baseball costume; and so at last I surrendered and bought a ticket. Shame.

The peddlers of flat beer and trichina-infested hot dogs sneered at me as I descended the aisle toward the outfield grass. My seat was out in the left field bleachers, and the players looked microscopic at this distance, teeny-weenies. Jonah Hardy, though, in left field, appeared almost life-size, and I could hear him trilling and chirping to himself. I had not known that he practiced birdcalls in his lonely outfield exile.

Just my luck: the seat was on the fringe of a group of little Little Leaguers, nine- and ten-year-old shorties, all dressed in their team uniforms and clutching balls and bats and gloves. None wore a red blanket around his neck. Fans in the seats behind me whistled and shouted insults. The kids gaped. I began to feel uncomfortable. My harmless mania fizzled. It is not easy being manic in a cookie-cutter paranoid society.

Third out. I glanced around for hostile ushers or security thugs, saw the coast was clear, went down a few steps and vaulted gracefully over the barrier. My cape filled like a parachute and wafted me gently to the ground. Fans at this end of the ballpark, even the kids, jeered. Someone threw a cup of beer on me. Fools. Slaves. Those dim peanut-eaters had made me a millionaire.

Jonah, chirping sparrowlike, jogged in toward the dugout. I followed. Lighten your stone-heavy hearts— here comes Baseballman.

The grass was wet. Each blade was sharply etched in the hard light. I saw clover, insidious crabgrass, filigrees of spittle, tobacco chaws that looked like dog turds. The great bowl of stands rose around me; and the light towers leaned inward, prepared to topple when the Richter scale reached 7.5.

Eddie Praeger was jogging out to left.

"Gonna smoke you, Eddie," I said.

He laughed. "Asshole! Where'd you get the cheap cape?"

When I reached the infield the big crowd, fifty thousand people, more, simultaneously rose and began clapping and whistling and cheering. A tribute to the plucky

Theodore Moon, heart-shot one night and valorously returning to the arena a mere twenty-four hours later. I stopped on the second-base bag, swept off my cap, and bowed to the cardinal points of the compass. The umpires screamed at me, and so I sprinted across the infield and slithered into the dugout.

"What a wacko," Bob Brieschke said. "Moon, you devil, you crazed goose, we hate you. Next time we'll chip in enough cabbage to hire a pro."

"You're steaming dung, Brieschke."

"Well? So? I'm comfortable with the dung concept."

I walked past all the smirks and sneers to the end of the dugout and said to Dickie Brackett, "Move over, rookie. You got my place."

There was a pouch of decayed Apache Chief in my back pocket; I clutched a mass the color, texture, and smell of old compost, inserted it in my right cheek, and bit off those tentacles that tried to flee. When the chaw was moistened and compacted, I said:

"Dickie, my heart stopped five times last night. Cardiac arrest. Finally they hooked the old pump up to a twelve-volt car battery."

"We was all hoping for arrest number six," he said sullenly.

"Listen. This nurse. Jesus. A cute, sexy little redhead, a nymphomaniacal pixie, came into my room and, pal, guess what?"

"They never was a nurse better looking than a toad," he said.

With a deft maneuver of my tongue I shifted the chaw over to my left cheek. A shred of chaw, or maybe a tobacco weevil, had crawled up into my nose's rear tunnel. A sneeze was conceived.

I looked out at the gently convex field. The grass was

jade-green and shiny with dew. And the light was hard, flat, cold—perhaps like the light shed by an atomic blast. Like the light, certainly, that I had seen on the desert a few nights ago.

"Nurses," Dickie said. "Don't tell me nothing about nurses. I married two of them."

At first the sneeze was not a certainty: it remained just a small, placid weevil lodged in my nose's back door; but then the worm wriggled and began to explore, and the sneeze ceased being provisional. My eyes watered. My sinuses fizzed.

"That bedpan stuff," Dickie said. "No, man, never mind. I growed up."

The players on the field froze just as the pitch was being delivered. They looked like marble statuary in the nuclear light. Stone figures, inert, but their strength and speed remained implicit in the stasis that separates action from action. Equipoise—half a tick's respite from the merciless unraveling of time and fate. Equipoise, or I had just been buzzed by a *petit mal* seizure, a "short stare."

A smirking TV cameraman directed his machine's cold glass eye down into the dugout and focused on the caped, square-jawed hero known as Baseballman. The little red light glowed. Thank you for inviting me into your living room. It was going to be a Force 12 sneeze, a veritable typhoon of chaw and mucus and saliva and squirmy tobacco weevils. Look out!

"I growed up," Dickie said. "Thinks you'll ever grow up, Moon?"

Author's Note

A long while ago I played professional baseball in the lower—class C—minor leagues. Subsequently I had from time to time tried to write a baseball novel, and each time quit after a few chapters.

One day, in December 1983, I decided to again try a conventional sort of baseball novel. There would be a pennant race, probably; a hero, naturally; the ninth inning of the final game of the World Series, no doubt: the usual sappy clichés. But then Theodore Moon emerged from some remote psychic recess and prompted me to write, "I am feared and loathed in certain quarters; I have powerful enemies."

I started the novel in December of 1983 and finished it late in the summer of 1984. My agent liked it. The first publisher to whom it was submitted offered a contract, which was refused for several reasons. And that was it for